A KISS BEFORE
THE APOCALYPSE

A REMY CHANDLER NOVEL

THOMAS E. SNIEGOSKI

A ROC BOOK

ROC
Published by New American Library, a division of
Penguin Group (USA) Inc., 375 Hudson Street,
New York, New York 10014, USA
Penguin Group (Canada), 90 Eglinton Avenue East, Suite 700, Toronto,
Ontario M4P 2Y3, Canada (a division of Pearson Penguin Canada Inc.)
Penguin Books Ltd., 80 Strand, London WC2R 0RL, England
Penguin Ireland, 25 St. Stephen's Green, Dublin 2,
Ireland (a division of Penguin Books Ltd.)
Penguin Group (Australia), 250 Camberwell Road, Camberwell, Victoria 3124,
Australia (a division of Pearson Australia Group Pty. Ltd.)
Penguin Books India Pvt. Ltd., 11 Community Centre, Panchsheel Park,
New Delhi - 110 017, India
Penguin Group (NZ), 67 Apollo Drive, Rosedale, North Shore 0632,
New Zealand (a division of Pearson New Zealand Ltd.)
Penguin Books (South Africa) (Pty.) Ltd., 24 Sturdee Avenue,
Rosebank, Johannesburg 2196, South Africa

Penguin Books Ltd., Registered Offices:
80 Strand, London WC2R 0RL, England

Published by Roc, an imprint of New American Library, a division of Penguin
Group (USA) Inc. Previously published in a Roc trade paperback edition.

First Roc Mass Market Printing, April 2009
10 9 8 7 6 5 4 3

ROC REGISTERED TRADEMARK—MARCA REGISTRADA

Printed in the United States of America

PUBLISHER'S NOTE
This is a work of fiction. Names, characters, places, and incidents either are the
product of the author's imagination or are used fictitiously, and any resemblance to
actual persons, living or dead, business establishments, events, or locales is entirely
coincidental.
   The publisher does not have any control over and does not assume any responsibility
for author or third-party Web sites or their content.

Praise for
A Kiss Before the Apocalypse

"The most inventive novel you'll buy this year . . . a hard-boiled noir fantasy by turns funny, unsettling, and heartbreaking. This is the story Sniegoski was born to write, and a character I can't wait to see again."

— Christopher Golden, bestselling author of
The Lost Ones

"Tightly focused and deftly handled, [*A Kiss Before the Apocalypse*] covers familiar ground in entertaining new ways. . . . Fans of urban fantasy and classic detective stories will enjoy this smart and playful story."

—*Publishers Weekly*

"This reviewer prays there will be more novels starring Remy. . . . The audience will believe he is on earth for a reason as he does great things for humanity. This heart-wrenching, beautiful urban fantasy will grip readers with its potent emotional fervor."

—*Midwest Book Review*

"It's kind of refreshing to see the holy side represented. . . . Fans of urban fantasy with a new twist are likely to enjoy Sniegoski's latest venture into [the] realm between humanity and angels."   —*SFRevu*

"Blurring the lines between good and evil, *A Kiss Before the Apocalypse* will keep readers riveted until the very end. This is an emotional journey that's sometimes filled with sadness, but once it begins, you won't want to walk away. Mr. Sniegoski defines the hero in a way that makes him very real and thoroughly human. . . . Fast moving, well written, and wonderfully enchanting, this is one that fantasy readers won't want to miss."   —*Darque Reviews*

continued . . .

For LeeAnne

ACKNOWLEDGMENTS

Burger King Crowns of Glory are awarded to Liesa Abrams and Christopher Golden for all their hard work and words of encouragement. I love you guys.

Thanks also to Mulder the Wonder Dog, Ginjer Buchanan, Kenn Gold, Mike, Christine and Katie Mignola, Dave Kraus, John and Jana, Harry and Hugo, Don Kramer, Greg Skopis, James Mignogna, Stephanie Lane, Joe Lansdale, Mom and Dad Sniegoski, David Carroll, Ken Curtis, Mom and Dad Fogg, Lisa Clancy, Kim and Abby, Jon and Flo, Pat and Bob, Pete Donaldson, Jay Sanders, Timothy Cole, and they who walk behind the rows at Cole's Comics in Lynn.

And for all those loved and lost.

CHAPTER ONE

It was an unusually warm mid-September day in Boston. The kind of day that made one forget that the oft-harsh New England winter was on its way, just waiting around the corner, licking its lips and ready to pounce.

Remy Chandler sat in his car at the far end of the Sunbeam Motor Lodge parking lot, sipping his fourth cup of coffee and wishing he had a fifth. He could never have enough coffee. He loved the taste, the smell, the hot feeling as it slid down his throat first thing in the morning; coffee was way up there on his top-ten list of favorite things. A beautiful September day made the list as well. Days like today more than proved he had made the right choice in becoming human.

He reached down and turned up the volume on WBZ News Radio. Escalating violence in the Middle East was once again the headline, the latest attempts for peace shattered. *Big surprise*, Remy thought with a sigh, taking a sip from his coffee cup. *When hasn't there been violence in that region of the world?* he reflected. For as long as he could remember, the bloodthirsty specter of death and intolerance had hovered over those lands. He had tried to talk with them once, but they used his appearance as yet another excuse to pick up knives and swords and hack one another to bits in the name of God. The private investigator shook his head. That was a long time ago, but it always made him sad to see how little things had changed.

To escape the news, he hit one of the preset buttons on the car's radio. It was an oldies station; he found it faintly amusing that an "oldie" was a song recorded in the 1950s. Fats Domino was singing about finding his thrill on Blueberry Hill, as Remy took the last swig of coffee and gazed over at the motel.

He'd been working this case for two months, a simple surveillance gig—keep an eye on Peter Mountgomery, copy editor for the Bronson Liturgical Book Company, and husband suspected of infidelity. It wasn't the most stimulating job, but it did help to pay the bills. Remy spent much of his day drinking coffee, keeping up with *Dilbert*, and maintaining a log of the man's daily activities and contacts. *Ah, the thrilling life of the private gumshoe*, he thought, eyeing the maroon car parked in a space across the lot. So far, Mountgomery was guilty of nothing more than having lunch with his secretary, but the detective had a sinking feeling that was about to change.

A little after one that afternoon, Remy had followed Peter along the Jamaica Way and into the lot of the Sunbeam Motor Lodge. The man had parked his Ford Taurus in front of one of the rooms, and simply sat with the motor running. Remy had pulled past him and idled on the other side of the parking area, against a fence that separated the motor lodge from an over-grown vacant lot, littered with the rusting remains of cars and household appliances. Someone had tossed a bag of garbage over the fence, where it had burst like an overripe piece of fruit, spilling its contents.

The cries of birds pulled Remy's attention away from Mountgomery to the trash-strewn lot. He watched as

the hungry scavengers swooped down onto the discarded refuse, picking through the rotting scraps, and
then climbing back into the air, navigating the sky with
graceful ease.

For a sad instant, he remembered what it was like:
the sound and the feel of mighty wings pounding the
air. Flying was one of the only things he truly missed
about his old life.

He turned his attention back to Mountgomery, just
in time to see another car pull up alongside the editor's. *Time to earn my two-fifty plus expenses,* he thought,
watching as Peter's secretary emerged from the vehicle. Then he picked up his camera from the passenger's
seat and began snapping pictures.

The woman stood stiffly beside the driver's side of
her boss's car, looking nervously about as she waited
to be acknowledged, finally reaching out to rap with a
knuckle upon the window. The man got out of the car,
but the couple said nothing to each other. Mountgomery was dressed in his usual work attire—dark suit,
white shirt, and striped tie. He was forty-six years of
age but looked older. In a light raincoat over a pretty
floral-print dress, the woman appeared to be at least
ten years his junior.

The editor carried a blue gym bag that he switched
from right hand to left as he locked his car. The two
stared at each other briefly, something seeming to pass
silently between them, then together walked to room
number 35. The secretary searched through her purse
as they stood before the door, eventually producing
a key attached to a dark green plastic triangle. Remy
guessed that she had rented the room earlier, and took
four more pictures, an odd feeling settling in the pit
of his stomach. The strange sensation grew stronger as
the couple entered the room and shut the door behind
them.

This was the part of the job Remy disliked most. He would have been perfectly satisfied, as would his client, he was sure, to learn that the husband was completely faithful. Everyone would have been happy; Remy could pay his rent, and Janice Mountgomery could sleep better knowing that her husband was still true to the sacred vows of marriage. Nine out of ten times, though, that wasn't the case.

Suspecting he'd be a while, the detective turned off his car and shifted in his seat. He reached for a copy of the *Boston Globe* on the passenger's seat beside him, and had just plucked a pen from his inside coat pocket to begin the crossword puzzle, when he heard the first gunshot.

He was out of the car and halfway across the lot before he even thought about what he was doing. His hearing was good—unnaturally so—and he knew exactly where the sound had come from. He reached the door to room 35, pounding on it with his fist, shouting for Mountgomery to open up. Remy prayed that he was mistaken, that maybe the sound was a car backfire from the busy Jamaica Way, or that some kids in the neighborhood were playing with fireworks left over from the Fourth of July. But deep down he knew otherwise.

A second shot rang out as he brought his heel up and kicked open the door, splintering the frame with the force of the blow. The door swung wide and he entered, keeping his head low, and for the umpteenth time since choosing his profession, questioned his decision not to carry a weapon.

The room was dark and cool, the shades drawn. An air conditioner rattled noisily in the far corner beneath the window; smoke and the smell of spent ammunition hung thick in the air. Mountgomery stood naked beside the double bed, illuminated by the daylight flooding in through the open door. Shielding his eyes from the sudden brightness, the man turned, shaken by the intrusion.

The body of the woman, also nude, lay on the bed atop a dark, checkered bedspread, what appeared to be a Bible clutched in one of her hands. She had been shot once in the forehead and again in the chest. Mountgomery wavered on his bare feet, the gun shaking in his hand at his side. He stared at Remy in the doorway and slowly raised the weapon.

"Don't do anything stupid," Remy cautioned, his hands held out in front of him. "I'm unarmed."

He felt a surge of adrenaline flood through his body as he watched the man squint down the barrel of the pistol. *This is what it's like to be truly alive,* he thought. In the old days, before his renouncement, Remy had never known the thrill of fear; there was no reason to. But now, moments such as this made what he had given up seem almost insignificant.

The man jabbed the gun at Remy and screamed, "Shut the door!" Slowly, Remy did as he was told, never taking his eyes from the gunman.

"It's not what you think," Mountgomery began. "Not what you think at all." He brought the weapon up and scratched at his temple offhandedly with the muzzle. "Who . . . who are you?" the editor stammered, his features twisting in confusion as he thrust the gun toward Remy again. "What are you doing here?" His voice was frantic, teetering on the edge of hysteria.

Hands still raised, Remy cautiously stepped farther into the room. As a general rule, he didn't like to lie when he had a gun pointed at him. "I'm a private investigator, Mr. Mountgomery," he said in a soft, calm voice. "Your wife hired me. I'm not going to try anything, okay? Just put the gun down and we'll talk. Maybe we can figure a way out of this mess. What do you think?"

Mountgomery blinked as if trying to focus. He stumbled slightly to the left, the gun still aimed at Remy. "A way out of this mess," he repeated, with a giggle. "Nobody's getting out of this one."

He glanced at his companion on the bed and began to sob, his voice trembling with emotion. "Did you hear that, Carol? The bitch hired a detective to follow me."

Mountgomery reached out to the dead woman. But when she didn't respond, he let his arm flop dejectedly to his side. He looked back at Remy. "Carol was the only one who understood. She listened. She believed me." Tears of genuine emotion ran down his face. "I wish we'd had more time together," he said wistfully.

"The bitch at home thought I was crazy. Well, we'll see how crazy I am when it all turns to shit." The sadness was turning to anger again. "This is so much harder than I imagined," he said, his face twisted in pain.

He lowered the gun slightly, and Remy started to move. Instantly, Mountgomery reacted, the weapon suddenly inches from the detective's face. Obviously, madness had done little to slow his reflexes.

"It started when they opened up my head," Mountgomery began. "The dreams. At first I thought they were just that, bad dreams, but then I realized they were much more."

The editor pressed the gun against Remy's cheek. "I was dreaming about the end of the world, you see. Every night it became clearer—the dreams—more horrible. I don't want to die like that," he said, shaking his head, eyes glassy. "And I don't want the people I love to die like that either." The man leaned closer to Remy. He smelled of aftershave and a sickly sour sweat. "Are you a religious man?"

If he had not been so caught up in the seriousness of the situation, Remy Chandler would have laughed. "I have certain—beliefs. Yes. What do *you* believe in, Peter?"

Mountgomery swallowed hard. "I believe we're all going to die horribly. Carol, that was her name." He jerked his head toward the dead woman on the bed. "Carol Weir. She wanted to be brave, to face the end with me. But she was too good to die that way."

He smiled forlornly and tightened his grip on the gun. "I would have divorced my wife and married her, but it seemed kind of pointless when we looked at the big picture. This was the nicest thing I could do for her. She thanked me before I . . ."

Mountgomery's face went wild with the realization of what he had done, and he jammed the barrel of the gun into Remy's forehead. The muzzle felt warm.

"Would you prefer to die now, or wait until it all goes to Hell?" the editor asked him.

"I'm not ready to make that decision."

Remy suddenly jerked his head to one side, grabbing the man's wrist, pushing the gun away from his face. Mountgomery pulled the trigger. A bullet roared from the weapon to bury itself in the worn shag carpet under them.

The two men struggled for the weapon, Mountgomery screaming like a wild animal. But he was stronger than Remy had imagined, and quickly regained control of the pistol, forcing the detective back.

Again, the editor raised his arm and aimed the weapon.

"Don't you point that thing at me," Remy snarled,

glaring at the madman. "If you want to die, then die. If you want to take the coward's way out, do it. But don't you dare try to take me with you."

Mountgomery seemed taken aback by the detective's fierce words. He squinted, tilting his head from left to right, as if seeing the man before him for the first time. "Look at you," he said suddenly, with an odd smile and a small chuckle. "I didn't even notice until now." He dropped the weapon to his side.

It was Remy's turn to be confused. He glanced briefly behind him to be sure no one else had entered the room.

"Are you here for her—for Carol?" Mountgomery continued. "She deserves to be in Heaven. She is—*was* a good person—a very good person."

"What are you talking about, Peter?" Remy asked. "Why would I be here for Carol? Your wife hired me to—"

Mountgomery guffawed, the strange barking sound cutting Remy off midsentence. "There's no need to pretend with me," he said smiling. "I can see what you are."

A finger of ice ran down Remy's spine.

With a look of resigned calm, Mountgomery raised the gun and pressed the muzzle beneath the flesh of his chin. "I never imagined I'd be this close to one," he said, finger tensing on the trigger. "Angels are even more beautiful than they say."

Remy lunged, but Mountgomery proved faster again. The editor pulled the trigger and the bullet punched through the flesh and bone of his chin and up into his brain, exiting through the top of his head in a spray of crimson. He fell back stiffly onto the bed—atop his true love, twitching wildly as the life drained out of him, and then rolling off the bed to land on the floor. His eyes, wide in death, gazed with frozen fascination at the wing-shaped pattern created by his blood and brains on the ceiling above.

Remy studied the gruesome example of man's fragile mortality before him, Mountgomery's final words reverberating through his mind.

I never imagined I'd be this close to one.

He caught his reflection in a mirror over the room's single dresser and stared hard at himself, searching for cracks in the facade. *Is it possible?* he wondered. Had Peter Mountgomery somehow seen through Remy's mask of humanity?

Angels are even more beautiful than they say.

Remy looked away from his own image and back to the victims of violence. *How could a case so simple turn into something so ugly?* he asked himself, moving toward the broken door, followed by the words of a man who could see angels and had dreamt of the end of the world.

He stepped quickly into the afternoon sun and almost collided with the Hispanic cleaning woman and her cart of linens. She looked at him and then craned her neck to see around him and into the room. Remy caught the first signs of panic growing in her eyes and reached back for the knob, pulling the door closed. In flawless Spanish he told her not to go into the room, that death had visited those within, and it was not for her to see. The woman nodded slowly, her eyes never leaving his as she pushed her cart quickly away.

Homicide Detective Steven Mulvehill stood beside Remy, as the team from the medical examiner's office prepared to remove the bodies from the motel room. Remy leaned against his car, arms crossed. The two friends were silent as they watched the activity across the lot.

A small crowd had formed, kept at bay by a strip of yellow crime-scene tape and four uniformed officers. The curious pack craned their necks, moving from one end of the tape to the other, eager to catch a glimpse of something to fill the misery quotient in their lives. It was something that Remy had never really understood but had come to accept: the human species was enthralled with the pain of others. Whether a natural disaster or a drive-by shooting, the average Joe wanted to hear every detail. Maybe the fascination stemmed from the fact that somebody else had incurred the wrath of the fates, and he, for the moment, could breathe a sigh of relief.

Mulvehill and his partner, Rich Healey, had already examined the scene in the motel room and released the bodies to the coroner. Healey was still inside, supervising the removal.

The detective took a long drag of a cigarette, expelled the smoke from his nostrils like some great medieval beast, then broke the uncomfortable silence. "You all right?" he asked. "You're kind of quiet." He took another pull from his smoke.

Remy stared straight ahead, his eyes focused on the entryway of the room across the lot. "He saw me, Steven. Right before that guy killed himself, he really saw me."

Mulvehill was a stocky man, average height with a wild head of thick, black hair. He was forty-seven years old, divorced, and living the job. Remy had met him more than five years earlier, when a homicide investigation had intersected with a missing-persons case he had been working on. The two had been friends ever since.

"He saw me for what I really am," Remy said again, truly disturbed by what he was saying.

Mulvehill looked at Remy, the last of the cigarette protruding from the corner of his mouth. "What, a shitty detective?" The cop smirked, taking the smoke from his mouth and flicking the remains to the ground.

The case that had first brought them together had ended badly, the murder suspect dead and Mulvehill with a bullet in his gut.

"You're a riot," Remy responded. "The stuff of Vegas floor shows. Really, if this cop thing doesn't work out . . ."

Mulvehill laughed out loud as he reached into his sports jacket for his pack of cigarettes. "And you're an asshole. Tell me again what you were doing here." He pulled one from the pack and placed it in his mouth.

"Very smooth, Detective." Remy grinned wryly. "It was simple surveillance," he explained. "Wife suspected he was having an affair. Nothing out of the ordinary."

Mulvehill lit up with an old-fashioned Zippo. He flicked the cover closed with a metallic click, then slipped it back inside his pocket next to the cigarette pack. He took a long, thoughtful drag. Smoking helped him think, he often said. Helped him focus. He'd tried to stop once, but it had made him stupid.

"So he shows up here with his secretary, they go in, and after a while you hear the first shot?"

Remy nodded. "That's about it. By the time I got in there, he'd already killed the woman. I think he was getting ready to shoot himself, but I interrupted him."

The homicide detective idly brushed some ash from the lapel of his navy blue sports coat. "So you think this guy could somehow see you—the real you."

Mulvehill had been near death when Remy found him lying in a pool of blood in an abandoned water-front warehouse. To ease his suffering and calm the terrified detective, Remy had revealed his true countenance. *Death is only a new beginning,* he had reassured the man.

Remy nodded, replaying the conversation with Mountgomery inside his head. "I didn't drop the facade at all, haven't done it in a long time. But the way he looked at me—and that smile. He was definitely seeing something."

The doctors said it was a miracle that Mulvehill had survived the shooting. After his recovery, the homicide detective had come looking for Remy, who had denied nothing—and offered nothing. But Mulvehill knew he had encountered something very much out of the ordinary, something that couldn't simply be attributed to loss of blood.

Remy knew that Mulvehill's mother and grandmother had been strict Catholics, and had tried to raise him in the faith as well. As a young man, he had gone to church to please them, but he had believed Christian doctrine to be nothing more than fairy tales, fantasies to relieve the fears of the devoted when faced with their own mortality. But since his own brush with death, and his encounter with a certain private investigator, the Boston detective wasn't quite sure what he believed anymore. In fact, he'd even started to attend Mass again. *Just to be on the safe side,* he'd told Remy.

But Remy had shown Mulvehill his true face by design. He had revealed himself on purpose. *This* was something else altogether. This dead man had seen beneath his mask.

"That ever happen before?" Mulvehill asked, interrupting Remy's brooding. "Besides when you wanted it to, I mean?"

Remy looked at his friend. "Not to me, but throughout the ages there have been holy men, visionaries, who could glimpse the unseen world and its inhabitants— usually before some kind of change in the world— something of great religious significance."

Mulvehill cleared his throat and fumbled for his cigarettes. "They're still alive, Remy," he said, the package crinkling from inside his coat pocket.

"That's impossible. I saw the woman's body, Steven. Mountgomery shot her in the forehead." He pointed to the center of his furrowed brow. "And just to be sure, he put another one in her heart."

Mulvehill was silent, glancing around at the several spots where blood had been spilled. It had already begun to dry, ugly dark stains that would never be completely washed away.

"I saw him put that gun under his chin and blow his own brains out." Remy pointed to the wing-shaped stain on the ceiling. "That's brain matter up there. They can't possibly be alive."

Mulvehill looked away from the ceiling and shrugged his broad shoulders. "Did you not see the ambulance take them out of here?" he asked. "They're alive. They both have pulses."

The feeling in Remy's gut grew more pronounced.

"Hey, it's not a bad thing—two people are still alive," Mulvehill reasoned. "Maybe it's a miracle or something."

"Or something," Remy repeated as he turned and walked from the motel room, leaving his friend to make sense of it all.

Though Remy looked and acted like a human being and chose to live like one, he was nothing of the kind. On occasion, his body functioned on another level entirely. He could feel things, sense things, that others couldn't. And right now there was something in the air that no one else could feel, something unnatural.

As he walked across the parking lot, he glanced at his watch and swore beneath his breath.

Late again.

Remy got into his car, knowing that what had

begun in room 35 of the Sunbeam Motor Lodge was far from over, and that two hundred and fifty dollars a day plus expenses wasn't going to come close to compensating him for what he feared was waiting on the horizon.

CHAPTER TWO

Remy stopped his car as a group of Northeastern University students crossed Huntington Avenue on their way to the dorms from afternoon classes. Impatiently, he glanced at his watch, angry with himself for being even later than usual. One last student cut across at a run to catch up with the gaggle, and Remy continued on toward South Huntington.

Well, at least something's going right, he thought, as he caught sight of a car pulling away from a space directly across the street from the Cresthaven Nursing Center. Remy performed an amazing feat of parallel parking, locked up his vehicle, and jogged across the street through a break in the dinnertime traffic.

He pulled open the nursing home's front door, and took a moment to compose himself as he was bombarded with a sensory overload the equivalent of storming the beach at Normandy. Smell, sound, emotion, taste; they all washed over him, pounding him, as they did every time he visited. The first time, he was nearly driven to his knees by the onslaught, but he quickly learned that a few deep breaths would help him to center, making the experience bearable.

"You are in some deep doo-doo, my friend," called out a large black woman dressed in a light blue smock and white slacks. She walked around the reception desk, waving some papers at him. "That poor woman's been waiting for you over an hour. I told her you were caught in traffic, but I don't think she's buying it."

Remy smiled as the woman playfully tapped him on the shoulder with the forms.

"I think she's catchin' on to us," she said conspiratorially, looking Remy up and down as she moved on through the lobby.

He waved to the receptionist, then stepped up behind the nurse. "No one must know of us, my Nubian goddess," he whispered in her ear.

The woman began to laugh, bending over and slapping her leg with the paperwork. "You are a crazy white boy, you know that?"

"Joan, you wouldn't have me any other way." Remy smiled. He paused for a minute, enjoying the sound of laughter in a place where the atmosphere could often be so oppressive. "How is she today—giving you a hard time?"

"If she's not careful, I'm going to toss her out on the street," Joan said, walking with him toward the ground-floor nursing unit. She moved away as a light came on outside a room on the opposite end of the hall. "Your mother's in the TV room," she called over her shoulder. "Why don't you go on and see her now so we can get some peace. Meet me in the supply closet at the usual time, and don't keep me waitin'."

Remy laughed as he turned, amused, but not only by Joan's invitation.

Your mother.

No matter how often he heard it, the lie always struck him funny. The staff at Cresthaven would never believe the truth, that Madeline Chandler was, in fact, his wife. The lie existed because of what *he* was, of course. He appeared human, but had never been that. And he did not age.

He stopped in the doorway to the TV room as an old man pushing a walker struggled through. He looked up at Remy with red-rimmed eyes, confusion and turmoil in his gaze.

"Have you seen Robert?" the man asked, his voice like the rustling of dry leaves. "He was supposed to take me home."

An aura of despair radiated from him in waves, nearly pushing Remy back with its strength.

"I have to get home. Who's gonna take care of the house? Have you seen Robert?" the poor soul repeated, already forgetting that he had asked that same question only seconds before. "He was supposed to take me home."

Remy gently touched the old man's shoulder and looked deeply into his aged eyes. "Robert will be here soon, Phil. Why don't you go see Joan, and ask her to make you a cup of tea?"

Phil smiled, his rheumy eyes slowly blinking away confusion. "Tea would certainly hit the spot." He licked his dry lips. "Why didn't I think of that? Must be getting old." He winked at Remy and continued on his way down the hall, a new strength suddenly in his step.

Remy watched his progress. He had spent many an afternoon talking with Phil about what the old timer called the good old days. Although his presence seemed to have a calming effect on these tortured souls ravaged by age, it still pained him to see the effects the years had on those to whom he had grown so close.

It was never more obvious than when he saw his Madeline.

Remy stepped into the doorway of the room that

tried hard to be homey but never quite overcame that institutional air, and spotted the woman he loved. She seemed so small and frail, sitting in a lounge chair in front of the big-screen television. There was an ache inside him, and he wondered why he had ever wished to be flesh and blood. It was a question he asked himself with every visit to Cresthaven.

Madeline hadn't noticed his arrival, and he watched her for a few seconds as she struggled to stay awake. Her eyes would flutter and close, her head slowly nodding until her chin touched her chest. Then she would come awake with a start, and the futile battle to remain conscious would begin all over again.

Remy moved farther into the room. It was set up to resemble a living room; a couple of couches and chairs—both recliners and rockers—covered in vinyl made to imitate leather. Soft lamp lighting and framed Monet prints from the Museum of Fine Arts gift shop down the street completed the attempt at coziness. The TV sat on top of a large, dark, pressed-wood cabinet, a VCR on the shelf beneath, its clock perpetually blinking twelve a.m. The local news was just wrapping up the weather—cooler, with a chance of rain by the end of the week.

He knelt beside his wife's chair as she drifted deeper into sleep, and touched her arm lovingly. Madeline lifted her head to look at him, her eyes dull, momentarily void of recognition.

"How are you ever going to keep up with current events if you're dozing?" he asked her and smiled, before leaning in to kiss her cheek.

The life was suddenly there, the dullness in her gaze burned away by the familiar mischievous twinkle. She smiled, reaching up to touch his face with an aged hand.

"Caught me," she said softly. "Now you'll make me go to bed first again."

It had been their nighttime custom; whoever fell asleep first while relaxing in front of the television had to warm the bed, while the other took out the dog, turned off the lights, and locked the doors. Madeline had been the champion bed warmer.

"How're you feeling today, hon? You look better."

She grinned and batted her eyes, patting the collar of her bright red sweatshirt. She knew he was lying. She had always been able to read his expressions. But she played along anyway, then changed the subject.

"You're late. Joan said you were caught in traffic. Was there an accident?" She started to stand.

Remy took her arm, helping her up. "No accident. Just the usual stuff. I was on a case longer than I anticipated." He guided her around the chair and toward the doorway.

"Anything interesting?" she asked, pausing, peering down toward the lobby, then back up the hall toward her room.

"Nothing all that unusual, until today." He was thoughtful as they slowly made their way up the hall. "The man I was watching killed himself and his lover in a motel on the Jamaica Way. No, let me correct that. I thought they were dead, but I was wrong."

Madeline stopped and stared at her husband. "You *thought* they were dead but you were *wrong*? What's the matter with you, Remy—getting senile?" She chuckled and patted his hand where he held her arm.

When they reached her room, Remy escorted his wife to the high-backed chair by her bed and helped her to sit.

"It was the oddest thing, Maddie," he said as he sat on the bed beside her. "I confronted him after he'd shot his lover. He talked about dreams of the end of the world. Claimed that was why he'd shot the woman and planned to shoot himself."

He stared through the window at the day care next door. It was dinnertime, but there was still a little Asian boy playing in the sandbox, and a little girl riding a bike in a circle, over and over again.

"But you know what the strangest part was, Maddie?" Remy asked. "He said he could see me. That he knew what I was." He looked at his wife and saw confusion on her face.

"Well, did you want him to see you?" she asked. "Did you let him—to stop him from hurting himself?"

Remy shook his head slightly. "No. It wasn't like that at all. It was as if he could see right through me."

Madeline looked disturbed, turning the wedding ring upon her finger. It was something she had always done when something upset her. Remy reached down, took her hand in his, and squeezed it affectionately.

"Hey, don't worry about it. The guy was pretty out of it. Maybe it was just coincidence that he saw me as an angel."

Maddie squeezed back, gazing lovingly into his eyes. "You're *my* angel and no one else's, do you understand? I can't bear the thought of sharing you with anyone."

She brought his hand up to her mouth and kissed it, and he knelt beside her chair, throwing his arms around her small frame. He felt her arms enfold him in a fragile embrace and was painfully reminded of a time when she could easily have hugged the life from him.

"You won't have to," he whispered in her ear. "I'm yours, now and forever." Remy stroked her gray hair and remembered the vitality of her youth.

When he'd first opened his agency back in 1945, he'd placed an advertisement in the paper for an office manager. Madeline had been one of the first applicants, fresh from secretarial college and overflowing with enthusiasm. And she was beautiful, inside and out. In their fifty-plus years together, Madeline Dexter had taught this earthbound entity more about being alive than he'd learned in six thousand years of wandering the planet.

He leaned in close and kissed her gently on the mouth. "I love you," he said, looking into his wife's gaze. It was his turn now to bring her hand to his mouth and gently plant a kiss upon it.

They were silent for a while, each basking in the warmth and love of the other.

"How's the baby?" Madeline asked, finally. "Does he miss me? You're not letting him have too much people food, are you?"

The baby was their four-year-old Labrador retriever, Marlowe, that they treated as if he were their child. They had had another dog, a German shepherd who went by the name Hammett, who lived to be more than fifteen. It was absolutely devastating to Madeline— and to Remy, surprisingly—when the old dog finally died. It took them years to get another, the memory of how much they loved Hammett, and how badly it hurt when he was gone, keeping them from making the next emotional investment.

It was the sad fact that they would never have children together that eventually swayed them to take another animal into their home. They had such an abundance of love that they wanted ... needed to share it with another life. There was nothing he would have loved more than to give her a child, but it wasn't meant to be. Others of his kind had done such things over the ages, and the results had been less than normal. There was something seriously wrong with children produced by the mating of human and angel.

Something unstable.

Remy grinned, pushing the sad thoughts aside.

"Marlowe's fine, and yes, he misses you a great deal. He always asks me when the female is coming back to the pack."

They both chuckled, Madeline reaching into her sweatshirt pocket for a wrinkled-up Kleenex. She wiped at her nose.

"I want you to bring him next time you visit," she said. "I need to see my boy."

Time was growing short for the woman Remy loved. It was something they were both very aware of—after all, no one came to Cresthaven to get well.

"I'll do that," he said softly.

She squeezed his hand and covered a feigned yawn with the other. "I'm tired, Remy. Would you mind? I think I'd like to lie down now."

He helped her to the bed, removing her slippers and swinging her legs onto the mattress.

"Do you want me to help you get undressed?"

She gave him a sly look. "Always at the most inopportune times," she told him weakly. "Maybe if I get a good night's sleep, I'll take you up on your offer tomorrow."

Grinning, she moved her eyebrows up and down, and Remy chuckled, giving her a wink.

"You go home. I'm sure the baby is ravenous and desperate to empty his tank. I'll see you both tomorrow."

Madeline waved him away and adjusted the pillow beneath her head.

She was getting weaker, and there wasn't a single thing he could do about it.

Remy leaned down and kissed her long on the lips.

"I love you. I'll see you tomorrow, then."

"I love you too. And don't forget Marlowe," she ordered as he turned to leave.

He was just stepping into the hallway when he heard her call his name.

"Yeah, hon?" he said popping his head back into the room.

Madeline had propped herself up against the headboard. "What do you think it means—that man seeing you?" she asked. "I can't shake the feeling that something isn't right."

Remy returned to her bedside and, leaning in, planted a reassuring kiss upon her forehead.

"I'm sure it means absolutely nothing," he told her. "It was just a fluke. The guy was so crazy he could have imagined me as the Easter Bunny. Now get some rest, and I'll see you tomorrow."

Remy flashed her a final smile as he stepped into the corridor and out of view. He passed through the lobby to see that the pretty young receptionist was on the phone, and he mouthed the words *Have a good night* as he passed.

Walking to his car, he was preoccupied with thoughts of his wife and her failing health. The poor woman didn't need anything else to worry her right now. He got behind the wheel and turned over the engine. In the theater of his mind he saw Mountgomery and his secretary entering the motel room, heard the clamor of the door slamming shut behind them like the sound of thunder.

Remy flipped on his blinker and eased out into traffic. Though he would have preferred otherwise, he couldn't help but remember Mountgomery smiling dreamily as he talked about the beauty of angels, just before putting the gun beneath his chin and decorating the ceiling with his brains.

He pointed the car for home, turning up the radio, hoping the music would distract him from further thoughts of the day's disturbing events. But it did little to drown out the sound of Mulvehill's voice repeating in his head.

They're still alive, Remy.
They're still alive.

Remy stood in the foyer of his Beacon Hill brownstone, sifting through the day's mail. From a basket attached to the inside of the door beneath the mail slot, he had plucked three envelopes and a grocery store circular. He tucked them beneath his arm and searched for his house key. On the other side of the inner door, Marlowe let out a pathetic yelp that suggested he was in great need of his master.

"Hang on, pally, help is on the way."

He let himself into the house and was immediately set upon by the jet-black Labrador with the furiously wagging tail. The dog's tail had become the legendary scourge of knickknacks up and down Pinckney Street, able to clear coffee tables with a single exuberant swipe.

Remy tossed the mail onto a hall table and bent down to rub the excited animal's big head, ruffling his black, velvety soft ears.

"Hello, good boy. How are you, huh? Were you a good dog today?"

Marlowe's deep brown eyes locked on to Remy's. And he responded. *"Good boy. Yes. Out? Out?"*

It was another angelic trait that Remy Chandler had chosen not to repress: the ability to commune with all living things upon the earth. If it had a language, no matter how rudimentary, Remy could understand and communicate with it.

"Okay, let's get you out, and then I'll give you something to eat," he told the dog as they walked down the hall and through the kitchen to the back door.

"Out. Then eat. Good. Out, then eat," Marlowe responded, his tail still furiously wagging while he waited for Remy to open the door into the small, fenced-in yard.

The dog bounded down the three steps, his dark nose sniffing the ground for the scent of any uninvited guests, as he trotted to the far corner and squatted to relieve himself. Remy smiled, amused by the expression of relief on the dog's face. Even though he was a male dog and nearly four years old, Marlowe still insisted on squatting to urinate. Maddie had suggested he was a slow learner and would be lifting his leg in no time. Remy wasn't so sure.

The dog started to poke around the yard again.

"Hey, do you want to eat?" Remy called from the doorway.

Marlowe looked up from a patch of grass, his body suddenly rigid. *"Hungry. Eat now, yes,"* he grumbled in response, then ran toward Remy, who barely managed to get the screen door open in time.

Marlowe hadn't eaten since six that morning and was obviously ravenous. But then again, when wasn't he?

Remy mixed some wet food from a can with some dry, Marlowe standing attentively by his side, closely watching his every move. A slimy puddle of drool had started to form on the floor beneath his hungry mouth.

"Almost ready, pal," he told the Labrador. "I hope you appreciate the time I put into the preparation of your meals."

"Appreciate," Marlowe replied. *"Hungry. Eat now?"*

"Yes, now," Remy confirmed, setting the plastic bowl down on a place mat covered with images of dancing cartoon Labradors. "Let me get you some fresh water."

He picked up the stainless-steel water bowl as Marlowe shoved his hungry maw into his supper. He emptied the bowl and rinsed it thoroughly, then filled it with cold water. In the seconds it took Remy to do that and return to the plastic place mat, Marlowe had already finished his meal and was licking the sides of the dish for stray crumbs.

"More?" Marlowe asked, looking up at his master.

Remy rolled his eyes and shook his head. "No. No more. Maybe later you can have an apple, if you're good."

He ruffled the dog's head and went to the counter to prepare a pot of coffee.

"Now better."

"What did I just say?" Remy said, scooping coffee into a filter. "Later, before bed."

Marlowe lowered his head and watched quietly as his master poured water into the coffeemaker. The dog carefully moved closer to Remy, casually sniffing at his pant leg.

Remy leaned down and thumped the dog's side. It sounded like an empty drum. "What do you smell there, big boy? Anything good?"

"Female," Marlowe answered. *"Smell female. Where?"*

Remy squatted in front of his friend and rubbed the sides of his black face. "Maddie is at the get-well place. I'll bring you to see her tomorrow."

The dog thought for a moment and then kissed Remy nervously on the ear. *"Get-well place? Get-well place bad."*

Maddie and Remy had called the veterinarian's office the get-well place, and the dog had never enjoyed his visits there. Marlowe was not happy in the least that Maddie was in the get-well place. She and Remy made up Marlowe's pack, and it confused the poor animal not to have her at home. No matter how Remy tried to explain that Madeline was sick and needed to be taken care of elsewhere, Marlowe could not grasp the concept. So, as he often did in instances like this, Remy changed the subject.

"Want an apple now?"

Marlowe snapped to attention, his missing pack member almost instantly forgotten.

"Apple now? Yes. Yes."

Remy grabbed a Red Delicious from a fruit bowl on the microwave table and brought it to the counter. He plucked a knife from the strainer, cored the apple, and cut it into bite-sized pieces. Marlowe followed him excitedly across the kitchen as he tossed the chopped fruit into the metal bowl.

"Here you go. Eat it slow so you don't choke."

Marlowe dug in. *"Apple good. Chew. Not choke. Good,"* he said between bites.

Remy returned to the coffeemaker and poured himself a cup. He leaned against the counter, watching the dog inhale his treat, and wondered how long it would be before Marlowe again asked for Madeline. *Not the best of situations,* he thought, his eyes going to the fruit bowl.

And they were almost out of apples.

It was after eight when Remy finally retired to the rooftop patio to unwind from the hectic day. It was getting cooler, but he didn't notice. He sat in a white plastic lounge chair, sipping his coffee and reading *Farewell My Lovely* for what was probably the tenth time. Remy never tired of Chandler. In fact, he'd chosen his *human* name and that of his "baby" as a kind of tribute to his favorite author. There was something about the man's prose, his keen observations of the mean streets of 1940s Los Angeles, that usually soothed the angel, but not tonight. He placed the paperback down on the patio table.

Marlowe lay on his side at Remy's feet, legs extended as if dropped by gunfire. He lifted his head and grumbled.

"Yeah, me too, boy. Even Chandler's not doing it tonight." Remy leaned forward in his chair and ran his fingers along the dog's rib cage. The Labrador laid his head back with a contented sigh.

Then, coffee mug in hand, he stepped over Marlowe and walked to the patio's edge, looking out over the city. He sipped at the cooling liquid as the day's disturbing events replayed inside his head. Mountgomery saw him in a guise he had not taken in years.

Remiel, an angel of the heavenly host Seraphim.

How he hated to be reminded of what he actually was.

The angel listened to the sounds of the city, of the night around him, knowing full well that if he so desired he could pinpoint the individual prayers of every person speaking to Heaven at that moment, but Remiel had given up listening to the prayers of others a long, long time ago. He didn't want to be something prayed to; he wanted to be like those he walked beside and lived among everyday. Remy Chandler wanted to be human, and until today, he was doing a pretty good job.

The door buzzer squawked below, and Marlowe climbed to his feet with a bark and bolted down the stairs, gruffing and grumbling threateningly. Remy took one last look at the city, wondering how many out there had asked for favors from Heaven tonight; then returned to the table for his book and followed the dog down the three flights.

He pushed the response button on the wall in the kitchen, leaning in toward the two-way speaker. "Yes?"

There was a bit of a pause. Then he heard the rustling of a paper bag.

"Hey. It's me. Let me in."

It was Steven Mulvehill, and it sounded like he had brought refreshments. Remy buzzed the man in and went to a cabinet for some glasses.

Marlowe watched his master with a tilted head.

"Who? Play?"

Remy pulled down two tumblers, running his finger along the inside of each glass to clear away any dust. "It's Steven," he said as he placed the glasses on the countertop.

The sound of the inner door opening sent Marlowe into spasms of barking fury. The dog bounded down the hall as Mulvehill entered, waiting patiently as the excited Lab sniffed him over.

"Hey, fella, how's it going?" Mulvehill thumped the dog's side with the flat of his hand as Marlowe leaned against him, as if starving for attention, his tail, of course, wagging crazily.

He straightened and strolled down the hallway to the kitchen, where he handed Remy the paper bag he was carrying. "I come bearing gifts. Make mine on the rocks, please."

Remy took the bag from his friend and removed the bottle of Seagram's whiskey. Marlowe lurked at Remy's side.

"Have?" he asked.

Remy tossed the paper bag down to the dog. "Rip it up in here. Don't get it all over the living room, okay?"

The Labrador quickly snatched up the satchel in his mouth and happily trotted into the living room.

Mulvehill laughed. "I'm always amazed by the amount of control you have over that animal."

"Marlowe does what Marlowe wants to do," Remy replied as he closed the freezer door and plunked a handful of cubes into each glass. "I can only make suggestions."

The homicide detective shook his head and looked toward the living room, where sounds of paper being torn to bits drifted out to them. "Spoken like a true pet owner," he chuckled. "Did you visit Maddie tonight? How's she doing?" the cop asked, suddenly serious.

Remy shrugged. "As good as can be expected. She wanted to know if you were coming by soon."

Mulvehill hadn't been to visit Remy's wife since she had entered the hospital more than six months earlier. He claimed he had a "thing" about hospitals, but Remy suspected it had more to do with the fact that Steven could not face the loss of a close friend in his lonely life. Even now he ignored the question, instead motioning toward the stairs that led to the roof.

"Shall we go up? I need a smoke."

Remy didn't allow his friend to smoke in the house. Madeline and Marlowe were both allergic, and besides, it left an odor on the furniture that the angel's acute senses found offensive. Mulvehill plodded up the stairs, and Remy followed close behind.

The detective took his usual seat with a grunt, and reached into his coat pocket for the first of what would likely be many cigarettes. Remy put the ice-filled glasses and the bottle down on the tabletop.

Lit cigarette dangling from his mouth, Mulvehill reached for the bottle of whiskey and cracked the seal. "Ain't a finer sound to be heard after a day like today," he offered.

Remy watched him pour the golden liquid over the ice in his glass, filling it halfway. "Should I hit you or do you want to do it yourself?" Mulvehill asked, gesturing toward his friend with the bottle.

Remy signaled with a wave of his hand for him to pour, as he sat down across from Mulvehill.

The detective offered a sinister smile. "I'm drinking with either a brave man or a stupid one."

The ice inside the glass popped and cracked as the whiskey drenched it. "Depends on what you're talking about," Remy responded as he reached for his drink.

Mulvehill set the bottle down, not bothering to screw the cap back on. He sampled his own drink with an eager gulp, and Remy could sense that something was bothering his friend.

"You sure you don't want this one too?" Remy asked, holding his glass out toward his friend. "I could get another glass and some more ice."

Mulvehill had already finished the first and was pouring a second. "Lousy day. Very long and lousy day." He finished filling his glass, avoiding Remy's eyes.

Quietly, Remy sipped his drink, allowing the alcohol to burn his throat as he swallowed. It had taken him many years to learn how to appreciate the effects of drink, but with the proper practice, he now did quite fine. Fire blossomed in the pit of his stomach as he let the whiskey enter his bloodstream and course through his body.

Marlowe came up the stairs to see what the rest of the pack was up to. He strolled over to Remy and nudged his master's hand with his snout, hoping for a pat.

"Did you make a mess with that bag in the living room?" Remy asked. "If you did, I'm afraid you'll have to go to the pound."

The dog made a pitiful sound of hurt and slunk dejectedly toward Mulvehill. The cop leaned forward in his chair to scratch behind the dog's floppy ears, as Marlowe licked his hand and the glass it held.

"Don't worry, boy," he told the dog. "You can live with me. How about that?"

Marlowe licked the man's cheek, and Remy laughed, taking another sip of his drink before setting it down.

"He'd have to go out for a walk more than once a month. Dogs are like that, you know."

Marlowe gave Remy a blistering look and laid his bulk down beside his new best friend. The animal wasn't about to forgive Remy so easily.

Mulvehill was in the midst of pouring his third drink

when Remy finally decided to pick up the conversation again.

"So, your day?"

His friend was silent for a moment, stirring his drink with his finger, the melting ice tinkling happily in the tumbler. "Mountgomery and his secretary? I checked on them tonight. They're both still alive."

The angel shook his head in disbelief, reaching for the bottle. "I still don't know how that's possible."

The cop lit another cigarette before he responded. "I have a buddy at Mass General, emergency room doc. He checked them out when they came in." He took a long drag, letting the smoke plume from his nostrils and mouth as he exhaled. "Said they were fatal injuries; no way those two should still be alive. He was pretty spooked by the whole thing."

Mulvehill fell silent and stared into space. Absently, he swirled the drink around in the glass, then drained the contents. "They should be dead, but they're not."

Remy was seldom affected by temperature, but he felt a sudden chill course down his back, and shivered.

His friend noticed, smiling thinly. "It's creepy, isn't it?" He plucked the smoke from between his lips. "I've seen a lot of weird shit on the job, but nothing quite like this." He took another substantial drag. "And you know what? It gets worse. Back at the station, I hear from other guys that shit like this is happening all over the city. People who should be dead, car wrecks, gang shootings, suicides—they're all hanging on. The hospitals are packed."

Mulvehill put his cigarette out in an ashtray littered with the remains of others he'd smoked in recent weeks. "Just like Mr. Mountgomery and his little girlfriend."

The two men were quiet again, each absorbed by their own thoughts, the rattling of Marlowe's snores filling the air.

Mulvehill had been looking out at the city, but now he met Remy's inquisitive gaze. "You said Mountgomery saw what you really are before he shot himself. Do you think there's any connection?"

Remy ran a finger along the rim of his empty glass, remembering the strangeness in the air he'd been feeling all day. "It's possible. But I haven't a clue as to what it means."

He reached for the whiskey. They were doing quite a job on it. The bottle was half-empty already. The angel poured about an inch of fluid into his glass. The ice was almost gone, and he thought about going downstairs for more.

"Leave it to you to get involved with another weird case," his friend said, as he leaned back in his chair, taking another cigarette from the pack on the table.

"They're not all weird," Remy said, feigning offense. "I've had some normal cases. The few bizarre moments just spice things up some."

Mulvehill had closed his eyes, letting the alcohol work its magic, but now scoffed loudly and opened them. "A few bizarre moments? Obviously you've lost your ability to distinguish, my friend." He sat up and ran his fingers through his mop of curly black hair with a sigh.

Remy downed what was left of his drink and made a face. He smiled in surrender. "Well, now that you mention it—"

They both laughed, and Marlowe came awake with a start, looking up from his place beside Mulvehill's chair to see if everything was okay. He grumbled deep in his throat, annoyed that he had been disturbed, and put his square head back down with a grunt.

"You are a fucking weird magnet, Remy Chandler," Mulvehill proclaimed. "Maybe being an angel makes you some kind of draw for this shit."

Remy had been allowing himself to feel the inebriating effects of the alcohol, but suddenly was stone-cold sober. He put his glass down. It was something he had often thought about, that his presence on the planet could somehow be responsible for these outbreaks of strangeness, that the unearthly was attracted to its like.

"That would certainly suck, wouldn't it?" He looked at his friend and smiled sadly. "When I first came here I didn't even want to be noticed. I just wanted to help when I could, but never interfere. I wanted to get lost in the crowd, to live like them—to be like them."

He got up from the chair, walked to the roof's edge. Marlowe also climbed to his feet, wondering if they were going somewhere. Mulvehill poured another drink and eyed his friend.

"Sometimes it's hard to remember I'm not human," Remy said softly. "And sometimes it's hard to forget."

Mulvehill sipped his drink and swished it around in his mouth. He swallowed, smacking his lips. "You're more human than half the scumbags I'm forced to deal with every day," he told the angel. "Shit, you're more human than everybody down at the Registry of Motor Vehicles."

Remy came back to the table but didn't sit.

"You always did know what to say to make me feel special."

Mulvehill raised his glass with a dopey grin.

"What are friends for?"

Remy fixed him with a serious gaze.

"There may be something to what you suggested— weirdness being drawn to me."

The homicide cop didn't respond.

"It's times like these when I wonder if coming here was the right idea. Am I being selfish—doing more harm than good? Gives me a headache if I think about it too much."

Remy picked up his glass from the table.

"Looks like I need more ice—want some?"

Mulvehill drained his and handed it to Remy.

"More ice would be good. Better bring up a bucket, to be safe. There's still a lot of drinkin' to be done."

Remy went toward the door, talking over his shoulder as he did.

"Don't start drinking from the bottle. I'll be right back."

Marlowe followed, just in case there might be a treat at the end of the journey, the possibility of food making him forget his earlier anger.

"Hey!"

Remy turned as Steven Mulvehill called to him.

The homicide detective was lighting up a new cigarette.

"I know it's probably none of my business, but I'm too drunk to give a shit, and to tell you the truth, I've been curious about this for years." He closed up his lighter and took a short drag before continuing. "Why *did* you come here?" he asked. "Why would an angel want to leave Heaven?"

Marlowe stared at his master and whined, sensing a sudden change in the man's mood.

The angel Remiel remembered the sounds of war, the screams of the vanquished as they were tossed down to the depths by the One they had always believed to be a merciful and loving Creator.

Remy stood there awkwardly, not wanting Mulvehill to see the hurt on his face. "Heaven isn't all it's cracked up to be," he said simply, driving the recollections from his mind. "Let's just leave it at that." He doubted there would ever come a day when those memories weren't agonizingly painful.

"I'll be right back with the ice."

He was almost down the first flight when his friend called out again.

"Listen, do you want ice or not?"

Mulvehill puffed casually on his latest cigarette.

"I don't mind you're here," he said, turning his head away to look out over Boston. "That's all. Go get the ice."

Remy nodded, sensing that it took a great deal of inner strength, as well as a substantial bit of whiskey, for the homicide detective to express those feelings. It was the closest thing to a declaration of friendship that was ever going to come from Steven Mulvehill, and at that moment Remy appreciated it greatly.

CHAPTER THREE

The drive to Salem from Boston was relatively easy.

Except for the usual traffic jam in the Ted Williams Tunnel, the ride through Revere and Lynn was free of congestion. It was 9:26 on Wednesday morning, and the entire trip had taken Remy a little more than an hour.

His appointment with Janice Mountgomery was for 9:30, and he pulled into the driveway of the home on Prescott Street right on time. This was the part of his job that he found most difficult—the final meeting with the client, where suspicions were either confirmed or denied. He reached for the manila envelope on the seat beside him and got out of the car. Dressed in black jeans, a white shirt, and wool sports coat, the private investigator climbed four orange brick steps to the front door, rang the bell, and waited.

He found himself listening to the noise of the suburbs. The sounds were different here than in the city; calmer, slower, less frantic. The angel opened his senses and heard light snoring, morning television, and young children at play. A dog angrily barked at a bothersome cat trespassing in his territory, and a trapped housefly buzzed in frustration as it bounced its tiny body against an unremitting pane of glass. Then Janice Mountgomery opened the door, and Remy tuned it all out.

The woman looked tired, even more so than the last time he had seen her. It was obvious she hadn't been sleeping. Her eyes were red, the skin beneath them puffy and dark. She looked as though she would collapse at any moment.

"Mrs. Mountgomery, if this is a bad time I could come back tomorrow—" Remy began.

"No. It's fine. Come in." The woman pushed the screen door open and motioned for him to enter. "I don't think there's ever a good time for something like this. Do you?"

She didn't seem to expect a response, and Remy offered none as he stepped inside his client's home.

The house reeked of cleanliness, the scents of several different cleaning products making his sensitive nose tingle. He followed her down a short hallway, past a den, and into a dining room. An oblong table made of dark cherrywood occupied the center of the room. Six chairs surrounded it. Framed family pictures hung on the walls, with watercolors of spring on Beacon Hill and the gold-domed state house as seen through Boston Common.

Janice stood beside a chair where she had obviously been working; stacks of envelopes, a calculator, and a ledger were neatly laid out. "I was doing the bills," she explained. "Have to have all my ducks in a row now that things are the way they are." She kept her eyes downcast as she spoke. "We've got a good health plan, thank God. Who knows how long he'll be in the hospital before he can come home."

She looked at Remy then, her red, watery eyes locking on to his for the first time. "If he comes home."

Remy held out the manila envelope to her.

"I know this is difficult. I'll try to be quick."

Janice took the envelope tentatively, as if expecting

it to be searing hot in her grasp. She held it for a moment, feeling the contents through the paper, and then set it down in the center of the table. She looked back to Remy, eyes swimming with sadness.

"Would you like a cup of coffee, Mr. Chandler? I've just brewed a fresh pot, and I really shouldn't drink the whole thing by myself."

Remy nodded and smiled.

"That would be nice. Thank you."

They sat across from each other at the dining room table, a plate of cookies that neither had touched between them. Janice blew on her coffee but didn't drink, and looked at Remy over the drifting steam.

"It doesn't surprise me at all, really." She laughed nervously, setting her mug down on a white paper napkin. "He was never really the same after the operation."

Remy sipped at his own coffee, his sixth that morning.

"Your husband mentioned something about surgery, and dreams he was having as a result. What was wrong with him, Mrs. Mountgomery?"

She picked up her mug again, holding it in both hands as if to warm them. "He had a brain tumor. They didn't think he would survive the procedure." She finally drank, quiet for a moment. "We even said our good-byes. Believe me when I tell you, there was a lot of praying in this house the morning he went in."

Remy wondered offhandedly whether any of his kind had been listening to the prayers of the Mountgomerys that day.

Janice continued. "They tell me he actually died on the table, but they managed to revive him." She drank some more, her eyes suddenly focusing on the thick envelope still lying in the center of the table. "Lately I've been wondering if it would have been better if they had let him die."

She dragged her eyes from the envelope.

"You probably think I'm awful. The bitter, spurned wife," she said with a nervous laugh. "But it's not like that at all. After the surgery he just wasn't the man I married anymore. It was like the operation made him into somebody else, like the tumor was really Peter and once that was taken away, he left too. I know it sounds crazy, but that's how it was."

Remy set his mug down on his own napkin and watched as Janice pulled a tissue from her pocket. Her eyes had begun to tear.

"I'm sorry, it's just been so much for me to handle."

The woman dabbed at her eyes and wiped her running nose.

"How was he different?" Remy asked.

Janice sat stiffly for a moment, thinking, remembering. "He became very distant, distracted. And there were nightmares. Every night, he'd wake up screaming, carrying on about the end of the world."

Remy leaned forward. "Tell me more about the nightmares."

Janice wiped the table in front of her with the side of her hand, sweeping away imaginary crumbs. "Something about seals being broken and horsemen coming. It was all quite disturbing."

Another intrusive chill ran down the length of the angel's spine. It was starting to become commonplace, and he didn't care for it in the least. Waxen seals being broken on scrolls in the possession of the Angel of Death would, in fact, stir the Four Horsemen of the Apocalypse and bring about the world's end, but any fanatic, or editor at a religious publishing house, would be aware of that.

Janice Mountgomery laughed bitterly and stood up from her chair, empty coffee mug in hand. "Of course, he was completely out of his mind at that point," the woman said. "The kids and I begged him to get help. But he just became more and more withdrawn. We hardly spoke anymore, and then he began sleeping in the guestroom. Said it was so his nightmares wouldn't wake me, but I knew otherwise."

She made her way into the kitchen with her mug, taking Remy's as she passed. He got up and followed her, standing quietly in the doorway as the bereaved woman placed the dirty mugs in the sink and ran water into each.

"He did go back to work, although I don't know how he managed it. That's where he got involved with that woman, his secretary, Carol something or other—Weir? Carol Weir, isn't it?"

She turned off the water and wiped her hands on a red-and-white checked dishtowel, which hung beneath the sink. "I guess she was a bit of a religious nut, at least that's what people tell me. She believed his stories about the end being near. Probably needed help as much as he did."

There was a simmering rage in her voice now, as she leaned against the sink, arms tightly folded across her chest. "It's funny. I knew it was going to be her. When I suspected that he was fooling around, I knew it was with his secretary. I met her once at an office function, a while ago, before Peter got sick. She gave me this look, and I knew she was going to be trouble."

Janice smiled sadly and glanced at Remy, still in the doorway. "Wives can sense these things." She chuckled nervously. "Listen to me—now I sound like Peter." Then her eyes began to fill and she quickly changed the subject.

"Are you married, Mr. Chandler?"

Remy nodded, though he was usually careful not to reveal too much of his personal life to his clients. Yet this woman was hurting so much that he allowed himself to share a little. "Yes. Yes, I am."

That was all he gave her, but it seemed to satisfy.

"You seem like a very nice man, Mr. Chandler. Your wife is a very lucky woman."

"Thank you, Mrs. Mountgomery." Remy turned and began to move through the dining room toward the hall. "If you don't have any more questions, I really should be on my way."

The woman came quickly toward him, an air of desperation about her.

"Should I pay you the remainder of your fee now, or will you bill me?"

"I'll bill you. That way you'll have a receipt for your records." Remy started down the hallway. "Thank you again for the coffee." He grabbed the front doorknob, pulling it open as he turned back toward her. "Please, don't hesitate to call me if there's anything else I can do for you."

Janice reached around him to help with the door. "I was pretty much set to leave him, before all this, before I called you. I . . . I just wanted to be sure I was doing the right thing. All that talk about angels and devils around every corner, it was enough to make me nuts."

Remy nodded, then turned back toward the screen door, recalling the expression of disbelief, then unbridled joy that spread across Peter Mountgomery's face before he'd shot himself. Had the man just been crazy, experiencing delusions as a result of some defect of the brain? The question gnawed at him. Remy couldn't be sure.

He pushed open the storm door and stepped outside. He could feel the woman's eyes on him as he walked toward his car. He half expected her to call out to him, to ask him questions that would keep him there longer, but then he heard the front door close. He focused again on the sounds of the suburbs around him: morning talk shows on television, the rasping snore of a restless sleeper, and a new sound—the pitiful sobs of a woman, more alone at that moment than she had ever been in her life.

It took him longer to get back into Boston. Remy sat in the late-morning traffic, listening to news radio and slowly making his way across the Lenny Zakim bridge. Something bothered him. No matter how hard he tried to shake it off, it wouldn't let go. The Mountgomery case was, for all intents and purposes, closed, done. But something would not allow him to think of it that way. The more he poked at the strange animal that was this case, the more it twitched to be noticed.

Remy decided to stop at the hospital, to see Peter Mountgomery for himself, hoping to still some of these strange feelings of unease.

Finding a space on Cambridge Street, he locked up his car, fed the meter a few quarters, and walked the short distance to Massachusetts General Hospital. He entered the main lobby through the revolving doors and willed himself invisible—another angelic trait he allowed himself to indulge in every so often. In his line of work, the talent frequently proved invaluable. Only the very young and the very old had the ability to glimpse the angel when he was in this state. He imagined it had something to do with being closer to the divine at those particular stages in the human life span.

Remy moved through the lobby and down the crowded corridor, following the signs for the Bigelow Building elevators. No one so much as looked in his direction. The center elevator chimed happily as its doors opened, and he joined a small crowd headed up.

While everyone else watched the numbers over the doors climb, Remy and a baby boy stared at each other. The child began to laugh, pumping his chubby arms crazily as drool trailed from his toothless mouth. Gently, the angel brushed the child's head with the side of his finger and mouthed the word *hello*. The boy laughed even harder, squealed loudly, and tossed his melon-shaped head back, flailing his arms. The mother glanced around nervously, looking for what had excited her baby so, but saw nothing out of the ordinary. She smiled and kissed the child, calling him her silly monkey, as they exited the elevator on the floor before Remy's.

He had little problem finding Mountgomery's room. Still unseen, he approached a tired-looking nurse who was doing paperwork at the nurses' station. He moved up silently behind him and whispered into his ear. The exhausted young man put down his pen suddenly, as though he had just thought of something he didn't dare forget again, and wheeled his chair over to a computer terminal. He began to type on the keyboard, and Remy watched as Peter Mountgomery's medical records appeared. He was in room 615. The nurse checked some information, nodded to himself in satisfaction, and went back to his paperwork. Silently, Remy Chandler thanked him and headed down the hall.

The angel heard it even before he'd reached the room he sought, the doleful, ethereal cries of a soul in distress wafting down the corridor. Remy entered room 615 and approached Mountgomery's bed, wincing as the man's life force screamed to be freed from its prison of flesh.

What is keeping you here? he wondered, staring down at the man, desperate for answers. *Why hasn't your soul been taken?* The man lay in the hospital bed, his head and neck swathed in bandages stained with blood and a yellowish discharge. He was hooked to a number of machines that monitored his condition and provided life support. Tubes of various sizes carried fluids to and from his body.

Remy took Peter's hand in his and gently squeezed. "Why are you still here?" he whispered, speaking directly to the spirit trapped within the broken body.

The imprisoned soul moaned all the louder, sensing the presence of a being who might free it from its confines. The anguished cries tore at the essence of Remy's true self.

"I'm sorry, but there's nothing I can do," he told it. "It's . . . it's not my job."

The soul continued to cry out, and the angel's thoughts turned to the one whose purpose it was to answer these plaintive cries. Remy let go of Mountgomery's hand, stepping back from the bed, watching the man's chest rise and fall with every breath—with life. Something was wrong.

Horribly, horribly wrong.

And then Remy heard the others.

The pleading wails of Mountgomery's soul rose in intensity, joining with other tortured cries from the intensive care unit, and it was almost more than the detective could stand. The accumulated misery was deafening, and he quickly left the room, making his way back to the elevators. He had to get away.

Tormented souls beckoned to him as he passed other rooms, begging for his divine attention, and he apologized to them all, sorry that there was nothing he could do to help them.

It isn't my job.

At the elevator he wondered, *Where is Israfil?* The question replayed itself over and over again as he practically threw himself into the elevator to escape the mournful pleas.

Where is the Angel of Death?

CHAPTER FOUR

Remy headed for his Beacon Street office, his brain feeling as though it were about to explode. For some reason, souls were not being collected. Life essences were trapped within bodies that should have been dead but were not.

Not good. Not good at all.

Remy climbed the steps to the converted brownstone and entered the lobby. He checked his mailbox and found that the postman had already been by with his daily dose of bills. This time it was electric and phone. Making his way to his office on the second floor, he swore that the utility companies had started billing more than once a month, for it didn't seem possible that the services had come due yet again.

The angel tensed as he pushed the key into the lock and turned it. There was no mistaking the smell wafting out from within his office. He listened to the clacking sound as the bolt slid back, unlocking his office door. It had been quite some time since he had last breathed in that thick, heady aroma. To the human nose, it would smell like a strange mix of cinnamon and burning tires.

To an angel, it smelled of power.

Remy turned the knob and swung open the door.

They were waiting for him. Four of them, each dressed in stylish suits of solid black with white shirts buttoned up to their throats. They stood before his desk, their broad backs to him, unresponsive to his entrance.

Remy entered the office just as he did any other day of the week, putting his keys back in his pocket and gently shutting the door. He placed his mail in a wicker basket that rested atop a gray file cabinet to the right of the door. The basket had once contained a plant sent to him as thanks from a satisfied customer, but not anymore. He had never been very good with plants.

His visitors still did not move, and Remy continued to act as if they weren't there, grabbing the glass carafe from the coffeemaker that sat on a small brown refrigerator on the other side of the file cabinet. He leaned over, opened the fridge, and removed a jug of springwater. He filled the carafe, then placed the water jug back inside. Allowing the refrigerator door to close by itself, he turned to finally acknowledge his guests.

"Coffee?" he asked, plucking a filter from a box. He placed it in the machine and filled it with several scoops of the rich-smelling brew, then poured the contents of the glass carafe through the plastic grill on top and flicked the switch to on. The machine gurgled to life.

He knew them, these silent visitors, each and every one of the strange figures who stood perfectly still before his empty desk, staring off into space. They were Seraphim, one of the highest orders of angels in the kingdom of Heaven. At one time, they had been his brothers.

One of the Seraphim slowly turned his gaze away from the wall and fixed the detective with an intense, unblinking stare. The eyes were large and completely black, the actual look of the human eyeball a detail considered trivial by its wearer. His name was Nathanuel, and he was their leader.

As he opened his mouth to speak, Remy knew it had been some time since the angel last wore the clothes of flesh, remembering the difficulty he himself had encountered after his decision to be human. "Coffee. Yes, I would enjoy coffee." The voice sounded wrong, the cadence off. Human speech was far more complicated than any angel knew.

The coffeemaker hissed and burbled loudly as the final drops of water passed through its innards.

"Hope you like it strong. It gets me through the day."

He was talking to them as if they were new clients—as if they were of this earth. That was a mistake.

Nathanuel laughed suddenly, harshly. It was how the angel imagined a human laugh should sound, but no human would have recognized as laughter the strange barking noise that sounded entirely bestial.

Remy looked over at the Seraphim leader.

"Something wrong?"

Nathanuel continued to stare at him. "You need coffee to keep you going. That is amusing."

Remy turned back to the coffeepot. "Yeah, a real riot." He set two mugs down, a black and an olive green, then looked toward the other Seraphim who were still engrossed in the empty wall behind his desk. "Anybody else? I've got a whole pot here."

None responded, showing as much life as department store mannequins.

"They are not as . . . daring as I," offered Nathanuel.

He watched as Remy, carrying the two mugs of steaming coffee, careful not to spill them, walked to his chair behind the desk.

"Please, take a seat." Remy motioned with his chin to the angel leader as he prepared to sit.

Nathanuel looked at the comfortable chair to the

right of the desk, his shiny, dark eyes taking in every detail.

"Yes, that would be fine."

The others were suddenly attentive, watching their leader as he sat, as fascinated with that act as they had been with the wall.

Remy had placed his cup on a cardboard coaster advertising the latest in light beers. He tossed another coaster in front of the Seraphim before placing Nathanuel's coffee mug atop it. "How do you like it? Cream? Sugar? I drink mine black."

The Seraphim leader studied the steaming mug on the desk in front of him. He reached out with both hands, gripped the cup, and brought it stiffly to his face. The angels standing around him leaned forward in unison.

"I will drink it as you do," Nathanuel answered.

The Seraphim leaned closer still, watching with rapt attention as their leader brought the steaming cup to his lips and gulped the scalding fluid.

"Careful, that's hot," Remy cautioned.

Then he watched the angel's expression turn from fascination to sudden pain and confusion as the hot liquid burned his throat. Coffee dribbled from the corners of his mouth, leaving angry red welts.

"You're supposed to sip it," Remy said shortly. "Coffee is for sipping."

"I do not see the enjoyment in this," Nathanuel said coldly, gently touching the seared flesh with his unusually long fingertips.

He set his mug down on the desk, ignoring the coaster, as the others hovered over him, studying his burns and nodding their agreement with his assessment.

Remy took a sip from his own cup. The angels now studied his every movement. "Practice," he said, savoring the hot refreshment.

Then he set his mug down and met Nathanuel's black, soulless gaze. "So, what are you doing here?" he asked. "I'm smart enough to know that this isn't a social call. Heaven doesn't work like that—or it least it never used to." He picked up a pen and tapped it impatiently on a notepad before him.

Nathanuel squirmed, the burns already starting to fade. "The experience of being human—it is not to my liking."

Remy shrugged, leaning back in his chair.

"It's not for everybody. What do you want?"

The angel leader smiled. It didn't look right; far too many teeth. It reminded Remy of a trip to the New England Aquarium, where he was given the opportunity to take a good, long look at a shark. He remembered staring at the gray-skinned beast as it gracefully cut through the water in search of prey—an animal to fear.

Nathanuel's smile was suddenly gone. "Masquerading as one of the Creator's special monkeys brings you pleasure. I do not see it."

Remy leaned forward again, his eyes blinking angrily. "I'm not asking you to. What I am asking, for the last time, is what you want."

The Seraphim leader seemed taken aback by Remy's open hostility, as he looked to his brothers and then back to the detective. "We have need of you, Remiel, not as an angel, but as what you pretend to be."

Remy didn't like the sound of that and quickly rose from his seat. He definitely needed more coffee. The Seraphim were silent, their heads turning smoothly, following his every move. He poured himself another full cup, set the half-empty container down, and took a sip.

"You need what I pretend to be? Explain," he demanded.

Nathanuel again tried a smile. It was equally as horrible as his first try. "Do not pretend that you have not felt something amiss in the natural world. You have not so completely disconnected yourself from your true origins."

The detective thought of the bizarre events of the past few days, his visit to the hospital that afternoon weighing especially heavily on his mind.

"You feel it as we do," Nathanuel continued. "You see it with your faux human eyes."

Remy placed his cup on top of the refrigerator and leaned back against an old steam radiator. "People aren't dying," he said quietly. "Souls aren't being claimed. Is that what this is about?"

"Israfil is missing," Nathanuel answered in a flat, emotionless tone. "The Angel of Death has disappeared."

Remy had already suspected the truth, but hearing it come from the mouths of creatures such as these made it twice as disturbing.

"The scrolls are missing as well," Nathanuel added, interrupting Remy's thoughts.

He didn't think it was possible, but the situation was actually getting worse.

"From the expression on your face, we see that you understand the magnitude of this problem," the Seraphim leader said.

Remy returned to his desk with his drink, not sure of how to respond.

"The scrolls—have any been opened?" he asked.

Slowly, Nathanuel shook his head. "But the forces that will be called down upon the world if they should be opened have already sensed that something is amiss. They are restless."

Remy looked down at the star shape he had doodled on his notepad earlier. He picked up his pen and drew a circle around it. He could feel the eyes of the Seraphim upon him, and looked up into their dark gaze. He knew why they had come—what they wanted from him.

"You want me to find Israfil."

Nathanuel brought his hands together in a silent clap and then pointed at Remy with a long index finger. He noticed the Seraphim leader's fingers had no nails, another unimportant feature of the human design.

"That is what your God wants, Archangel."

"Why me?" he asked. "Last time I checked, I wasn't quite in favor with the Heavenly powers."

Nathanuel thought for a moment, cocking his head, birdlike, to one side. "You are the best of both worlds, so to speak. You are of Heaven, but you also know the ways of man."

Remy laughed nervously, tapping the notepad with his pen.

"You mean to tell me that with all your power, you can't find one of your own?"

There was a flash of something in Nathanuel's black eyes. Anger, perhaps. The angel did not care to be questioned. He never had.

"Israfil is one of our most powerful. For reasons unknown, he has chosen to hide his presence from us."

Remy was getting close to the meat of the problem.

"Why?" he asked. "Why is the Angel of Death hiding? Why has he forsaken his responsibilities? You must know something more."

Again there was a spark in those horrible, incomplete eyes. The corners of Nathanuel's mouth began to twitch. The others watched their master, alert to the growing intensity of his mood.

"As you are well aware, this world has an adverse effect on certain members of our kind. It makes them take leave of their senses."

The other Seraphim again nodded in agreement with Nathanel's words.

"We believe that Israfil has grown too enamored with this place and the human animals that populate it. There is a chance he may have gone so far as to don human form and move amongst them."

Remy smiled, but there was little humor in it.

"Heaven forbid."

"There are even rumors that he may have become romantically involved with one of the natives," Nathanuel said, a look of disgust spreading across his long, pallid features. "It's almost more than I can bear."

A spark of anger ignited in Remy.

"The way you talk and look at me, Nathanuel, it's as if you blame me for Israfil's actions."

The Seraphim chief slowly rose from his seat. The others stepped back, allowing their leader his space.

"In Heaven, you are looked upon as a rebel, Remiel of the host Seraphim. And for reasons unbeknownst to me, some find what you have done . . . attractive."

Remy stood as well, placing the tips of his fingers on the desktop and leaning forward.

"What if I were to tell you that I don't want anything more to do with our kind, now or in the future? What if I told you to find the Angel of Death yourself?"

Nathanuel smiled yet again. There may have been progress there, but it disappeared too quickly to tell.

"You play the part so well, Remiel, so full of righteousness and anger. You must be enjoying yourself."

The detective had had enough. "Get out," he told them. "You and the news you bring have nothing to do with me. I'm not part of that world anymore. I'm sorry, but I can't help."

Nathanuel's stare grew more intense, the wet surface of his shiny black eyes seeming to roil. "And what world will you be part of when the seals are broken, the scrolls unfurled, and the Horsemen rain death and destruction down upon this one? Will you then seek the forgiveness of Heaven? I'm curious."

Remy bit his tongue as he attempted to keep his anger in check. Nathanuel turned and slowly made his way toward the door. The other Seraphim followed. At the door, he stopped and looked back at Remy.

"Find Israfil or don't—it matters not to me. The Creator dispatched us with this message for you, and we have performed our appointed task. He always did have a soft spot for this miserable ball of dirt and its filthy inhabitants."

The door had not opened, but the other Seraphim were suddenly gone.

"Hey, Nathanuel," Remy called, taking his seat again.

There was genuine annoyance on the angel's human countenance.

He certainly is learning quickly.

Remy picked up his coffee mug and drained the last of its contents. It was cold, bitter. Similar to how he was feeling. He gestured to the angel chief with the empty mug.

"We didn't discuss my fee. You don't expect me to work for nothing, do you?"

"Fee, yes," Nathanuel answered thoughtfully, slowly nodding his head. "Is averting the Apocalypse not payment enough?"

Remy leaned back in the chair, putting his feet up on the desk. "Sounds fair to me," he said with a wry smile. "Pleasure doing business with you."

The afternoon was shot.

Remy still sat at his desk, chair pushed back as far as it could go. Hands behind his head, he gazed up, deep in thought, at the cracked plaster ceiling. Everything that had happened since yesterday now made a twisted sort of sense.

The Angel of Death was missing. It explained everything: Mountgomery and Carol Weir, the cries of the trapped souls at Mass General, pleading to be set free.

He thought about how huge this was, how everything that lived upon the planet, everything that exhibited some form of sentience, human or not, had a soul and would be affected. Without Israfil, nothing could die; no matter the level of suffering, the solace of death would remain unattainable.

And then it hit him like a ton of bricks dropped from the Prudential Tower.

"Shit," he said, putting his hands over his face as he sat forward in the chair, the enormity of what had been dropped into his lap finally sinking in. "Shit. Shit. Shit."

Remy grabbed his mug and stood, heading to the coffeepot for a refill. His hand was shaking as he picked up the carafe, and it took a concentrated effort for him to keep from spilling the hot drink.

He replaced the pot on the burner and slowly brought his hand up to his face to gaze at the still-trembling digits. He could feel his heart rate quicken, the blood pound through his body. It was times such as this when he truly felt like them.

When he believed that he really understood what it was like to be human.

But this . . . this is all so much bigger than that.

Remy carefully picked up his mug, leaning forward for a large, slurping sip so as not to spill coffee on himself. He returned to his desk, mind racing. The more thought he put into it, the worse the situation became.

As if it wasn't bad enough that the Angel of Death was missing, but with the five scrolls gone as well . . .

Remy shuddered, trying to force thoughts of the Apocalypse from his mind.

He had some more of his coffee and then tried to distract himself with work. He turned on the computer that sat on the corner of the desk. He had to finish the estimate on a surveillance job he'd been offered, as well as the final bill for services to Mrs. Mountgomery, but no matter how hard he tried, he just couldn't get it together.

Remy couldn't stop thinking about the Angel of Death, and the Horsemen galloping toward the end of the world.

Exasperated, he finally switched off the computer and gathered up his things, resigned to the fact that nothing was going to be done in the office that day. Whenever he felt this way, there was only one thing that could help him focus.

As he shut off the office light and closed the door behind him, Remy noticed that he could still smell a lingering scent of the angelic, and made a mental note to bring a scented candle from home, just in case the loathsome stink was still there when he returned to the office tomorrow.

First he would stop off at home to pick up Marlowe.

His mind a jumble with thoughts of Seraphim, angels of death, and a possible apocalypse, Remy knew he had to see Madeline.

He needed to see his wife.

Marlowe tensed, his dark brown eyes riveted to the yellow-green tennis ball clutched in Madeline's bony hand.

She made the gesture to throw, once . . . twice, before finally letting the ball fly across the well-kept lawn at the back of the Cresthaven Nursing Center.

Her laugh is the most wonderful thing to hear, Remy

mused as they both watched the black dog bound across the grass in pursuit of his prize.

The weather was warm again, with just the slightest tease of the cooler months to come, but Madeline still pulled her sweater tight about her dwindling frame as she sat in the green plastic chair.

"He looks good," she said to Remy standing beside her, watching as the dog happily snatched up the ball and rolled around in his mouth. "Thought for sure he'd be fat with all the crap you give him."

"Me?" Remy said with a laugh. "Who's chair did he sit beside every morning, waiting for toast?"

"Oh, those were just little pieces of bread," Madeline said, and clapped her hands together, summoning Marlowe back to her. "That never hurt him."

She gave Remy a smile and that sly look out of the corner of her eye that even after fifty years of marriage still got to him. He put his arm around her and she leaned into his side, resting her head on his hip.

"I miss him terribly," she said wistfully.

Marlowe trotted back toward them, ball held proudly in his mouth. Until suddenly, something distracted the goofy animal, probably a smell in the grass that he hadn't noticed before, and he dropped the ball, sniffing furiously.

"And don't even get me started on how I feel about being away from you," Madeline continued quietly.

Remy felt an invisible fist squeeze tightly around his heart. "Then come home," he said, watching as the dog rooted around in the grass. "We'll go in right now, gather up your things, and bring you back to Beacon Hill."

"I'm sick, Remy," she said, head still resting against his hip.

"I'll take care of you."

Madeline raised her hand to his butt and patted it lovingly. "You're a good guy," she said, sounding weaker than he ever remembered hearing her sound. "But it wouldn't be fair to you, or to Marlowe. The kind of care I need . . ."

"I told you I'd take care of you."

"And you would. I haven't a doubt in my mind about it, but that's where the trouble would start."

Remy looked down at her then, seeing past the illness that was slowly stealing her life away, staring into the eyes of the woman who had taught him the beauty and power of love, and to whom he had so willingly given his heart.

"I can't have you sitting around watching me die," she told him with a slight shake of her head.

Remy looked away, hating to hear her talk about the inevitable. Marlowe had found a new friend. An old man in a heavy winter jacket sat in his wheelchair, patting Marlowe's big head while the dog did everything he could to try and lick the old-timer's face.

Madeline took Remy's hand in a disturbingly icy grip, pulling his attention back to her. "I know you don't like to hear me talk about it, but it's all right," she said with a small smile. "I know I'm going to die, Remy, and I accept that, but I don't want you to die with me."

He was suddenly thinking about Nathanuel's visit to his office—about the missing Angel of Death, and what it meant to the world.

What it means to me.

"What if I told you that you weren't going to die," he said aloud, before he even knew the words were coming out of his mouth.

"I'd say that you were kidding yourself. I am dying, Remy. No matter how much you hate to think about it. I have cancer, and I will die soon."

One of the nursing assistants had picked up Marlowe's ball and was playing with him now.

"Nathanuel came to visit me today," Remy said, holding Madeline's hand tighter, willing some of his own warmth into her icy grip.

"Nathanuel ... the angel Nathanuel?" she asked with disbelief. His wife was fully aware of his past dealings with the Seraphim, how they felt about him, and his feelings toward them. "What on earth did he want from you?"

"Israfil is missing," he said, looking back to her.

"Israfil," she repeated. He could tell she was playing with the name inside her head.

"The Angel of Death," he clarified. "The Angel of Death has gone missing, and there's nobody doing his job."

Madeline let go of his hand suddenly, grabbing at the collar of her sweater, pulling it up closer around her neck as if protecting herself from a sudden chill. "Does this have anything to do with the case you were talking about yesterday? The one where the man could actually see you?"

Remy nodded. "It does," he explained. "Before he shot himself, he said that he'd been dreaming about the end of the world."

"Then he killed himself," she stated, her voice almost a whisper.

Remy slowly shook his head. "He tried ... but he hasn't died."

And then it seemed to hit her. He could see the meaning of his words flooding into her expression. She reached for his hand again, pulling herself to her feet.

"Nobody is doing his job," she repeated, her stare intensifying. "Nothing is dying."

He took her into his arms, hugging her close to him, not caring if anyone noticed the intimacy in the embrace between the supposed mother and son.

"They want you to find him, don't they?" Madeline

said, her cheek pressed against his chest. "They want you to find Israfil."

"Yes." Remy held her tightly.

She pulled away from him slightly, looking up, trying to find his eyes, but Remy was looking elsewhere, focusing on the dog at play, doing everything he could to not think of the repercussions of what he had been asked to do.

"You're going to do it . . . right?" Madeline asked.

Remy remained silent.

"Remy?"

He lowered his gaze to finally meet hers and saw that she was crying.

"I know what you're thinking," she told him, her voice trembling with emotion. She raised a hand to his face, cupping his cheek. The hand was freezing, but at the moment Remy could feel nothing.

"And I want you to stop."

Remy brought his hand up to hers, taking it from his face and kissing it softly.

"I love you," he said, the words almost excruciatingly painful as they left his mouth.

"And I love you too," she told him. "But I don't want to live if it has to be this way. I need to go soon, darling," Madeline said. "I don't want to, but I'll need to. Do you understand?"

He nodded, understanding completely, but not wanting to accept it.

"I love you now, and will always love you, Remy Chandler," Madeline said, smiling at him wistfully. And he was reminded of his wedding day, when she had said the very same thing to him.

"And I love you now, and always will, Madeline Chandler."

"That's nice," she said, and hugged him again.

Remy hugged her back, kissing the top of her gray

head. And they stood there like that for quite some time, breaking apart only when Marlowe finally found his way back to them, tennis ball in his mouth.

"There he is," Madeline said happily, and Marlowe's tail began to wag. She squatted down, putting her arms around the black dog, hugging him close, pressing her face to his. "Thank you so much for coming to visit me, you goofy thing."

Marlowe licked her face, and she began to laugh.

Again, Remy thought of how much he loved that sound.

And how much he would miss it when it was gone.

CHAPTER FIVE

"Maddie come home?" Marlowe asked from the back-seat of the car, tilting his head and pointing his moist, jet-black nose toward the flow of air coming in from the partially open windows.

"No," Remy responded more sharply than he meant to as he tried to navigate Huntington Avenue's rush-hour traffic.

It had to have been the fourth time the dog had asked about Madeline since they'd left Cresthaven. Remy understood exactly where the pup was coming from, which just made it all the harder for him to explain why Marlowe's favorite female wasn't going to return to the pack.

Remy brought the car to a gradual stop at a traffic light near the Pru and casually looked into the rear-view mirror to check on his buddy. He found himself staring into the dark, reflective eyes of the Labrador.

"Why?" the dog asked.

Remy sighed, turning the corner as the light changed to green.

"You know why," he told the animal. "Madeline's sick and needs to stay at the get-well place, where they'll take care of her."

The dog's head suddenly turned, zeroing in on a

particularly interesting scent as they made their way down Boylston Street toward the Public Garden. Remy hoped that he would lose interest in the discussion of Madeline, but that wasn't the case.

"When?"

They always ended up in this uncomfortable place. He could tell Marlowe just about anything: tomorrow, two weeks from tomorrow, a year from next Tuesday, and to the simple animal it all meant pretty much the same thing. The dog, as with almost all animals, had no real concept of the passage of time. He lived for the moment, the now. That was what Marlowe truly wanted. He wanted Madeline home with them now, probably just as much as Remy himself did. Marlowe wanted the pack to be whole again, wanted life to be how it used to be.

How it was *supposed* to be.

But things had changed, and life never would be the same again. And how did he explain to this simple, loving animal that what it desired most could never be? Remy was the alpha male . . . the master, the provider. How could he not make this happen?

Instead, Remy ignored the dog, concentrating on getting home as quickly as possible. The remainder of the ride was filled with silent tension as Remy waited for the animal to press the issue, but Marlowe chose not to. In fact, he seemed more concerned with barking a greeting through the open window every now and again as they passed people walking their dogs.

The gods of parking must have been feeling especially benevolent, for Remy managed to find a space right on Hancock Street, near the State House. With a dazzling display of parallel parking—*one of the most difficult things I've had to master as a human*—Remy parked the Toyota for the night.

After a leisurely walk back to the brownstone, Remy

retrieved his mail from the basket in the foyer and, unlocking the inner door, let them both into the hallway. The house was stuffy, and he walked around opening the windows to let in some fresh air. Marlowe followed at his heels, sniffing the influx of air for anything of interest.

Remy glanced at the wall clock as he left the living room, and saw that it was past the dog's supper time.

"Hey, pal, want to eat?" he asked, going into the kitchen. He got the dog some fresh water and then went to a cabinet beneath one of the counters for the container of Marlowe's food. With a plastic measuring cup he filled the dog's bowl and turned to put it down.

Marlowe still stood just inside the doorway, his stare intense. Normally the Lab would have been pushing Remy out of the way to get at his supper, but tonight something was different. There was a look in the animal's eyes that the angel immediately understood— the conversation that had begun in the car was not yet over.

"When?" Marlowe said pointedly.

Remy set the bowl down on the place mat next to Marlowe's water. The Labrador still didn't move, showing a self-control that he'd never displayed before.

The dog continued to stare, and finally Remy knelt, calling the Labrador to him. Tentatively, Marlowe approached, head low, ears flat, obviously thinking he was in trouble.

"Not bad," he grumbled.

"No, not bad," Remy said with a sad smile. He pulled the dog closer and lovingly rubbed the animal's ears. "You're a good boy, a very good boy."

He took Marlowe's blocky head in his hands and held his face close to his own. The dog's pink tongue shot out, licking Remy's face affectionately.

"I am good boy," he agreed, tailing wagging. *"I am."*

"Yes you are, but we need to talk about Madeline."

Marlowe's tail slowed, dropping down, only twitching slightly. *"When coming home?"*

Remy gently held the dog's face, gazing into his deep, brown eyes. "She's not," he said firmly, feeling his own heart break with the words. "Madeline has to stay at the get-well place, Marlowe. They are going to take care of her there, because we can't do that here."

The dog whined sadly. *"No. Want Maddie. Now. Want Maddie. Home."*

"I'm sorry," Remy said. "But she is not coming home. She's very sick and . . ." He paused, trying to find the right words. There wasn't any easy way to say it, so he simply let the words come. "She's going to die, Marlowe."

The animal tried to pull away, but Remy held him in place.

"No die," he whined, the nails on his feet clicking upon the tiled floor. *"No die."*

Remy let the dog go and he left the kitchen, tail tucked between his legs. "I'm sorry," he called after the animal, and no truer words were ever spoken.

"I'm so, so sorry."

Remy thought he might be able to relax a bit by watching some of his favorite home-improvement shows, but he never got that far.

The evening news caught his attention, every story worse than the one before it. Escalating violence in the Middle East, hunger and disease running rampant in the African nations, and then the disconcerting report on how scientists from all over the world had begun to take note of a sudden decrease in death rates, and how dangerous it was becoming to an already strained ecosystem.

Dangerous isn't the word, Remy thought with a sigh, picking up the remote from the arm of his chair and turning off the set before yet another story could send him plummeting further into the depths of depression.

The evening had become pretty much a wash, and Remy decided that he might as well go up to bed. Maybe a few more chapters of *Farewell My Lovely* would help ease his funk.

He headed for the kitchen, calling Marlowe, for one last trip outside. When the canine didn't answer, Remy strolled down the hallway to the spare room that the dog had claimed for his own. The black Labrador was curled into a tight ball on his tattered blanket, the floor about him strewn with stuffed toys.

"I'm going to bed now," Remy said. "Do you need to go outside?"

"No outside," the dog mumbled, not even lifting his head.

"Are you sure?" Remy asked.

"Sure," the dog answered, obviously still very upset over the news that Madeline was not returning to his pack.

"Well, good night, then," the angel said, waiting to see if the dog was going to join him in bed, as he often did. But Marlowe remained in his own place, closing his eyes with an elongated sigh. He didn't even want his bedtime snack.

"I guess I'll see you in the morning."

In all actuality, Remy didn't have to sleep, but he had learned to do so out of boredom and loneliness during the early morning hours while he waited for the rest of the world to awaken. It hadn't taken him long to teach himself, and he soon found that he quite enjoyed the act of shutting down to recharge his batteries. It felt good to escape the constant conflict between his angelic nature and the human guise he worked so hard to maintain, even if it was for just a short time.

Once again Remy found it difficult to focus on Chandler's words, and finally decided that it was time to call it a night. He laid the book facedown on his bedside table and was reaching to turn off the light when he sensed that he was no longer alone.

Marlowe stood in the doorway to the bedroom, staring.

"What is it, bud? Do you have to go outside?"

"Leave pack too?" the animal asked. *"Leave Marlowe like Maddie?"*

Remy sighed, a wave of empathy for the animal's sadness passing over him. "No, Marlowe," he said gently. "I won't leave you."

He patted an area of bed beside him, and the Labrador bounded from the doorway up onto the bed, tail twitching nervously. Remy rubbed the dog's floppy black ears, allowing the animal to lick his face.

"You're the best boy," Remy told him. "How could I ever leave you, huh? How could I?"

"Marlowe best," the dog said, happily panting. *"Marlowe best boy ever."*

"Yes, you are," he told the animal. "Why don't you lie down now?"

The dog plopped heavily beside him, and even though there was plenty of room for both of them, his butt was pressed firmly against Remy's leg as he settled down.

"That's a good boy." Remy patted Marlowe's side. "We'll get a good night's rest and be able to look at things more clearly in the morning. How does that sound?"

"Love Remy," Marlowe said, tail thumping upon the mattress, looking, with deep, soulful eyes, over his shoulder at the angel.

"I love you too, pal," Remy answered, reaching over to turn off the bedside light. "Now let's get some sleep."

Remy lay in the darkness, the rhythmic changes in Marlowe's breathing as he gradually drifted off helping him to relax.

It wasn't long before he too was asleep.

And dreaming.

It was like something out of a spaghetti western.

Remy found himself standing in front of an old train station. The wood of the place was weather beaten and dry, and the floorboards creaked noisily as he shifted his weight.

The angel was alone.

He looked out across the broad expanse of desert, following the dark, metal tracks as they curved off into the horizon, where an angry orange sun was just starting to rise. A sudden wind kicked up, blowing thick clouds of dust and sand off the desert, and Remy shielded his eyes from the grit and grime. He looked down at himself and saw that he was wearing his Brooks Brothers suit—his best suit—the one that he wore to weddings and funerals. Offhandedly, he wondered what the occasion was.

At first, he mistook the sound for the wind, a low, moaning sound that seemed to come up out of nowhere, filling the empty expanse around him. But then he heard it in tandem with another sound, and he knew exactly what it was.

A train was coming.

He put a hand upon his brow and squinted into the morning light.

The train appeared as an unsightly blotch against the orange of the rising sun, a thick plume of black smoke trailing from its smokestack.

Remy walked down the length of platform toward the

oncoming locomotive. It was big, larger than any train he'd ever seen before, its metal body blacker than the smoke that plumed from its unusually tall stack. But it wasn't just its appearance that was strange; the way the train moved along the track was almost as if it were somehow more than just a machine—strangely alive, like some huge, prehistoric predator, slithering down the length of track, following the scent of its prey.

He knew then, as he stood upon the lonely platform, that the train coming into the station carried no more than four riders. And each of these riders brought with them a means by which to begin the Apocalypse.

The Horsemen were coming.

And the end of all things followed them.

Remy awakened with a start, the image of the fearsome locomotive barreling toward him as he stood upon the station platform seared into his mind's eye.

His heart was racing, and a fine sheen of sweat covered his entire body. He lay in bed, staring up at the ceiling, an occasional car passing by on the street below causing oddly shaped shadows to slide across the white surface. But he paid them little attention; his thoughts replaying the events of the bizarre dream.

He heard the train whistle, moaning somewhere in the back of his memory, the rhythmic pulse of the locomotive engine as it drew closer.

The Horsemen on the way.

It was then that he realized he was alone. He turned his head on the pillow, looking for Marlowe where he'd normally be, curled up into a tight ball near his head. But the dog wasn't there.

He sat up, looking down at the foot of the bed. He wasn't there either.

Remy was about to call out the dog's name when he heard a soft whimper from somewhere in the room.

"Marlowe?" Remy asked in the darkness.

Something scrabbled beneath the bed, nails scraping across the hardwood floor. Remy rose and knelt down, lifting the blanket and sheets that hung over the side of the bed and peering beneath. Marlowe's dark, glistening eyes stared back at him.

"What the heck are you doing under there?" Remy asked the animal.

"Scared," the dog told him.

"Scared of what?"

"Something coming . . . something big."

Remy felt an electric jolt of surprise. Had the animal shared his dream? "A train?" he asked. "Did you dream about a train?"

"Train," the dog agreed. *"Train coming. Bad. Scared."*

Remy reached into the shadows and scratched the dog behind the ear. "You don't have to be afraid," he soothed him. "Come on out."

"Scared," the dog said again.

"Well, okay, then," Remy said, dropping the sheets and beginning to stand. "Guess I'll just have to go for a walk by myself."

"Walk?" Marlowe barked, creating a racket as he clambered to extract his seventy-five pounds from the cramped confines beneath the bed.

"I thought you were too scared," Remy said, slipping on a pair of dark gray sweatpants.

Marlowe emerged from his hiding place, standing alert, tail wagging furiously, his fear already forgotten.

"Yeah," Remy chuckled as he pulled a sweatshirt on over his head.

"Walk."

CHAPTER SIX

Remy loved the dawn.

If the day before was lousy, it was a chance to try it all again. And if the new day didn't work out, well, there was always tomorrow.

A fresh start every day.

Before he had abandoned his angelic nature, there had been no dawn, no todays or tomorrows for him. After all, what was the passage of time to a being that would live forever? If nothing else, his decision to live as a human among them had made him realize how precious each new day really was.

Marlowe trotted along beside him, his chain collar jingling cheerfully. They stopped at the corner of Joy and Beacon streets, and Marlowe's tail began to wag happily as he caught sight of the Boston Common across the way.

"*Common,*" he said, over and over again, his pink tongue flopping from the side of his mouth as he panted excitedly.

"Can't pull the wool over your eyes, can I, pal?" Remy said, eyeing the early morning traffic.

A yellow *Boston Herald* truck slowed down with a squeal of old brakes, and the driver motioned for them to cross.

Remy waved his thanks, then gave a gentle tug on the leather leash. "C'mon," he said to Marlowe, and the two sprinted across the street and down the granite steps into the Common.

It was still relatively dark in the park, the sun not yet high enough to penetrate through the trees. Remy scanned the shadows, and seeing only a few joggers on the paths here and there, reached down to unclip the leash from Marlowe's collar. There was a leash law in Boston, but as long as it wasn't crowded and the dog didn't bother anybody, Remy didn't see the harm in letting him run a bit.

"Don't bother any of the joggers," he reminded, releasing the Labrador.

"No bother," Marlowe agreed, and trotted off through the trees. His black form merged with the shadows, the glint of the chain around his neck sometimes the only thing separating the dog from the darkness as he darted from tree to tree, nose pressed to the grass.

Marlowe was searching for rats. There was nothing the retriever loved more than chasing rats in the early morning hours on Boston Common. Remy didn't have to worry about his four-legged friend catching any of the vermin that prowled the public park; it was all about the chase with Marlowe.

The Boston Common and adjacent Public Garden formed Boston's equivalent of New York's Central Park. It was the oldest public park in the United States, and Remy could actually remember when its land was used for cattle grazing, and when British troops had camped here before marching out to face Colonial resistance at Lexington and Concord.

It seemed like only yesterday to him, but then again, so did the fall of the Roman Empire.

A sudden excited bark drew him from his memories, and Remy searched the darkness for his dog, finding him in the distance in hot pursuit of a decent-sized rat. "Careful!" he called out to the animal, but he needn't have worried.

At the sound of Remy's voice, the dog abandoned his chase and ran to him. *"Rat!"* Marlowe exclaimed, his normally soulful brown eyes wild with excitement.

"Certainly was," Remy replied. "And a big one at that."

"Big rat," the dog agreed.

"Listen, I'm going over to the bandstand to look for Lazarus. Why don't you see if you can find some more rats?" Remy suggested.

Marlowe was off in a flash, nose to the ground in search of new prey.

Remy turned and headed for the far corner of the Common. It was lighter now, and the city on either side of the park was slowly coming alive. There were more people in the park: walkers; runners; bike riders; a gaggle of old Chinese women doing t'ai chi; a few businessmen, briefcases in hand, walking with robotic purpose down the twisting paths toward the financial district or the Park Street T station.

As Remy neared the bandstand, he could see an encampment of sleeping bags, blankets, and shopping carts filled with all manner of refuse near its base. It would be getting colder soon, and the Common would no longer supply the city's homeless with the freedom they so craved. Some would rather die than spend a night in a shelter, and the bitter New England winters often obliged.

A man wrapped in a heavy green blanket was leaning back against a tree, smoking a cigarette. He was the only one of the group that appeared to be awake, and he eyed Remy suspiciously as he approached.

"Morning," Remy said cheerfully. "Lazarus around?"

The man snarled, showing off a set of yellowed

teeth. "Who wants to know?" he asked, finishing his cigarette and pulling his blanket closer around him.

"A friend," Remy replied, and he could almost feel the man's eyes scrutinizing him, searching for any sign that he wasn't telling the truth. "Is he at the bandstand?" Remy continued, reaching into the pocket of his sweatshirt and pulling out a twenty-dollar bill.

The man slowly nodded.

Stepping closer, Remy bent down and held out the folded money to the transient. "Why don't you buy some breakfast for you and your buddies," he said. "Bagels and coffee would be good. It feels like that kind of day."

Without a word, the homeless man's hand snaked out from beneath the blanket and snatched the offering.

Remy rose and headed down the brick walkway toward the Parkman Bandstand. His thoughts again drifted to the past, memories of warm summer nights with Madeline, the music of Mozart and Beethoven wafting from the circular concrete structure while they sat upon a blanket, sipping wine from paper cups.

A bittersweet smile played at the corners of his mouth; this memory seemed even farther away than revolutions and the fall of empires. He made a mental note to call Cresthaven, just to hear his wife's voice, as soon as he went home.

It was dark on the bandstand.

"Hey, Laz?" Remy called into the shadows as he climbed the steps to the stage. "It's Remy. Are you up here?"

And then he smelled it, the sharp, metallic odor of spilled life. How many times had it filled his lungs in his countless years upon the planet?

He searched the darkness and found Lazarus on the floor, back pressed against the wrought iron railing that surrounded the structure, head slumped to his chest, arms splayed on either side of him. Then he noticed the bloody knife resting in his lap, and the dark, glistening puddles of crimson that had expanded outward from beneath the man's slashed wrists.

"Son of a bitch," Remy hissed in disgust.

When is he going to learn?

He leaned his hip against the railing and crossed his arms, looking out over the Common for a sign of his dog as he waited. He caught sight of Marlowe in the distance, sitting before an elderly couple who appeared to be eating their breakfast on one of the park benches.

Remy brought his fingers to his mouth and let out an ear-piercing whistle. The Lab glanced over his shoulder at Remy, then turned his attention back to the poor couple. Of course, they had food, and if there was one thing to say about Labrador retrievers, it was that they certainly had healthy appetites.

"Marlowe," Remy yelled. "Leave them alone and get over here."

Clearly, the dog was torn, but finally he stood, wagged his tail, and headed for the bandstand.

"That whistle could rupture eardrums," Lazarus suddenly said, and Remy looked at the crumpled figure still slumped upon the ground.

The blood that had pooled around his slashed wrists was gone, and he was closely examining the new lines of scar tissue that adorned his flesh, along with the remains of so many others.

"Any different this time?" Remy asked, pushing off the railing and walking over to Lazarus. He reached out a hand to help the man up from the ground.

Lazarus took hold of the offered hand in a powerful grip, allowing himself to be pulled to his feet. "Not really," he said, scratching at his short, black beard. "But you can never tell. . . . This could've been the time it stuck."

Remy felt the same pangs of sympathy he had when he'd first met the man nearly two thousand years before. Stricken by leprosy, Lazarus had lain dead in his tomb for four days, until the Son of God raised him.

"Lazarus, come forth."

At first, the miracle had been a blessing, but soon after, Lazarus began to realize that he was no longer aging. And finally, as he watched everyone he loved wither and die, he began to think of the Lord's gift as a curse.

Lazarus had been trying to kill himself for centuries, and who knew? Maybe someday he would succeed. But there was certainly no chance of that now, not with Israfil among the missing.

"Not this time, Laz," Remy said, slowly shaking his head. "We got big troubles brewing."

Lazarus leaned back against the metal railing, fishing through the pockets of his Navy pea coat. "Thought something might be up," he said, pulling out a crumpled pack of cigarettes. He tapped one from the pack and placed it in his mouth. "I can feel the change in the air—that's why I thought it might work this time." The unlit cigarette bobbed between his lips.

Both men glanced at the knife still lying on the ground, and Remy reached down to pick it up. It too was clean of blood.

"That's not the change you feel, I'm afraid," he said, flipping the blade in his hand to give it back to his friend, handle first. "Israfil has dropped off the radar."

"No shit," Lazarus said, carefully taking the blade and slipping it inside his coat with the pack of cigarettes.

"You're not dying, and neither is anybody—or anything—else."

Lazarus reached up and took the unlit smoke from his mouth. "Got a light?" he asked.

Remy shook his head. "Sorry."

"Things'll kill me anyway," he chuckled, shoving the cigarette back inside his pocket. There wasn't a hint of humor in the laughter, only a deep, tortured sadness.

Lazarus was tired of living, and Remy had even gone so far as to promise the man that if ever there came an opportunity to find the solution to his problem, he would help him—free of charge. It was the least he could do, for Lazarus had helped him out on a number of cases. He had a real knack for hearing things on the street, which was why Remy had sought him out this morning.

"So the Angel of Death is missing," Lazarus said, running his hands through his long, matted black hair. "That's bad, man . . . real bad."

Remy nodded. "I had a visit from the family and everything."

"No shit," Lazarus said again. "Seraphim?"

"Nathanuel and the boys came by the office, coerced me into finding our wayward angel."

Lazarus leaned out over the railing of the bandstand, lifting his face to the early morning light. "I knew something was up," he said, eyes closed, sniffing at the air. "Smells all wrong. Out of balance. Now it makes sense."

"I was hoping you might have heard something," Remy said, before the jangling of Marlowe's collar interrupted the two men. Remy turned as the dog bounded up the stone steps. "There he is," he said, a smile that he couldn't have stopped even if he had wanted to spreading across his face.

Marlowe's tail wagged as he headed toward Remy. "Catch anything?" he asked, rubbing the panting dog's neck.

Lazarus clapped his hands together and squatted down as the dog trotted over to him. "How's my boy?"

He rubbed and patted Marlowe as the Lab twisted and turned, making sure Lazarus hit all the hot spots, before finally stopping as the man began to scratch that spot just above his tail.

"How come I always end up scratching your ass?" Lazarus asked.

"Like it," the dog answered, as he wiggled his hindquarters, claws clicking on the cement floor of the bandstand.

"What did he say?" Lazarus asked Remy.

"He says that he likes it."

"Then that's good enough for me," the immortal said, scratching with both hands now.

"As I was saying before we were interrupted for more important things," Remy said sarcastically, his dog looking up at him with hooded, pleasure-filled eyes, "I was hoping that you might've heard something."

Lazarus gave the dog a final pat before rising to his full height, knees cracking noisily. "Nothing," he said. "But I'll see if I can't flip over a few stones. Might be able to find something."

"I appreciate it," Remy said, reaching into the pocket of his sweats again and coming out with some more folded bills, which he handed to the man.

"Ditto," Lazarus said, slipping the money into his own pocket. "I'll be in touch."

Remy looked to his dog, who was now lying beside Lazarus' feet. "You hanging with Lazarus today, or are you coming with me?"

Marlowe tilted his head curiously. *"Going now?"*

"Yeah, you coming?"

"Coming," Marlowe answered, climbing to his feet and following Remy, Lazarus already forgotten.

They had just reached the brick path when Remy heard Lazarus call out to him. He turned to see the immortal man leaning over the metal railing.

"Have you talked to *them* yet?"

"Them?" Remy asked, before realizing who it was that Lazarus meant. "Oh, them," he said, shaking his head. "No, I haven't."

"Might not be such a bad idea. They usually have a good handle on what you Heavenly types are up to. You know, birds of a feather and all that shit."

Remy nodded. "Yeah, birds of a feather," he repeated, turning away with a wave.

And all that shit.

Remy and Mulvehill sat on either side of a small metal table outside Starbucks at the corner of Cambridge and New Chardon streets. Remy sipped his coffee, watching Mulvehill over the brim of his cup.

"Are you all right?" he asked, as his friend reached for his own cup, not quite able to hide the tremor in his hand.

"I'm fine," Mulvehill said, making an annoyed face. "Why wouldn't I be? I hear this kind of shit every day." He carefully sipped at the hot coffee. "Could use something a little stronger than cream in this, though."

Remy remained silent, tearing a piece from a cinnamon-raisin bagel and feeding it to Marlowe, who was lying at his feet under the table.

"Last night," Mulvehill finally began, "I caught a case—guy took an aluminum baseball bat to his five-year-old daughter. Beat her so badly that nearly every bone in her body was shattered, and even though there wasn't any logical reason for it, she was still alive. Crying for her mommy, and still alive." He shook his head. "Christ, I need a cigarette. Goddamn city—pretty soon it'll be illegal to smoke in your own house." Instead, he took a long drink from his coffee cup.

"How the fuck could the Angel of Death walk away

from his job?" Mulvehill asked, leaning forward and dropping his voice.

Remy ripped another hunk of bagel away and fed it to the drooling dog. "I don't know," he replied. "But the Seraphim have their suspicions."

"Suspicions?" Mulvehill asked. "What? Better benefits package? More time off?"

Remy drank from his large cup of coffee. "They didn't come right out and say it, but they're blaming me."

"What do you have to do with it?"

"They suspect that Israfil may have been seduced by the ways of humanity, like they believe I was."

"What do you think?"

Remy shrugged. "I don't know."

"So this could all be your fault?"

"If you want to look at me as some kind of angelic role model, then yeah, I guess it is."

Mulvehill was silent for a few moments, staring off into space. "The other guys on the job are talking. They're all freaked out by what's happening around the city—around the world—and here I am with the answer to the fifty-thousand-dollar question." He paused before continuing, as if weighing what he was about to say. "You know, I shouldn't know about this shit."

A woman with a baby carriage walked by, and a sudden cry from within the stroller sent a spasm through Mulvehill's hand, causing him to knock over his coffee cup, what little remained inside it spilling over the table. "Son of a bitch," he hissed, grabbing up some napkins from an empty table nearby to absorb the mess.

Remy stood, adding his own napkins to the spill. His eyes locked with Mulvehill's and he could see the fear there. "It's going to be all right," he tried to reassure him.

The cop smiled, picking up the saturated napkins

and putting them inside his cup. "See, I wouldn't be having such a fucking hard time if I didn't know what was actually going on." He waved a hand in the air. "All this shit would be just that—weird shit that I wouldn't know a damn thing about . . . just as much in the dark as the next guy."

It was his turn to stare into Remy's eyes.

"I know too goddamned much," he said, looking away before Remy could even respond, taking the trash to a nearby barrel.

Remy stood, grabbing Marlowe's leash as Mulvehill returned to the table. The Labrador watched him with dark, excited eyes, his muscular tail wagging.

"Let me know if I can help," Mulvehill said. "Anything at all." He gave Marlowe one last pat. "There's not that much for a homicide cop to do when nobody's dying."

Perhaps he's right, Remy thought, watching as his friend walked away from him.

Maybe he does know too much.

CHAPTER SEVEN

He knew what he had to do, and the knowledge nagged at him for the remainder of the morning.

Remy returned to his Beacon Hill brownstone, called Madeline to wish her good morning, showered, dressed, and got Marlowe settled for the day, leaving him a banana and a couple of cookies to hold him over until supper.

Marlowe lay on his back on the couch, front paws sticking straight up into the air, back legs splayed.

"I should be back around dinnertime," Remy told him, pausing in the living room doorway on his way out.

Marlowe stared at him, upside down, with complete disinterest. Remy was interfering with his nap time.

"If I can't make it by then, I'll call Ashlie and ask her to feed you and take you out."

Marlowe's tail thumped happily on the cushion. He loved the teenaged girl who lived on the next street over. Remy thought she was pretty awesome himself, lucky that he had been able to find somebody he could trust completely with his four-legged pally.

"Don't work too hard today," he called over his shoulder as he left the house, locking the door behind him.

It was a beautiful day and Remy decided to walk the few blocks to his office. It would give him a chance to think, and he wouldn't have to waste time trying to find a parking spot on the congested Boston streets— one less thing to worry about.

He still didn't have any leads on the whereabouts of Israfil and the scrolls. He had hoped Lazarus might have heard something in his travels, but that hadn't been the case so far, and now he was left with only one other option.

He turned the corner from Charles Street onto Beacon Street and felt his irritation prickle. He hated the Watchers with a passion; and they were none too crazy about him.

In Heaven, they had been called the Grigori. They were a host of Heavenly guardians charged with safeguarding the development of the Almighty's most beloved creations—humanity—and preventing them from straying off the path of righteousness.

Yeah, that worked out well.

Remy reached his office building near the corner of Mass Ave., stepping through the door into the lobby. He took his keys from his pocket and opened up the mailbox, just in case the delivery had come early. It hadn't, so he slammed closed the rectangular metal door and headed for the stairs.

Instead of protecting humanity from corruption, the Grigori themselves had become corrupted, seduced by the primitive human ways, going native, so to speak. They began teaching the fledgling human race things they were not yet mature enough to know. And it wasn't long before humanity had mastered the art of making weapons: swords, knives, and shields—instruments of violence. But the Watchers didn't stop there, the dumb sons of bitches had actually introduced the joys of jewelry and makeup to the early females.

Remy shook his head. A lot of guys would want to see the Grigori get their asses handed to them for those reasons alone.

And get their asses handed to them, they did.

Remy reached the top of the stairs, glancing at the keys in his hand, finding the one for his office.

The Almighty was not amused. He had lashed out at the Grigori, stripping away their wings. If they so badly wanted to be human, then let it be so. He banished them to Earth, and they had been here ever since.

Remy was just about to slip the key into the lock on his office door when he felt a sudden chill, the temperature in the hallway dropping by at least ten degrees. He glanced up, curious, and noticed that the lights at the end of the hall near Rolanda's Beauty Supply had gone out, plunging the end of the corridor into total darkness. *Better give the super a call about replacing those fluorescents*, he thought.

And then the darkness began to spread, flowing toward him, swallowing the light as the wave of shadow picked up speed.

Remy didn't even have a chance to react before it was upon him.

Before *they* were upon him.

The first punch nearly broke his neck, dropping him to his knees, the taste of blood filling his mouth. The attackers were strong, inhumanly so, and their use of the darkness implied something demonic in nature. Totally blind in the sea of inky black that engulfed him, Remy couldn't be sure how many there were; it could have been two or twenty. What he did know was that if he didn't act fast, they would kill him.

He took a deep breath and surged to his feet, swinging his fists, hoping to hit something. And hit something he did, feeling his knuckles connect with dry, rough skin and listening to the satisfying grunts of pain as he lashed out again and again with strength far greater than the average human's.

Suddenly, Remy could feel his angelic nature begin to stir. Locked away, deep inside, it was roused to the brink of wakefulness as his instinct for self-preservation kicked in. It had been a long time since last he'd felt that power, and immediately he pushed it back, allowing his attackers to gain the upper hand.

That was not him anymore, and he couldn't imagine any amount of pain would ever force him to be that way again.

They were kicking him now, driving him back against the cool plaster wall. He struggled to block the blows, but he was sore and lost in the darkness, and it was becoming harder to stay focused.

And just when he thought he could take no more, the beating stopped; but within the sea of shadow, he could still hear them breathing.

"Had enough?" Remy asked, cracking wise, wiping a stinging trickle of blood from his eye.

One of them laughed, a high, wheezing sound that ended in a low, wet gurgle. "Look at you," the voice rasped, echoing in the artificial shadow. "A soldier of the Heavenly host Seraphim, beaten and bloody, cowering in the darkness. Is this what you have abandoned so much to become?"

Remy shifted his back against the wall, every joint and muscle screaming in protest as he tried to stand. He could still feel it within him—stirring—deep in the hole where he kept his true nature locked away.

That's not me anymore.

"Sorry to be such a disappointment," he grunted, sliding up the plaster wall.

"We could kill you now," the voice said coldly, and Remy could feel each word, a gentle movement against his battered cheek.

"Yeah, you probably could," he agreed, staring in the direction he imagined his attackers would be. "But I think if you were really going to, you would've done it by now."

His comment was met with a resounding silence.

"Thought so," Remy said. "Why don't you tell me what you want, so we can all get on with our day." He straightened, keeping his back against the wall, its firmness providing an anchor in the ocean of black.

"Is this how you do penance, Remiel of the Seraphim?" the voice asked. "Is this how you pay for your sins?"

The words hurt more than any of their physical blows, but Remy gritted his teeth and stared defiantly into the shadows. "What the fuck do you want?" he demanded.

Again there was laughter, only this time much closer. The voice was right in front of him, close enough to reach out and strangle.

"We strongly advise that you cease your current investigation."

"And which investigation would that be?" Remy asked, playing dumb. He knew exactly why they were here, and the implications were already filling his mind, threatening to burst his skull like an overripe melon.

"Stop it," the voice snapped, so close now that Remy could smell the stink of corruption on its breath, like it had just finished a heaping bowl of murder for breakfast. "Continue to play your human games, moving amongst them, pretending to be one of them, but leave the Death Angel to us—after all, it would be in the best interests of those to whom you have grown close and hold so very dear."

Those final words chilled Remy to the bone, and he found himself doing something all too stupid—all too human. He sprang off the wall, raising his fists to strike at his enemy, but they were ready. They avoided his blows with ease, and then they were hitting him again, knocking him back against the wall, pushing him down to the floor, the savagery of the blows bringing him close to the brink of oblivion.

And just as he was about to spiral down into the arms of unconsciousness, they stopped, and he felt the cold words of his attackers' spokesman gently teasing the flesh of his ear, making it feel as though maggots were crawling inside it.

"Stay down, Seraphim," it said, chased with a wet chuckle. "Think of this as just another form of penance."

And then the darkness was gone, like thick smoke dispersed by the wind.

Remy pushed himself up on his elbows and, with his one good eye, gazed up at the buzzing fluorescents that now illuminated the hall outside Rolanda's, as clear as day.

Guess he wouldn't have to call the super after all.

He was driving down Huntington Avenue much faster than he should have been, the ominous words of his attacker echoing inside the hollowness of his skull.

Remy picked up the cell phone resting in his lap and tried Cresthaven again. He'd been calling every five minutes since he'd left his office, and he still couldn't get through.

Speeding through a yellow light in front of the Museum of Fine Arts, he narrowly missed a group of tourists who had foolishly stepped out to catch the T across the street.

The phone continued to ring in his ear, but no one answered. Images of violence filled his mind—death and destruction hidden in an undulating fog of total darkness, falling upon the convalescent home, all the lives within threatened because of him, because of the life he had so selfishly chosen.

And because of the task with which Heaven had charged him.

"Damn it," Remy hissed, tossing the useless piece of technology onto the passenger's seat. He was almost there. His eyes scanned the horizon for smoke and flames, but everything appeared to be perfectly normal. He, of all people, knew that appearances could be deceiving.

Luck was with him, and he found a parking space easily. He was out of the car and running across South Huntington Ave. at full speed, distantly aware of parts of his body aching in protest.

He charged through the doors of Cresthaven and into the lobby. Everything seemed perfectly fine, except for the look on the receptionist's face. Her eyes were wide, mouth hanging open, as she stared at him.

"Are . . . are you all right, Mr. Chandler?" she asked, her voice high and wavering, as she slowly began to stand.

And then he realized what he must look like. He glanced down at the front of his light blue button-down shirt, spattered with stains of drying blood. His knuckles were scuffed and bleeding, and he could only imagine how his face appeared after the beating his enemies had given him.

"Yes," he said, not really sure how to continue. "I was trying to call, but . . ."

"The lines have been down since early this morning," the receptionist explained. "I called the phone company with my cell and they said they're working on the problem. I guess there was a fire on Center Street this morning and . . ."

Remy felt his legs grow wobbly, and he thought he just might need to sit down.

"What the hell happened to you?" a familiar voice bellowed, and he looked to see Nurse Joan coming around the corner. She was wearing bright red scrub pants and a top decorated with the characters from *Looney Tunes*.

He felt himself begin to sag, but then Joan's strong arm took hold of his, preventing him from falling.

"Do I need to call the police?" she asked in a hushed tone.

Remy shook his head and wished he hadn't, as the lobby began to spin. His attackers had taken more out of him than he imagined, and the surge of adrenaline that had gotten him here was waning.

"No, I'm fine. Job hazard; had a little run-in with some folks who don't appreciate a case I'm working on." And before Joan could respond, he added, "Madeline, is she okay?"

Joan nodded, holding firmly onto his arm, escorting him out of the lobby. "She's fine," the woman explained. "Had a rough night, but she's resting now. I was just down with her."

Remy nodded. "Good. That's good. As long as she's all right. I need to see her."

He started to pull away, but met with firm resistance.

"You go down there looking like that, your momma's gonna get sicker than she already is," Joan said, dragging him toward the nurses' break room.

He was desperate to see his wife, but he knew Joan was right, so he allowed himself to be escorted through the doorway into the small room. There was a table in the center with chairs around it, a watercooler in the far corner, and a refrigerator on the other side. To his left was a sink with cabinets above it.

"Sit," Joan ordered, and he did. "I'll be back in a minute."

Remy didn't argue, actually glad to be seated. He looked at his knuckles, at the torn skin, and flexed his hand. He was already starting to heal. In a day or so he'd be as good as new.

If only his pride would heal so quickly.

Joan came back into the room, arms loaded with medical supplies. "And I don't want to hear any complaining from you," she said, setting the stuff down on the tabletop. "This is probably gonna hurt like hell, but what did you expect?"

She started by cleaning the gash over his eye, and then moved on to the other cuts and abrasions. There was nothing she could do about the bruising.

"Tell me one thing," she asked, stepping back to look at her handiwork. "Does the other guy look as bad?"

Remy laughed, his ribs hurting sharply with the movement.

"Don't know," he gasped. "It was too dark to see."

"By the looks of these, you done all right," Joan said, cleaning off his knuckles with an alcohol wipe.

She tossed the used supplies in the barrel, then, putting her hands on her broad hips, she gave him the once-over again.

"Well, you still look like hell, but at least you won't be giving the poor old thing a heart attack."

Remy stood. "Thanks, Joan," he said, pushing his chair back beneath the table. "I owe you one."

"One? Then you can't count," she said, gathering up the unused supplies and turning to leave the break room.

Remy followed her through the door, turning in the direction of his wife's room.

"And don't you go waking your mother up," Joan called out. "If she's still asleep, you leave her alone. She needs her rest."

"Gotcha, and thanks again." Remy waved over

his shoulder and continued on to Madeline's room. The nurse said nothing more, her rubber-soled shoes squeaking noisily as she went.

He passed the doorways of other residents, some asleep, others watching television from their beds, or simply sitting in chairs in their rooms. And from somewhere down the long hallway, a soul cried out for release.

Remy reached Madeline's doorway and slowed as he entered the room, not wanting to startle her if she was awake. But he needn't have worried. She was fast asleep, lying on her side, and he was reminded of the thousands of times he'd watched her sleep, sometimes for hours at a time. He used to find a certain peace in the act, a special solace, but now it only made him feel sad.

Careful not to make a sound, he moved a chair closer to the bed. He felt a certain amount of relief seeing her alive and unharmed by his mysterious foes, but there was also despair. She looked paler than usual, an expression of pain permanently present on her features. He reached out, moving a stray lock of gray hair from her sweat-dappled forehead, then reached beneath the covers to take her hand in his. It was cold, the chilling sensation worming its way to his heart.

And as he watched her lying there in the hold of sleep, he knew that it was only a matter of time before the illness claimed her. *It would be so easy,* he thought, his thumb lightly caressing the soft flesh of her hand. To ignore the Seraphims' request—to do what his attackers had demanded of him—to lie down and do nothing.

To have more time with her would be wonderful, but at what cost?

Madeline groaned, the discomfort of her illness etched upon her face, even in sleep.

But at what cost?

He couldn't do that to her.

Remy let go of his wife's hand, placing it beneath the covers, and got up. He put the chair back where he'd found it and returned to Madeline's bedside, allowing himself just a minute more to stare before bending down and kissing her on the forehead.

He had to go. There were things he needed to do—people he needed to see—if he had any hopes of finding Israfil.

Though it pained him to do so, he had to speak to the Watchers.

Remy removed his bloodstained shirt and threw it on the bed.

"I'm fine," he told the Labrador standing in the doorway, as he grabbed a clean shirt from his closet. "I got a little bit banged up, but I'll be all right. Okay?"

He slipped the shirt on, ribs aching sharply as he moved.

"Hurt bad?" Marlowe asked, tilting his head in curiosity.

"Little bad," Remy answered, as he buttoned up the cream-colored dress shirt. "Some bad people were waiting for me when I got to work."

"Attack you?"

"Yes, they did. Worked me over pretty good, I'm sorry to say," he said, buttoning his cuffs.

"Marlowe bite them," the dog said, lowering his head and letting out a low, rumbling growl that actually managed to sound quite menacing.

"I'm sure you would have, but I'm glad you weren't there. I wouldn't have wanted you to get hurt." He bent over in front of the dog and rubbed Marlowe's ears. "And besides, I went to see Madeline, and Nurse Joan fixed me up."

The dog's tail wagged, hitting the doorjamb. *"Like Nurse Joan."*

"Yeah, she's something special." Remy walked over to his dresser mirror and checked his reflection. The cuts on his face were healing, and the bruises fading. Before long, no one would ever be able to tell that he'd had the crap kicked out of him by demonic entities.

As if it wasn't bad enough that the Angel of Death was missing, now there were demons involved. This case just kept getting better and better, and he suddenly found himself longing for the simplicity of spousal infidelity.

Marlowe bounded up onto the bed and sat down. Remy watched him from the mirror.

"What are you up to?" he asked.

"Go with?" Marlowe asked, now resembling a sphinx as he lay fully alert upon the bedspread.

Remy turned to face the animal. "Nope, sorry, pal," he said. "Wouldn't wish where I'm going tonight on my worst enemy, let alone my best friend."

He motioned for the dog to follow him and the two left the bedroom, heading downstairs to the first floor.

"Marlowe protect," the dog explained.

"I appreciate your concern," Remy said, going into the kitchen. "But I'll be fine."

"When come back?"

"Not long," Remy answered, getting the dog's supper together. "But until I get back, Ashlie is coming over to stay with you."

He hated to leave Marlowe alone. It just wasn't fair to the animal, after being by himself all afternoon, to be alone at night as well. And that was where Ashlie entered the picture.

The dog barked happily, tail wagging again.

"Yeah, I know all about you and Ashlie," Remy said,

putting the dog's food down onto the place mat along with some fresh water. Marlowe went to his bowl and started to eat.

The weather had taken a turn for the worse that afternoon, the temperature plummeting, a cold, dismal rain falling.

Appropriate, Remy thought, taking his raincoat from the hallway closet and slipping it on.

Marlowe had finished eating and was standing in the center of the kitchen, watching him with cautious eyes.

"Ashlie will be over in a little while," he told the dog. "She's going to take you for a walk and then play with you. I shouldn't be too late."

"Go with," Marlowe said, coming to stand beside him at the door.

"No, Marlowe. I need to go alone. I'll be fine. There's no need to worry."

The dog sniffed at Remy's hand. *"Not smell fine,"* he whined.

He couldn't fool Marlowe. The dog could read his moods with ease, and he had nailed it once again. Remy wasn't crazy about going to see the Grigori, especially with all the weird stuff that had been going on lately.

It was anybody's guess what he might be walking into.

"Okay, I'm a little nervous, but it should be okay," Remy explained. "I'm just going to talk to some *special* people," he said, using their code name for anybody of a supernatural nature. "Ask them some questions, that's all."

"Who?" the dog asked. *"Special people? Who?"*

"You don't know them," Remy replied. "The Grigori . . . they're angels."

He opened the door, then turned back, ready to remind Marlowe to be a good boy.

"*Angels,*" the dog said, sitting attentively by the door, smiling as only a Labrador could. "*Like you.*"

"No," Remy said with a serious shake of his head. "Not like me at all."

CHAPTER EIGHT

Western Asia, 9000 B.C.

Remiel drifted down from the star-filled night sky, his golden wings gently beating the chill desert air, slowing his descent.

He could sense them, others of his kind, and was drawn to their presence like a thirsty animal to water. He did not recall exactly how long it had been since he last communicated with others of his ilk, but he longed for the special rapport that only others of the Heavenly host could share.

The angel touched down upon coarse desert sand that mere hours before had burned like fire, but was now cool beneath his bare feet. He reveled in the sensation, enjoying the feeling of the damp granules between his toes, hiding the memories away with the many other experiences he had sampled since abandoning Heaven, and coming to the world of the Almighty's most sacred creations.

Remiel remembered Heaven sadly, how it used to be before the war—before the fall of the Morningstar.

A howl of excitement, followed by the sounds of primitive music, drifted across the desert toward him, pushing away the memories of how things had been but would never be again.

Remiel gazed across the drifting sands toward what

seemed to be a settlement of some kind; the multiple structures made from piled stone and bricks of mud and hay. The angel smiled at the simplicity of the buildings, seeing, perhaps, an attempt by man to duplicate some divine, barely accessible memory of Heaven's glorious edifices.

Withdrawing his wings beneath his robes, the angel crossed the sands toward the encampment and the sounds of life, the music growing louder as he was drawn to the revelry.

His sense of others like himself grew stronger as well, and his curiosity was piqued. Since the Great War, angelic presence in this world had been frowned upon, and he wondered who of his kind would dare risk rousing the ire of the Lord.

A huge bonfire blazed in the center of the encampment, the inhabitants performing some kind of strange dance around the roaring fire. Remiel took note of the humans' bodies, their exposed flesh—men and women—adorned with colorful markings, and upon their backs, the strangest of things, crude representations of wings woven from local vegetation.

Remiel continued to watch the strange ritual that seemed to depict the act of flying. He was mesmerized, moving closer to the performance, oblivious to everything except the bizarre ceremony.

Their feet pounded the dirt to the rhythmic beating of drums. Trilling flutes made from the hollowed bones of livestock added a voice to the primal cacophony.

And then the rite stopped abruptly—the world going to silence as the participants froze, glinting eyes locked upon the flames leaping skyward. One by one they tore the makeshift wings from their backs, tossing the mock appendages into the hungry fire. Then each and every one of them fell to their knees, crying out in a display of crippling despondency.

What does this mean? the angel wondered, the intensity of his curiosity almost causing him to forget the niggling, angelic presence that had first brought him here.

Almost.

Remiel looked across the writhing bodies of the desert settlers locked in the grip of hysteria, and saw them. They sat alone, away from the humans, and at once he knew their breed.

Remiel approached, stepping over the bodies of those who cried and writhed as if in the embrace of some invisible torment.

The eleven of his brethren stood as he drew closer, their solid black eyes shining in the firelight, faces distorted in such a way as to bare their teeth at him. A show of emotion, he knew, but was not sure which. *Happiness? Sadness? Anger?* There was still so much he did not know about this inhospitable place he had chosen above the kingdom of God.

So much still to learn.

"Welcome, brother," the obvious leader of the eleven proclaimed, his voice booming above the cries of the humans still in the throes of emotion. They all bowed to him, and Remiel returned the gesture, shedding his human guise to reveal his true form to those who addressed him.

"Greetings, my brethren," he stated, his wings of golden yellow unfurling majestically, their movement stirring the dust of the desert around his bare feet. "I am Remiel of the most holy host Seraphim."

"Of course you are," said the leader, his hands folded before him. "We've anxiously awaited your coming."

Remiel looked upon the eleven with curious eyes. None had assumed their true forms, as was the proper response to his own revelation.

"I am Sariel," the leader informed, motioning to the

others who loomed attentively behind him. "And we are the host Grigori."

Remiel's wings spread wide, carrying him away, repelled by the accursed name of Sariel's host. "Pariahs!" he spat, drawing a sword from a sheath hidden beneath his robes. "Defilers of God's most holy trust!" He stared down the blade forged in the center of the sun, that glinted even in the darkness of night.

The Grigori were outcasts, defilers of the Almighty's holy word. They had been charged with the guardianship of the human species, to watch over God's flock and protect them from sin, but it was they—the Grigori—who had become seduced by the ways of mankind.

The human settlers began to scream at the sight of Remiel. The Grigori fell to their knees, bowing to an authority that he no longer possessed.

"Soldier of Heaven," Sariel said, lifting eyes his toward him. "We knew that it would be only a matter of time before you returned, that our prayers for forgiveness would be heard."

Assigned the task of protecting His prized creations from evil, it was, in fact, the Grigori that shared with the fledgling species secrets that God believed they were not yet ready to know. They were taught about the constellations and the resolving of enchantments, of agriculture and the refinement of metal, which led to the creation of weapons for war.

And for this wicked behavior they were banished to live among the young race, and to never lay eyes upon the glory that was Heaven again.

The humans had gathered around the Grigori, as if shielding the defilers of the Creator's wishes from His wrath.

"They remember the first time.... When the Archangels came," the Grigori leader explained, the humans now surrounding the eleven, pawing at their robes, pulling them down to expose the angels' pale, almost translucent flesh.

"Our wings . . . our beautiful wings torn from our backs as punishment for our transgressions."

The Grigori turned, showing him how they had been defiled by God's wrath. The scars where wings had once sprung were red and angry, tears of yellow infection dribbling down their exposed backs. The humans swarmed around the Grigori's wounds, using their own garments to wipe away the running discharge.

"Imprisoned in these fragile, human bodies of skin, blood, and bone." Sariel gazed over his shoulder. "But now you have come. Our prayers have been answered, and we will at last be allowed to beg His forgiveness."

Remiel descended, furling his wings as he touched down upon the earth. "You are mistaken, watchers of humanity," the Seraphim said, sheathing his heavenly blade. "I have not the power to grant you absolution."

Sariel appeared startled by this revelation. "Have you not been sent by the Almighty?"

The other Grigori began to murmur among themselves, angrily pushing away the inhabitants of the settlement who now groveled about them.

"I no longer represent Heaven or my host," Remiel said sadly, feeling the distance between this world and the world that he had known before the war yawning ever wider. "I am alone now."

The Grigori leader looked to his brothers and then back to Remiel. "Then why are you here?"

The Seraphim looked to the sky, hoping to find an answer there. But the night and the multitude of twinkling stars remained silent, keeping their secrets to themselves.

"I once believed that serving Heaven was all I needed for fulfillment," Remiel said, his thoughts filled with the images of the Morningstar and those who followed him as they were cast down into the fires of the abyss. "But I learned that wasn't true."

Four human women clung to Sariel's legs, gazing up at the angelic being with adoration in their eyes, their hands stroking his legs through his flowing robes.

"And you have come to this place . . . to this world, seeking answers?" the Grigori asked, looking about in disbelief. He turned to his followers and began to laugh. "Shall we attempt to provide him with what he seeks, brothers?" Sariel asked.

The Grigori laughed, and Remiel could hear the madness there. Denied the light of Heaven and the glory of God, the angels had succumbed to insanity, he feared.

Sariel looked back to Remiel, eyes wild. "There are no answers here, brother Seraphim," he snarled. "This world of man is a cruel and harsh place, populated by beasts not much better than primates, but for some reason, they have been given the gift of *His* love."

The Grigori leader reached down to one of the women lying at his feet, holding her chin in his hand as he lifted her to stand beside him. Sariel gazed deeply into her eyes as if searching for something.

"*He* gave them something," Sariel purred. "A gift denied to us—His Heavenly servants—the first of His creations."

The woman squirmed in the leader's grasp, attempting to pull away, but it was for naught.

"Into each of them He put a bit of Himself . . . a divine spark that marked them as His chosen ones.

Why, Seraphim? Why do you think He did that for them?"

Remiel knew not the answer to that question either.

"We thought we'd learn the answer—my brothers and I—by living amongst them ... living *as* them. But they can tell us nothing."

The woman began to cry as Sariel's grip on her face tightened. She struggled feverishly in his grasp as he pulled her face closer to his, and then she lashed out at him, clawing bloody furrows into the pale, delicate flesh of his wrists.

Sariel drew in a hissing breath, sounding like a serpent preparing to strike. Savagely, he twisted the female's head sharply to one side, breaking her neck with a muffled snap.

"So special, and yet so fragile," he said softly, letting the woman's broken body slump to the ground.

Immediately, it was picked up and carried away by others of the settlement.

"You come here seeking answers, Seraphim," the Grigori leader snarled again. "As you can see, we have none to give."

The cold drizzle turned into a downpour as Remy drove slowly down LaGrange Street in what was once lovingly known by the residents of Beantown as the Combat Zone.

Centered on Washington Street between Boylston and Kneeland streets, extending up Stuart Street to Park Square, the Zone, so christened by a series of newspaper articles published in the 1960s, was once Boston's thriving adult-entertainment district. *Of course they'd be here*, Remy thought as he pulled into a metered space in front of an adult bookstore. The Grigori gravitated toward the old and abandoned—deconsecrated churches, closed-down movie palaces from days gone by, decrepit factory buildings.

He locked his car and headed up LaGrange in the hissing downpour. The streets were deserted, and he remembered a time when even the rain wouldn't have kept the perverts away.

The Zone had come about when city officials razed the West End and former red-light district at Scollay Square, near Faneuil Hall, to build the Government Center and revitalize the area. Urban renewal, they'd called it. Remy smiled as he pulled the collar of his raincoat up over his neck against the cold touch of the weather. Places such as this grew up like weeds; tear it down to the ground, and they'd just spring up somewhere else along the road.

The Combat Zone was dying now. It had been since the early eighties, as rising property values made the downtown locations all the more attractive to developers. Most of the strip clubs and adult bookstores had already been replaced by shiny new office buildings and hotels. It would be completely gone soon, and Remy had to wonder where it would turn up next.

But there were still some places, here and there, that belonged to the older time. Remy stood in front of one such place at the end of LaGrange Street, between Washington and Tremont. It used to be a factory of some kind, and it looked abandoned, but Remy knew better.

Even after all this time, he could still sense them. They were inside, the Grigori. The Watchers.

Remy pulled open the heavy metal door, the stink of urine wafting out to say hello. An old man wrapped in a filthy comforter stared up at him from the bottom step of stairs that climbed into shadow.

"Rainin' like a son of a bitch," the old-timer slurred,

his glassy eyes blinking repeatedly, as if he were having a hard time focusing. A filthy hand appeared from inside the flowered cover holding a bottle of cheap whiskey. He leaned back his head, sucking on the bottle, the golden liquid contents sliding down his thirsty throat.

"Though I hear tomorrow is supposed to be nice," Remy responded.

The man belched wetly, and the bottle disappeared again beneath the comforter.

"Tha's good," the man slurred. "Got things to do tomorrow."

Remy moved toward the staircase, the old-timer's head following him jerkily. "You goin' up there?" he asked, his eyes flashing briefly toward the darkness at the top of the stairs.

"Yeah."

The whiskey bottle appeared again. "I wouldn't if I was you," he said, before having another drink.

"And why's that?" Remy asked.

The man shrugged. "Jus' doesn't feel right," he said. "Whole place don't feel right. If it wasn't so fuckin' wet I'd be out on the street instead'a in here."

"Thanks for the concern, but I've got some things I need to take care of," Remy said, taking the first two steps toward the pool of blackness.

"They know you're comin'?" the man asked, suddenly sounding more sober.

Remy turned on the second step to look down at him. "No, they don't," he said. "I thought I'd surprise them."

The drunk made a noise that Remy guessed was a laugh. "Yeah, tha's good," he gurgled, bringing the bottle up to his mouth once again. "They jus' love fuckin' surprises." The man held the whiskey in one hand while his other snaked out from beneath the cover, waving Remy on with a dismissive flourish.

Without further hesitation, Remy climbed the stairs into the darkness, holding on to the greasy metal banister. Floor after floor he ascended, feeling himself getting closer.

Closer to them.

His stomach roiled with the thought of being in their presence, and he would rather have been just about anywhere else at that moment, but he knew that this was necessary.

The Grigori knew things about the city and its more unique residents, and he was willing to bet that they could give him something that would start him on the road to finding Israfil and his scrolls before things got even more out of hand.

As he climbed, Remy's thoughts drifted to the strange dream he'd had the other night, the monstrous train coming down the track. Now, standing in front of a metal door, its surface painted a flat black, he had to wonder how close that train was.

How much closer are the Horsemen?

Steeling himself, he raised his fist and pounded upon the door. Remy could feel the corrupted presence of the Grigori emanating from the other side, and he had no doubt that they could feel him as well.

He didn't have long to wait before he could hear the sound of locks being turned and dead bolts sliding across the other side. The heavy metal door opened slowly, the shriek of the hinges giving the impression it had been quite some time since it was last opened. An older man dressed in a starched white shirt and black bow tie stood at attention, his milky, cataract-covered eyes gazing out at Remy, seeing nothing but at the same time seeing everything.

Blind.

"This is a private club, sir," the man said, his voice dripping with disdain. How dare Remy befoul their doorstep. "I suggest you leave before you arouse the ire of my masters."

He started to close the door, but Remy placed the palm of his hand firmly upon the cold black surface. "I'm here to see Sariel. Tell him that Remiel is here," he stated flatly, hand still pressed upon the door. "And that I'm still looking for some of those answers."

The blind man went away for a bit.

Remy had allowed him to close the door, leaving him in the darkness on the landing while the servant went off in search of his master.

It won't be long.

Despite the fact that they hated one another, there was still a connection between Remy and the Grigori—an unearthly bond, a brotherhood that could not be denied. They were all a part of something so much larger.

The sound of the dead bolt interrupted his thoughts, and the door creaked open again.

"This way, Master Remiel," the old, blind man said with a bow, motioning for Remy to enter.

He passed through the doorway from the dark factory landing that stank of dampness and age, into an opulent lobby that made the Four Seasons look like a Motel Six. Another man stood there, dressed in a crisp white shirt, black bow tie, and black slacks. This one was younger but also blind.

There was something about the handicapped. Almost as if to make up for their physical or mental deficiency, some were given another gift, the ability to recognize heavenly beings for what they actually were. The blind were the most sensitive of all, and the Grigori loved nothing more than to be recognized for what they used to be.

"Your coat, sir?" the young man asked, reaching out in Remy's general direction.

"No, thank you," he responded. "I'll hold on to it. I'm not planning to be here that long."

The doorman led him toward a dark mahogany door at the far end of the lobby. "This way, Master Remiel."

Remy bristled at the use of his true name, but knew if he wanted to talk with the Grigori leader, it had to be this way.

The doorman found the carved ivory handle and pushed it down, allowing the door to glide smoothly open, and for the sound of revelry from within to escape.

There was a party going on, and Remy wouldn't have been in the least bit surprised to see a bonfire with people wearing fake wings dancing around it.

But this appeared to be a much classier affair.

A full orchestra, all blind, performed a beautiful piece by Mozart from their station in the corner of the room, but those present really didn't seem to notice, or care. Booze flowed from two bars set up on either side of the room; the pungent aroma of marijuana wafted through the air; and on tiny side tables scattered about, Remy could see crystal dishes piled with what could only have been cocaine and various multicolored narcotics.

Grigori and a few chosen humans—both male and female—carried on as if this really was the night before the end of the world.

Remy felt suddenly sick at the thought that they might know something he did not.

Looking about the room at the decadence, he saw that even after all these years—*thousands of years*—the

Grigori were exactly as they were the first time he'd met them, unchanged by the passage of time.

Poor bastards.

But he did have to give them points for consistency.

"Remiel!" a voice called out over the sounds of the festivities, and Remy turned to see a grinning Sariel heading toward him.

The Grigori leader was dressed impeccably in a suit that probably cost more than what Remy had made the previous year before taxes. The angel wore his white hair long and slicked back, and his skin had an odd orange color like that of an artificial tan.

Sariel strode across the room, snatching two flutes of champagne from the serving tray of a blind waiter as he moved.

"So nice to see you again," he said, leaning forward to kiss Remy on the side of the cheek.

Remy's senses were nearly overwhelmed by the aroma of expensive cologne, and something else just beneath the strong perfume—the scent of decay. He stepped back, resisting the urge to wipe at his face.

The Grigori leader offered him one of the two flutes he was holding.

"No, thank you," Remy said, shaking his head.

Unfazed, Sariel downed one and then the other. He smacked his lips noisily, and then tossed both of the empty champagne glasses over his shoulder. They shattered on the hardwood floor, and for a moment the silence in the room was deafening, but then the band resumed its play and the buzz of conversation began again.

"To what do I owe the pleasure of this visit?" Sariel asked, an unnatural smile creeping across his angular features. "Your aversion to mingling with our kind is quite well-known, and it's killing me to know what could be so pressing."

One of the blind waiters had appeared with a dust-pan and brush, dropping to his knees, gingerly moving his hands across the floor in search of the razor-sharp slivers of Sariel's glasses. The Grigori watched the man with great interest, their eyes twinkling maliciously each time the man's groping hands encountered a piece of glass.

"Why are you here, Remiel?" Sariel asked again.

The waiter suddenly yelped in pain as he knelt on a jagged fragment of the flute. The Grigori burst out laughing, applauding the injured man as he pulled the bloody glass from his knee.

"Is there someplace where we can speak in private?" Remy asked, not able to keep the tone of distaste from his voice.

"Oh, my," Sariel said, bringing a hand to his mouth in mock horror. "This sounds serious."

Remy said nothing, waiting.

"Very well." Sariel finally motioned for him to follow. "This way."

They started across the room, the Grigori and their human guests parting to let them through.

"Missed a piece," Sariel said, gently stroking the top of the waiter's head as the angel passed him. The man's body trembled, as if in the throes of ecstasy, at the touch of the Grigori leader's hand, and he continued his search for stray bits of glass with increased vigor.

Sariel led Remy to another wooden door at the far end of the ballroom, then stopped, turning to look out over the expansive room. "They hate you," he said as casually as if he were commenting on the weather.

Remy was a bit taken aback, but not surprised. "You'd think they'd be over it by now," he said, feeling their suspicious gazes on his back.

"They'll never be over it," Sariel replied, opening the

door and gesturing for him to move through. Remy entered, the Grigori leader following, closing the door on the hate-filled eyes.

"You can go back any time," Sariel continued, crossing the room toward two overstuffed chairs in front of a marble-and-wood fireplace. A cozy fire burned within. "Back to the glory that is Heaven . . . back to *Him*, but you choose not to. You're actually here because you wish to be."

Remy chose a chair and sat down as Sariel did. It was warm and comfortable, the fire chasing away the chill that had resided in his bones since heading out into the rain tonight.

"They're jealous," Remy said, mesmerized by the flames.

"Perhaps they were once, but now they're simply angry," Sariel responded.

There was a knock on the door, and a waiter came into the room.

"May I bring you anything, master?" the man asked, his blind eyes rolling uselessly in their sockets.

"Remiel?" the Grigori leader asked him.

It was a moment of weakness, and he blamed it on the comforting effects of the fire. "Scotch on the rocks," he said, but regretted the words as soon as they left his mouth.

"Excellent idea," Sariel responded. He turned toward the waiter. "Two Scotches."

The waiter bowed and carefully left the room, closing the door behind him.

"I didn't come to make anybody angry," Remy said, still gazing into the fire. His felt his face flush, his eyes growing heavy as the fire worked its comforting magic upon him.

"I wouldn't concern yourself with that. They hate

you all the time." The Grigori chuckled. "Your disregard for what they want most of all infuriates them. . . . Infuriates me."

The waiter returned with their drinks, placing a silver tray down upon a small wooden table between the two chairs.

"Will there be anything else, sir?" the servant asked, standing at attention.

Sariel ignored the question.

"I think that's it," Remy told him, feeling uncomfortable with the man's attentive presence.

The man didn't move.

"Go," Sariel finally barked.

The waiter bowed again and left them alone in the study.

The Scotch was good. *Steve would gladly give up his mother's soul for a bottle of this*, Remy thought, savoring each sip.

"You actually respect them," Sariel said, shaking the tumbler in his hand and causing the ice within to tinkle merrily.

"Who? Them out there?" Remy pointed to the wall with his glass. "The people beyond these walls, out in the real world? You bet your ass I respect them." He took a large sip from his drink, swishing it around in his mouth before swallowing. "It's not easy being human," he added.

"And you would know," Sariel said, slowly bringing the glass to his mouth.

The fire snapped like the crack of a bullwhip, and one of the logs tumbled from its perch upon the burning stack, a plume of fire and burning embers momentarily flaring up into the flue.

"Why have you come here, Remiel?" Sariel asked, repressed anger obvious in his tone.

Remy had some more of the fine Scotch before answering.

"I had a visit from Nathanuel the other day," he finally said, looking into the dancing flames.

He could feel Sariel's eyes suddenly upon him.

"Seems that the powers that be have lost track of Israfil." Slowly he turned his head, tearing his gaze away from the mesmerizing flames to meet the intensity of the Grigori's stare. "And they've asked me to find him."

It seemed to take Sariel a moment to process the information.

"The Angel of Death is . . . missing?"

Remy nodded, taking the last of his drink. He wiped his lips with his fingers and set the glass down on the table between them.

"And I was hoping that you might have some information to help me take care of this business and restore the balance before . . ."

"Nothing is feeling his touch?" Sariel interrupted.

"No," Remy answered. "So I'm sure you can see why the Seraphim are so interested in finding him as quickly as possible."

"And they haven't any idea as to where he has gone?" the Grigori asked.

"No."

And with those chilling words, Sariel started to laugh. It was an awful sound, like the excited cry of a hungry raptor as its eyes fell upon unsuspecting prey. "One of their most powerful has escaped their watchful eyes," he said shaking his head.

Then he dropped his empty glass onto the table and stood, moving to the fireplace, where he leaned against the mantle, staring down into the flames. At last he turned to look at Remy, his face shaded in the shifting shadows of the dancing flames.

"You spoke of restoring the balance. How bad is it out there?"

Remy thought of the past two days, his experience at the hospital, the stories on the news and in the daily papers.

It's bad.

And then there was the dream, the train pulling into the station, carrying the bringers of the Apocalypse.

It's real bad.

"It's horrible, and it's only going to get worse." Remy leaned his head against the back of the chair, eyeing the angelic being standing at the fireplace across from him.

"The scrolls?" Sariel asked, black eyes twinkling inquisitively.

"They're missing too."

"Well, this *is* quite a predicament." The Grigori returned to his chair. "But it makes sense now."

Remy's ears perked up. "What does?" he asked, looking toward the angel. "Do you have something for me?"

"Perhaps," Sariel replied. "It happened some time ago."

"What happened?" Remy questioned, the potential for his first lead pulling him out of his seat to stand in front of the Grigori leader.

"I'm not sure how long ago, exactly," Sariel said, rubbing his brow as if attempting to stimulate his brain. "I have such difficulty with the passage of time. A week, a decade, they all seem to flow together. Do you find that as well, Remiel?"

Remy surged forward, grabbing hold of the arms of Sariel's chair, leaning into his face.

"What happened, Sariel, and what does it have to do with Israfil?"

The Grigori smiled at Remy's intensity.

"We were so excited to see him," he said. "Thinking that maybe . . . maybe he had been sent to tell us that we were at last going home.

"After all, why else would the Angel of Death come to visit?"

CHAPTER NINE

Between a week and ten years ago

They were having a celebration.

Sariel did not remember exactly the reason for the festivities; perhaps it had something to do with the changing of the seasons, perhaps not.

Whatever it was, the leader of the Grigori did not feel the need to pursue it any further. They were celebrating.

It was better than slipping into madness.

The blind musicians were playing something lively. Sariel thought it was probably something by Beethoven. Of all the human composers, *he* was the one that actually came the closest to duplicating the music of the spheres, of the celestial choirs of Heaven.

The shrill sound of human laughter stirred him from his reverie.

The Grigori leader opened his eyes. From his seat in the corner of the recently renovated space, he saw that Araquiel had returned, and that he had brought along women.

Sariel smiled, overjoyed at the potential for distraction. *What's a celebration without females?* he thought, pushing himself from his seat and crossing the room toward where his brothers had congregated around their visitors.

The Grigori had a weakness for the fairer sex—just one of the damning reasons they had ended up in the situation they were in, and had been in for countless millennia. What was it about humanity that had seduced them so, that continued to seduce them?

How many times had he and his brothers asked themselves that very question? *As many times as there are stars in the sky*, the leader thought, admiring the women.

They were quite attractive . . . for humans. Dressed in gowns of the finest material, faces painted alluringly and adorned in jewelry of silver, diamonds, and gold, there was little that separated them from their primitive ancestors.

Harlots, each and every one, enticed here with the promise of payment. *They'll earn their reward*, Sariel thought.

"Welcome, ladies," he said, as his brothers stepped away from the women so that he could view them unhindered.

They were just what the moment called for.

A distraction from the pain of exile.

And they served their purpose well, as did the alcohol, the drugs, and the food specially prepared for their distinctive palates. But in the end it was all so horribly fleeting.

Because of their angelic physiology, nothing remained with their systems for long. They tried to kill the pain of their tortured existences with excess, and in the end, it was never enough.

But it never stopped them from trying.

Sariel had his way with all of the women, the stink of their sexual acts hanging heavy in the air, reminding him again of how far he—how far *they*—had fallen. His brothers were still lost in their decadence, their indulgences, but he'd had more than enough for now.

Leaving his brethren to their lustful antics, Sariel rose from the pillows on the floor and strolled naked across the space toward their renovated living quarters. Already he could feel the guilt of his wanton acts wearing on him, reminding him of the reason for their banishment.

He had reached the far end of the grand room turned den of iniquity, when he realized that the sounds of revelry had ceased. He turned, curious, and saw him standing in the center of the room.

Instinctively, Sariel knew who it was. He could feel the power radiating from him.

"Brother Israfil!" he called, suddenly frustrated that he was unable to spread his wings and glide through the air to their powerful visitor's side.

The Angel of Death appeared as human, but he was so much more than that. The power of Heaven throbbed beneath the masquerade of flesh and bone. Israfil remained eerily silent, his eyes riveted upon the Grigori in their various stages of immorality.

Sariel slowly approached the angel, head bowed in reverence. "Holy Israfil," he said, painfully aware of his nakedness, the scars throbbing with pain where his glorious wings had once sprung. They had never stopped hurting—never fully healed. "This is indeed a great honor. May I ask the occasion?"

His thoughts raced with the possibilities as he waited for the angel to respond. But Israfil's gaze remained upon his brothers and the examples of their debauchery.

Even those who served the needs of the Grigori were drawn to the heavenly power, the blind servants emerging from the back rooms, their useless eyes somehow able to perceive the divinity of the visitor.

Israfil finally turned his haunting gaze to Sariel, the intensity of the look dropping the leader to his knees.

"I wanted . . . wanted to see," the Angel of Death said in a voice that seemed to tremble with emotion. "I needed to know if it really is possible."

Sariel did not understand the angel's words. "Excuse my ignorance, brother," he began carefully. They did not need Israfil angry with them; that would be disastrous in so many ways. "But if what is possible?"

Israfil was looking at his Grigori brothers again. The human females, wallowing in the euphoric grip of the abundant narcotics, had no idea of what was truly transpiring here, no idea of the power this visitor held.

"To truly be with them . . ." he began, his voice little more than a whisper. "To be *like* them."

Sariel still did not understand, and was about to attempt further discussion when one of his own, the Grigori Armaros, rose from his pillow on the floor, his eyes glazed, a twisted smile on his drug-addled features.

"You want to be with them?" Armaros slurred, reaching down to pull one of the prostitutes up from where she had started to doze. It was the redhead, and Sariel did not remember her name. He could never remember their names.

"Take this one," the Grigori said, pushing the naked woman toward Israfil.

The woman stumbled, her large breasts flopping grotesquely as she fell to the ground in front of him.

And Armaros began to laugh, a high-pitched keening that filled the hall with its irritating sound.

Sariel felt it before it happened. The temperature in the room dropped dramatically, and he saw the strangely troubled expression on Israfil's face turn to one of fury and revulsion.

The Angel of Death extended his arm toward the giggling Armaros, as the other Grigori seemed to become immediately lucid, scrambling away from their brother. The females appeared to sense trouble as well and crawled away to hide behind an overstuffed sofa.

"You think it's funny?" Israfil asked, his voice shaking with barely contained rage.

Sariel reached out to Israfil in an attempt to calm his ire, and felt the flesh on his hand grow numb as his fingers entered a field of severe cold that surrounded the angel. With a hiss, he withdrew his nearly frozen limb, clutching it to his chest.

"You think you're special?" Israfil asked Armaros.

The Grigori dropped to his knees, averting his gaze and begging for mercy. But Israfil's anger had rendered him as blind as their servants.

And then Armaros began to scream, his naked body flopping to the ground, writhing in agony.

"It is they who are special . . . they who are the chosen of our Holy Lord."

Armaros' body began to wither and cracks appeared in his flesh. Still the Grigori screamed, his cries for mercy falling upon deaf ears.

There was a sudden flash of light as a sphere of pulsing energy exploded out from within Armaros' desiccated body. The glowing orb drifted across the room to Israfil's extended hand, and as it came close, the Angel of Death closed his fingers upon it, extinguishing the light.

And then Israfil turned his angry gaze toward the others. Sariel and his remaining brethren quickly averted their eyes so as not to further feed his anger. They waited for a sign that they were to die, or be spared the angel's wrath, but it did not come.

Finally gathering up his courage, Sariel raised his head, only to find Israfil gone.

The reason he had come to them, and his behavior, a mystery.

The lingering stench of an angel's death hanging heavy in the air, the only evidence that he had even been there at all.

To truly be with them . . . to be like them.

Sariel's account of Israfil's visit replayed in Remy's mind. Over and over again he heard the Grigori's words, painting a picture that served only to intensify his growing sense of unease.

It was raining harder now in Boston, and he was having a difficult time concentrating on navigating the wet city streets. Thankfully, no one was about, as if the deluge had washed away anyone foolish enough to venture outside.

Remy hated to admit it, but the Seraphim's suspicions might actually have meant something, that Israfil had somehow become enamored with humanity, thus making it difficult for him to do the job that the Almighty had assigned him.

It's crazy; this is the freakin' Angel of Death, for Pete's sake.

But if what Sariel said was true, Israfil had come to the Grigori looking for some sort of affirmation that it was possible to be of both the Heavenly host and humanity.

It made Remy's head hurt to think of it. The two states of being were polar opposites, which was why he himself had chosen to suppress his true nature . . . at least as much as he was able. He could only imagine the ferocity of the struggle as the two conflicting natures attempted to exist at the same time, which was probably why the world was in its current situation.

It was actually Sariel's disturbing supposition as Remy had been preparing to leave the Grigori den that had left him chilled to the bone. He heard the leader's words again, filled with a breathless anticipation.

"Do you suppose that if the Apocalypse is called down— that if all is laid to waste—the Heavenly father will finally allow us to return home?"

Remy was so taken aback by the question he hadn't known how to reply. He had simply left the building as quickly as he could.

He turned up Charles Street between the Public Garden and the Common and reached for his cell phone. Holding it up, keeping one eye on the road, he scrolled down his listing of most used numbers. He found the one he was looking for and dialed it.

"Yeah," came Lazarus' familiar voice on the other end.

"Just getting back from seeing our friends," Remy said. "Israfil paid them a visit not too long ago . . . seemed a bit out of it. The implication being that he wanted to be human."

"Ouch," Lazarus said.

"Yeah, ouch as in 'Ouch, this whole Apocalypse thing could really put a crimp in my day.' Do you have anything for me?" Remy asked as he turned onto Derne Street and began the chore of looking for a parking space.

"Nothing, really. Everybody's pretty quiet. It's like they know something big is coming and they're all holding their breath."

"Have you seen anything of a demonic nature?"

"I try and stay clear of those types. Why?"

"Had a run-in outside my office with some individuals of definite demonic persuasion. They tried to convince me to give up on the case."

"They kick the shit out of you?" the immortal asked.

Remy could hear the amusement in his voice.

"Pretty much. There had to be at least four of them, maybe even more."

"Sure," Lazarus chided.

"Yeah, go screw." Remy had just about given up on finding a space when he remembered that he still had to give Ashlie a ride home anyway.

"So you think there are demons involved with this business now?" Lazarus asked.

"I think there are parties interested in seeing Israfil stay lost, and in conjunction, bringing about the end of the world. Isn't that friggin' cheerful?" Remy pulled up in front of his house, driving the car onto the sidewalk so as not to block the narrow street any more than he had to.

"Sounds it," Lazarus agreed. "Well, I suppose the night's still young. I'll see what I can dig up."

"Thanks," Remy said, turning off the engine. "Call if you come across anything."

The immortal broke the connection, and Remy returned his phone to his belt, taking a moment to collect his thoughts as the rain thrummed on the hood of his car.

Finally, he bit the bullet and exited the car.

Out into the storm.

Remy heard Marlowe bark as he slipped his key into the door. It was followed by the sounds of the jangling tags and clicking toenails as the dog raced to greet him.

The nails sounded long; he would have to cut them again soon.

"Hey, buddy," Remy said, closing the door, the dog happily sniffing him up and down.

"You're home! You're home!" Marlowe chanted, barely able to contain his excitement. Remy reached down to pet him, his movement causing the water that beaded on his coat to rain down upon the happy pup.

"Wet!" he yelped, licking up some of the drops that spattered the hallway floor.

"Yep, it's pouring. Where's Ashlie?" he asked, looking for the teenager, guessing that she'd probably fallen asleep in front of the television.

"*Ashlie gone,*" Marlowe said, turning and bounding down the hallway, back to the living room.

"What do you mean she's gone?" Remy asked, following the animal. "Ashlie?" he called out. "Hey, Ash?"

Remy rounded the corner and stopped as he caught sight of the stranger sitting on his couch. He stared at the young woman, not sure of what to do next. It was obvious that he had woken her up. Her shoes were on the floor in front of the couch, a mug that looked as though it might have once contained tea resting on the coffee table in front of her. She looked at him with large, fear-filled brown eyes. She was attractive, a brunette with shoulder-length hair and fair skin.

Marlowe had hopped up onto the couch next to her, leaning back and waving a paw at Remy as he panted loudly.

"Who the hell are you?" Remy asked.

"*Casey,*" Marlowe barked.

"I'm not asking you, I'm asking her," he said, his eyes shifting from the dog to the woman.

"I'm Casey, Mr. Chandler. Casey Burke. I'm so sorry about this. I must've dozed off."

"How did you get in here. . . . Where's Ashlie?"

"*Ashlie go home,*" Marlowe said, leaning back even farther so that both paws were now flapping in the air. It looked as though he was doing the wave at a football game.

"I told you to hush up," Remy scolded the dog. "I want answers from you." He pointed at the woman from the doorway. He didn't sense any danger from her, but it still didn't change the fact that she was a stranger sitting on his couch in his living room.

"I came by to see you, and Ashlie told me that you

had gone out for the evening. I must've looked really pathetic because she asked if I wanted to come in and write you a note."

Remy scowled, upset that the teenager could have been so foolish.

"Don't be mad at her," Casey said quickly, putting her feet down and slipping into her shoes. "I started explaining my situation a little and got kind of upset. She thought that maybe I should hang around until you got back."

Remy sighed, exasperated, and leaned against the door frame. "Where is she now?"

"She wasn't feeling too good," Casey explained, making a sort of embarrassed face. "You know, female problems."

"So she just left you here? A stranger, in my house with my dog?"

"No stranger. Casey," Marlowe informed him.

"I know it's Casey," he said, annoyed.

The woman started to laugh, abruptly stopping when she realized that Remy was staring at her.

"I'm sorry," she said. "It's just that somebody I'm very close to used to do the same thing with our cat."

Remy tilted his head, frowning quizzically.

"You know, the whole talking-to-the-animal thing, as if they know what you're saying."

He sensed her mood suddenly darken as she lowered her head, looking down at her hands. Marlowe moved closer, nuzzling her arm in hopes that petting him would cheer her up.

"That somebody is actually why I'm here, Mr. Chandler," Casey said, rubbing Marlowe's ears. Remy could hear the dog rumbling with pleasure. "My fiancé . . . Jon Stall is missing . . . has been missing for the last few weeks."

Feeling his ire start to subside, Remy shucked off his still-dripping coat. "Ms. Burke . . ."

"Casey," she interrupted him. "Please call me Casey."

Remy sighed. "Fine, Casey." He quickly went out into the hallway, hung the coat on the closet doorknob, and came back into the living room.

"Casey, this type of thing is usually handled at my office," he explained. "And even then . . ."

"I've been to the police and they had me fill out all the proper paperwork, but I really don't think they took me all that seriously, and besides, he told me to come to you if anything happened to him."

Remy was surprised by the revelation. "You said his name is Jon Stall?"

The pretty woman nodded. "Jon Philip Stall. He's a professor at Mass Tech. . . . Biology."

He repeated the name again. It didn't ring any bells. "I'm sorry, but I don't recall the name," he said as he walked through the living room toward the kitchen. "Listen, I'm going to make a pot of coffee, would you like some?" he asked her.

"I would love another cup of tea, if that would be all right," she said, getting up from the couch and following, Marlowe close behind.

"*Apple?*" the dog asked.

"I'll get you an apple in a minute," Remy told the dog as he filled the teakettle and placed it on the stove. He then started to prepare his coffee, deciding on a full pot. He suspected it was going to be one of those nights.

"The week before he . . ." Casey paused. It was obvious that she was taking her boyfriend's disappearance quite hard. "The week before Jon went away, he talked about you a lot."

She was standing in the kitchen doorway, arms folded across her chest.

"He talked about me?" Remy asked with surprise as he scooped freshly ground Dunkin' Donuts coffee into a filter.

She nodded, pushing back a strand of dark hair that dangled in front of her pretty, oval face. "He talked about how much he admired you and what you had done with your life."

"I don't know what to say." Remy shook his head, leaning against the counter as the coffeemaker began to hiss and gurgle. "I honestly don't know who your boyfriend is."

Marlowe barked once from his spot in the middle of the kitchen floor.

"Right, your apple," Remy said, grabbing a Red Delicious from the fruit bowl and bringing it to the counter.

"Did Jon say anything specific, Casey? Anything as to how he knew me or where he knew me from?"

Remy finished cutting the apple into strips and brought them over to Marlowe's bowl. The dog bolted up from the floor, pushing Remy's hand out of the way to get at his treat.

"He said you two had come from similar backgrounds—the same town I think."

And suddenly a recognizable image began to take shape in Remy's mind. *Is it possible?* he wondered. Had something ridiculously fortuitous dropped into his lap . . . ? *Or is there something else going on here?*

The tea water had started to boil, screeching to be noticed. Casey made a move toward it, but Remy was already on the way.

"Sorry," he said, taking the mug from her and placing a tea bag inside it. "Lost in thought there. So where was Jon from?" Remy asked, pouring the steaming water into the mug.

"Some little town north of here called Paradise."

Remy's arm twitched and he spilled hot water all over the countertop.

Paradise.

He grabbed a dishcloth and started to mop up the spill. "Sorry about that," he apologized, handing the steaming mug to Casey.

"Is that where you're from, Mr. Chandler?" she asked him, watching him intently. "Are you from Paradise?"

Images of a place that as far as he was concerned didn't exist anymore began to take shape inside Remy's head.

It was so long ago.

CHAPTER TEN

Heaven, a very long time ago

The sword in his hand grew heavier with each passing moment, the stench of burning flesh and blood almost palpable in the air.

Remiel looked about the battlefield. What had once been golden fields of high grass that sang with joy when the celestial breezes moved through them were now trampled flat, and everywhere he looked his eyes fell upon the fallen.

He knew them all, whether they be friend or foe, for not long ago they had been brothers under God. But that was before the Morningstar gathered his forces about him and challenged the will of the Almighty.

Before the war that turned Choir against Choir, brother against brother.

It was drawing to a close now, the followers of Lucifer Morningstar either vanquished or awaiting capture. But looking about the battlefield, at the twisted wings and broken bodies of those who had died fighting, Remiel knew it would never be the same again.

Standing there, in what had once been golden fields, he made up his mind, letting his weapon fall from his hand to lie uselessly upon the blood-soaked ground. Remiel closed his eyes, committing to his memory how it once had been.

Slowly, he removed his armor, shedding the raiment of warfare, letting that too fall useless to the ground beneath his feet.

"It is over, brother," said a voice from nearby, and Remiel slowly turned to gaze upon the visage of the angel Israfil as he walked among the dead, their bodies disintegrating to dust, carried away upon the winds as he passed.

As if they'd never been there at all.

"The legions of the Adversary have been driven to their knees before His most holy glory," Israfil told him.

"And what of the Adversary—what of Lucifer Morningstar, who was once the favorite of our Lord?" Remiel asked the angel.

"He is to be cast down," Israfil replied. "A fitting punishment for one who dared try to usurp the will of the All-Father."

At first Remiel did not respond, gazing out across the field and the bodies of those who had not yet been removed by the power of the Angel of Death, but he could keep it inside him no longer.

"Haven't we all been punished enough?" he asked. And then he began to walk across the field-turned-battleground, on his way to the golden gateway that separated the Kingdom from all else.

Remy knew that Jon Stall was Israfil.

For some reason, he had chosen to don a human form and live among humanity. Now it was up to Remy, an angel who had done something very similar so long ago, to locate the wayward Angel of Death and convince him to return to the life that Remy himself never would.

And, oh yeah, he couldn't breathe a word of it to his girlfriend.

"When did you and Jon first meet?" Remy asked.

They had returned to the living room, and he was sitting in a chair across from the couch where Casey sat, Marlowe practically in her lap.

She took a careful sip from her mug of steaming tea before she answered his question, clearly reliving the past in her mind. "It was about a year ago. I was doing some temp work in the psychology department." She made a face and then smiled. "Not the psychology department . . . the Department of Brain and Cognitive Sciences."

Remy returned the smile. "There's a difference?"

Casey laughed. "I guess so. He was just a nice guy, y'know?" She smiled warmly with the memory.

Remy drank his coffee, his silence urging her to continue.

"We really hit it off . . . both of us coming off some pretty rough times and stuff."

"Rough times?" Remy asked.

She put her mug down on the table, doffed her shoes, and pulled her legs up beneath her. "I had lost my mother a little less than a month before to breast cancer, and Jon had been quite sick himself."

"I'm sorry about your mom."

"Thanks," Casey responded with a sad smile. He could see emotion welling in her eyes.

"Jon had been sick as well?" he prompted after a minute.

The woman nodded. "From what he told me, I guess it was pretty bad. They'd given up on him. He had inoperable brain cancer and they'd given him less than a year to live."

Remy felt a cold knot of fear twist in his stomach.

"So he survived, then."

"Yeah." She nodded enthusiastically. "I guess they looked at him as a sort of miracle. The cancer went into remission and he was fine after that."

Casey picked nervously at a piece of skin on one of her fingers. Her voice started to tremble. "You wouldn't even know he used to be sick. It was amazing."

"Did he talk about his past much?"

She was petting Marlowe's head as he snored by her side. "Not at all, really . . . other than the stuff about you. I know he doesn't have any family or anything—both his parents were deceased and he was an only child. He used to say that the cancer gave him a chance at a new beginning," she explained. "That it enabled him to start all over again."

The icy knot in Remy's belly twisted tighter. Outside, the wind was whipping, spattering the heavy rain against the windows. Israfil had become this Jon Stall, assuming his identity, his life.

But why? Why had he abandoned his work, and why had he then gone missing?

"Tell me everything leading up to Jon's disappearance," Remy said, gulping down the last of his drink. He rose from his chair, heading toward the kitchen for another cup.

"More tea?" he asked her.

"No, thanks. I'll be peeing all night if I do."

Marlowe lifted his head. *"Treat?"*

"You've had enough," Remy said, and the dog's large head dropped between his paws with a heavy sigh.

"Was Jon acting strange? Was there anything to make you think that something might be wrong?" Remy asked, returning to the room with a fresh cup.

He could see that she was thinking hard. "It's all hindsight now," Casey said. "I really didn't think anything of it at the time—it was just Jon being Jon."

"And what does that mean?"

She shrugged, changing her position so that now she was leaning against Marlowe. "He would get very quiet, then go into his study and lock the door and not come out for hours. Stuff like that."

"So you lived together?"

"Yeah, he had a two-bedroom in Southie. I moved in not too long after we started dating. Most of the time it was great, just toward the end there it got a little hard. He was drinking a lot more and I think he might've been . . ." She paused.

"Drugs?" Remy finished for her. "You think he might've been taking stuff?"

"Yeah," she sighed, the memories of the bad times weighing heavily on her. "He said that it was to help him sleep, but I don't think he was sleeping inside his study all that time."

"What do you think he was doing in there?"

"I used to think it was school stuff, y'know, for the classes that he taught, but then I started hearing him talking to himself . . . and crying."

Marlowe lifted his head and looked at her with his deep brown eyes. He could sense that she was troubled, and laid his head consolingly upon her thigh.

"He's so sweet." Casey leaned down to kiss the top of his head.

"Yeah, he's a good boy," Remy confirmed.

Marlowe's tail thumped on the couch.

"Did you confront Jon about his behavior?" Remy asked, turning the conversation back to the problem at hand. He had to get every little bit of information he could to piece together the entire picture of the situation.

"Oh, sure. And that was when he started talking about you, and how much he admired you and everything that you'd done in your life, and how I was to get in touch with you if anything happened to him."

Casey suddenly stopped talking, putting all her concentration into petting the dog.

"Why do you think he thought something was going

to happen to him? Did he give any indication that he was in trouble?"

"Jon wasn't himself at that point, Mr. Chandler," Casey explained. "He'd become very paranoid, certain that he was being watched and followed. He even stopped going to work, spending all his time locked in his study."

The warmth from the coffee cup felt good on Remy's hands. Even though he'd been out of the rain for well over an hour now, he could still feel the chill of the nasty weather.

"And when did you suspect he was gone?"

"Pretty much right away," she answered. "He said he was going out for a while. He hadn't been out of the house . . . out of his study . . . for days. I just knew that something wasn't right."

Casey started to cry. Remy got up and brought a box of tissues over from a side table.

"Thank you," she said between sniffles. "It's just that he didn't even kiss me good-bye." And then she began to cry all the harder. "I'm sorry," she finally managed, plucking another tissue from the box beside her.

"It's all right," Remy said. "I can see how this would be hard for you."

She dabbed at her eyes and nose. "Was I right to come to you?" she asked, crumpling the tissue in her hand. "Will you help me, Mr. Chandler?"

Marlowe lifted his head and woofed at him. *"Yes."*

"Marlowe says I should." Remy rested his empty mug on the arm of his chair. "How can I argue with that?"

She smiled sadly. "Thank you."

"Jon's things are still at the apartment, correct?" he asked.

Casey nodded. "I haven't touched a thing."

"Good. I'd like to look at them. . . . If that's all right with you."

"Sure," Casey said, nodding. "You can come over tomorrow and . . ."

"Now," Remy interrupted.

The clock was ticking, and he couldn't afford to waste any more time.

A handful of dog cookies and a promise to be back in time for Marlowe's breakfast, and they were off.

The weather was still bad, alternating between torrential downpour and deluge, and Remy had to seriously wonder if this was some sort of precursor to the end.

"You never really answered my question," Casey said, above the sounds of the storm: the heavy patter of rain as it landed upon the roof of the car, the rhythmic swish from the wipers as they barely kept up with the water on the windshield.

"What question was that?" Remy asked, as he headed down Atlantic Avenue toward Summer Street, the rain so heavy he could hardly see the harbor on the other side of the hotels.

"What's Jon's connection to you?"

He had to think a bit on how to answer. The truth was obviously out of the question, but he didn't want to lie to her either; the poor woman had already been through enough.

"Jon has changed," Remy began, carefully picking his words as he navigated the Toyota through the rain-drenched streets. "He isn't who I remember him to be. . . . But then again, neither am I."

He could sense her sudden agitation.

"So what're you saying: that you do know him, that the two of you have changed your identities or something?"

"No, nothing like that," Remy said, trying to stifle her growing unease. "Let's just say that we both have . . . complicated pasts, and leave it at that."

Casey gazed into the darkness through the rain-spattered passenger's window. "That's probably what he meant about starting fresh after his illness."

Remy wanted to agree. The illness had indeed allowed Israfil to start fresh, providing him with an established identity—a life—that he could slip into like a comfortable suit of clothes. And then it hit him. Casey had never known Jon Stall at all; it was Israfil that she had fallen in love with.

She looked away from the window and at him. "Just tell me that you didn't do anything wrong . . . you or Jon."

Remy remembered the war in Heaven, wings spread as he dropped down from the skies, his sword cutting a bloody swath through the forces of the Adversary.

Killing his brothers.

She waited for an answer that he wasn't sure how to pose, when he was saved by the ringing of his cell phone.

"Excuse me." He reached for his phone, and she turned back to the window.

"Hello?" he said.

"It's me," said the unmistakable voice of Lazarus. He always sounded exhausted, like he had just woken up from a nap. Living as long as he had was obviously very tiring.

"Hey," Remy answered, avoiding a particularly nasty-looking pothole behind the Industrial Park. "Do you have something for me?"

"Nothing," Lazarus said sleepily. "But it isn't that I'm not trying. I hit a few hangouts . . . some demon social clubs. I asked about your beating and nobody was fessing up. They all thought it was pretty funny, though."

"A riot," Remy answered. "Nothing about the other thing?"

"Israfil? Nope, but they all sense something's up. The last place I was in was pretty wild. Lots of heavy drinking and fights. The natives were most definitely restless. Had to spread some serious cash around in order to get anybody to even look at me."

"I'll reimburse you." Remy glanced over at the girl. She was drawing a smiley face in the window fog. "I might actually be on to something about that."

The phone was quiet, and for a moment Remy thought he might have lost the connection. "You still there?"

"Yeah," Lazarus answered. "Sorry about that. Do you think you know where he is?"

"Maybe. I'm on my way to a place on Dorchester Street."

"The Angel of Death was living in Southie?" the immortal asked incredulously.

"Maybe," Remy told him.

Again there was silence, and Remy had to wonder if Lazarus was watching television or something.

"Well, good luck," the immortal finally said. "Give me a call if you need anything."

"Yeah, you do the same."

"Was that about Jon?" Casey asked, as Remy returned the phone to its holder on his belt.

"Sort of," he replied. "It's a little complicated right now. I'll fill you in a bit more after I have a look around his study, all right?"

He looked over at her to see she was staring directly at him. There was trust in her dark eyes as she nodded in agreement.

"Good. Now, why don't you guide me the rest of the way. We have to be getting close now."

Casey did as he asked, directing him toward an olive green two-family building on Dorchester Street. He managed to find a parking space relatively close, on the other side of the street, among the bumper-to-bumper

SUVs. Somebody had broken a bottle in the spot, making it unattractive, and Remy got out and kicked the glass around a bit with his shoe before parking.

Collars pulled up against the rain, the two hurried across the street. She pulled her keys from a tiny purse and opened the front door. The entryway was warm and dry. The house, like many older buildings, smelled like food, like the hundreds of meals cooked there over the years. It was a good smell. A comforting smell.

Casey put a finger to her lips, telling him to be quiet as they climbed the carpeted steps to the second floor. "The landlady's a pretty light sleeper," she whispered, searching her key chain again. "I'll be hearing about it for days if I wake her up."

She found her apartment key and let them both in, switching on a ceiling light as they entered.

"This is it," Casey said, taking off her wet coat and throwing it on an old wooden chair that sat by the door. Remy left his coat on, casually checking things out.

The door opened into their living room; mismatched furniture around an old television set, tasteful watercolors of what looked to be a beach house on Cape Cod decorating the walls. Beneath that was a framed and yellowed photograph, of what looked to be the same location captured by the watercolor artist, only in the photo there was family—mother, father, and son, dressed in the clothing of the time period, the early seventies, Remy believed—standing out in front of the cottage. He guessed that the child was Jon.

In a recliner in the corner, a large tiger cat rose to its feet, arching its back in a quivering stretch. The animal eyed Remy curiously with large, yellowish eyes.

"Hello," Remy said to it.

"Who?" the cat asked.

"Who am I? I'm Remy. I'm a friend of your master."

"No master," the cat proclaimed indignantly, then began to lick its paw, ignoring him.

"Sorry," Remy apologized. Cats always had the worst attitudes.

"Feed?" it suddenly asked between licks.

"Not me," the angel answered it.

Then, as if on cue, Casey returned with a dish in her hand.

"Are you talking to Tyger?" she asked, a hint of a smile playing around the corners of her mouth.

"She'll feed you," Remy told the animal, hooking a thumb toward her.

The cat meowed loudly, jumping down from the recliner, walking around Casey's feet, rubbing against her legs.

"Come on," she said to the cat. "I've got your supper here." She turned back to the kitchen, Tyger following, complaining all the while that he shouldn't have had to wait so long to eat.

Just beyond the living room was a short hall, and down the hall, a door. "Is this Jon's study?" Remy asked, raising his voice so that Casey could hear him in the kitchen.

She came back to the living room, wiping her hands on an old dish towel. "Yeah, but I think it might be locked."

Remy grabbed the doorknob and tried to give it a turn. It was.

"I'd really like to take a look inside," he said to her.

"I don't have a key," she said. "Maybe you could open it with a screwdriver?" She started back down the hall. "There's one in the kitchen that we use to . . ."

"I could open it with a minimum amount of damage," he called after her.

Casey stopped, slowly turning back to him. "Just try not to make a lot of noise, all right?" she warned.

Remy put his shoulder against the door, and using only a portion of the strength that he possessed, pushed upon it, breaking the lock and a bit of the jamb. "I'll pay for that," he said, as she joined him in the doorway.

Remy allowed her to enter first. She reached up to pull a chain hanging from a fixture in the ceiling, illuminating the tiny room.

"There isn't much to see," she said, looking around the cramped space.

And she was right. The room was small, with an old metal desk the dominant piece of furniture, squatting in the room's center. There were no pictures on the walls, no shade upon the naked bulb hanging from the ceiling. The room was coldly sparse.

"Do you mind?" he asked her, pointing at the desk.

"Go ahead."

Even the top of the desk was bare, except for a single ballpoint pen resting upon the flat surface, as if waiting to be used.

Used for what? Remy wondered. He pulled out the desk chair and sat down. There were two drawers on either side. He opened one and found it completely empty. Not holding out much hope, he checked the larger drawer below it.

"Hello there," he said with surprise, reaching down and lifting out a stack of notebooks. "Do you know what these are?" Remy asked Casey as he placed the books on top of the desk.

She shook her head, moving to stand beside him. She reached down and opened one. The notebook was filled with writing, page after page of writing, but not in a language she could understand.

"What is this?" she asked, flipping the pages, as if hoping to find something that she could decipher, but Remy knew it would be impossible, for there were very few who could still read angelic script.

"Is this . . . Latin?" she asked, frowning in confusion.

"It's older than that," Remy said.

"You can read this?" she asked him.

He nodded.

"What's it say?"

Remy took the last notebook from the bottom of the stack.

And he began to read.

CHAPTER ELEVEN

Remy found himself sucked down into the ancient script—Israfil's thoughts and feelings in his own words. And the angel's worst fears about what was happening became realized.

It's even more than I suspected. Sensations and stimulations that threaten to overwhelm me every waking moment.

How do they deal with it? How do they function? The sights, sounds, and smells; the bombardment is both terrifying and exciting all at the same time.

If this is how it is for them even a fraction of the time, my admiration for them and for what the Almighty has created grows with leaps and bounds.

The human species is even more remarkable than I originally believed.

The body that I assumed for my experiment is now free of illness, and I can feel my new physical form growing stronger every day as I become acclimated to this new state of being.

Jon Stall was a good man, afflicted with an incurable illness; he sought to live out the remainder of his existence attempting to understand the meaning of life . . . and of death.

How many times did I listen to him as he spoke aloud of his condition, and how much he despised his affliction? He cursed the Creator for what was happening to him, but soon came to accept his inevitable fate, blaming no one and choosing to make what remained of his fleeting existence as rewarding as he possibly could.

For a reason that I still do not fully understand, I was drawn to this example of humanity, grew more connected to him than to any of the other countless millions that I have assisted on to the next phase of existence. How I loved to watch him, to experience life as he did in his final days. But I knew that I could never hope to understand the full meaning of what I had come to admire so.

The human experience; how attractive it had become.

Jon Stall's life force was nearly expended, thanks to the disease that wracked his human frame. All he could do was wait for the inevitable . . . wait for me to release him.

And he was ready, oh yes. He was waiting for my touch when I had the most ridiculous of ideas. Even as I write these words now, I cannot believe them. It was the most insane of thoughts, and yet seductively exciting.

I would take his body, wear it like the finest of garments, and I would live as both human and angel, experiencing all that humanity had to bestow upon me, while still maintaining my function as God's Angel of Death.

Oh, what an experiment that would be, I imagined, thrilled as I had never been before in my long years of being.

And I was right.

I was so right.

Remy flipped through more of the journal, finding entry after entry about Israfil's experiences with being human. There was something frighteningly familiar about the words the angel had written; if Remy had kept journals during his time on earth, they would—he imagined—have read very much like these.

But there was a difference. Israfil had appropriated a preexisting human body, merging with the dying college professor. Quite literally, Jon Stall's form, and everything that defined him, had been assumed by the Angel of Death.

Remy had stifled his true nature, basically forcing his angelic essence to configure to a more human form. Yes, he was still an angel, but mostly all that defined him as such had been locked away deep inside.

What Israfil had become was something altogether different, something unique, something both human and angelic attempting to live within a single form.

It seemed like a recipe for disaster.

And as Remy read through more of Israfil's journal entries, he began to see that his suspicions were right.

I've assumed Jon's life . . . his job as a teacher of life functions . . . of biology. Tapping into his memories, I've found everything I need to continue his existence.

Every day is more and more fascinating. I have even met a woman. Her name is Casey.

Not long before the beginning of my study, I had taken her mother. What a small world. She is providing me with such insight.

As far as humans go, I find her more outstanding than most.

I think Jon would have liked her.

I've become . . . involved. Romantically involved.

I did not intend for it to happen, but it did.

They are the strangest of things, these emotions and desires. I can barely contain them. Sometimes I wonder if I am actually in control.

It's absolutely irrational, I know this, but I'm feeling a nearly overpowering need to apologize to her—for performing my purpose—for taking her mother.

There appears to be a sort of conflict developing between my new humanity and my angelic function. This bears watching.

I would hate to see it evolve into something unmanageable.

Remy closed that journal and removed the last from the pile. Even the condition of the notebook gave a chilling insight into Israfil's deteriorating state. It was tattered and wrinkled, as if something had been spilled on it. A part of him did not want to open it, afraid of what he might find.

Tyger padded into the study, hopping up onto the desk and sniffing at the various journals.

"Where's your . . . ?" Remy almost said *owner* before changing his mind midsentence. "Where's Casey?"

"Couch," the cat said, rubbing the side of his face and neck against the corners of the stacked notebooks, marking them with his scent.

Remy reached out to pet the animal and it reared back, avoiding his hand.

"No touch," Tyger warned.

Remy pulled back his hand. If only Israfil . . . had remained so aloof, maybe they wouldn't be in the situation they currently found themselves in.

Ignoring the animal, he turned his attention back to the last journal and slowly opened the cover.

It was as he suspected.

As he feared.

It's becoming so hard.
To shed this skin of humanity . . . to assume the form and purpose of what I was.

Am.

It's all so very sad. To end their lives. None of them want to die; they cling so desperately to what little life remains. What right do I have?

It's my job; that's what I keep telling myself, over and over, but it's getting so difficult.

I know what they're feeling—how they think. They fear death . . . me, most of all. They fear my design. . . . They fear what I can do.

There's so much pain, but still they hold on with both hands. Fighting to survive. Fighting to live . . . even for a second more . . . they fight.

They fight.

The alcohol and narcotics help to numb the pain, giv-ing me the ability to see things clearer.

At least I believe that I am seeing more clearly.

I have gone to the Watchers, to see if it is possible to be as I am and still live amongst them. Out of all of us drawn to the allure of humanity, I assumed that they would know best.

I was wrong.

They know as little now as they did when they first arrived upon the world of God's man; still wallowing in excess and perversity, waiting . . . believing that they will someday be allowed to return to Paradise.

The Watchers will not be forgiven, and if I had not managed to control my anger, they would have all been destroyed.

There has been enough death for now.

Tyger had lain down at the edge of the desk beside Remy, the cat's contented purrs providing him a mo-mentary distraction from what he feared he was about to read.

The two natures were at war, the angelic struggling

against the human, and in reading Israfil's words, Remy was made privy to the mental collapse firsthand.

He flipped to the last page in the journal.

> *The jackals gather.*
> *They know that I am weak. My thoughts troubled. I am not thinking clearly . . . correctly.*
> *They want it all to end . . . for all the sadness to die.*
> *They say all I need do is stop.*
> *I know that it is wrong . . . but to end the pain.*
> *It would be glorious.*
>
> *They want the scrolls . . . to break the seals.*
> *To begin the end times.*
> *I know I'm not thinking clearly. I must escape their influence . . . hide what they seek from me. It's the only way.*
> *I'm not sure how much longer I can remain strong.*
> *They tell me that this is what He desires.*
> *To end it all.*

Remy looked up, icy fingers of fear running up and down his spine.

The jackals gather.

He had some answers, but now even more questions.

They want it all to end.

Who? Who are the jackals and why do they want it all to end? Remy's thoughts spun.

They want the scrolls. . . . To begin the end times.

He felt as though he might jump out of his skin. The cat was still purring, and he resisted the urge to chase it away.

The scrolls.

He began to rummage through the two remaining drawers on the other side of the desk. Pulling open the larger bottom drawer, he found only a psychology text-book, some office supplies, and a few empty folders.

"I must've fallen asleep," Casey's voice said as she came into the room. "Did you find out anything useful?"

Remy didn't answer. He had just opened the top drawer and knew what he had found. He carefully removed the ancient object, the aroma of age wafting from the soft leather sack that had once contained the scrolls.

"What's that?" Casey asked, reaching across the desk to feel it. "Some kind of leather pouch or something?"

Tyger lifted his head toward her hand, wanting then to be petted.

Cats.

"Have you ever seen this before?" Remy asked.

Casey shook her head. There was a hint of confusion—of fear—in her eyes, and he wasn't sure how much longer he could keep the truth from her.

He was about to ask if there was any other place in the apartment where Jon might have hidden some-thing when Tyger's body went rigid on the desk. The cat hissed, lashing out at Casey, his claws scratching the back of her hand.

"What the hell did you do that for?" Casey whined, bringing the injured hand to her mouth.

"Danger!" the cat said, his fur puffed, eyes wide with fear. Then he sprang from the desk with a growl, his back legs scrabbling for purchase on the wood floors as he fled the room.

Remy started to sense it also, a sudden chill in the air as the light gradually began to dim.

"Is it getting darker in here?" Casey asked, injured hand still pressed to her mouth as she glanced around the room. She reached out with her good hand, tap-ping at the hanging bulb.

Remy grabbed most of the notebooks and shoved them into the leather casing. "We need to leave," he said, putting the satchel under his arm and grabbing Casey as he moved around the desk.

"What's wrong?" Fear had crept into her voice.

The tiny office was darker now, as if the light cast by the bare bulb was slowly being drained away. Remy dragged Casey behind him down the hallway and toward the living room. It was dark there as well, an unnatural inky blackness flooding the room.

"What is it? What's going on?" Casey shrieked, on the verge of hysteria. And he couldn't blame her.

He had come up against those who traveled in the darkness earlier today, and he had no desire to deal with them again.

"A back door," he said, giving her a sudden, violent shake. "Is there a back door?"

She stared at him, eyes welling with tears, lower lip trembling. It was colder now and the darkness was beginning to coalesce around them. Something moved inside the black.

"Is there a back door?" Remy screamed at her again.

A bit of focus seemed to return to her eyes, and she moved toward the kitchen. They darted across the linoleum toward the forest green door in the corner, as a wall of solid black spread out behind them.

Remy reached the door first, grabbing hold of the knob and giving it a turn. It didn't open. He saw the dead bolt and grabbed for it, the sound of the latch slipping back deafening in the eerie silence that suddenly filled the kitchen.

Casey gasped from behind him. Hand still on the doorknob, Remy turned to see that a skeletal hand, its flesh pale and mottled, had emerged from its sea of gloom and grabbed hold of the woman's hair.

"Help me," Casey begged, her eyes wide in horror as she was violently yanked back.

Into the hungry darkness.

Remy grabbed hold of Casey's flailing hands.

She was screaming now, her head bent awkwardly backward as she struggled to keep from being drawn into the shadows.

"Don't let go!" she shrieked at him. "Please!"

But he did, shutting out her wails of despair as the darkness pulled her in. Remy's focus was on the counter and what he could see glistening seductively in the dish rack. He lunged, snatching up the butcher knife and turning back toward the advancing wall of black. Steeling himself, Remy threw himself into the inky darkness.

He was blind, but had expected as much. Holding the knife aloft, he called upon a portion of the power inside him. He hated to do it, but another's life was on the line now, not just his own.

Eagerly it surged forth, energy so great that it caused his almost-human facade to violently tremble. Remy pulled back on the Heavenly force, focusing its power, allowing it to flow up his arm and into his hand. The pain was excruciating, his fleshy form barely able to contain the power, but the knife suddenly glowed like a miniature star, dispelling the darkness.

Remy gasped at the sight of the creatures within. There were at least six that he could see. They were humanoid, thin, pale, and tightly muscled. Wings with a decidedly leathern, batlike appearance sprang from their hunched backs.

A horrible amalgam of the demonic and angelic.

They shielded their eyes from the brightness of Heaven's light, letting the petrified Casey go.

"Come to me!" Remy ordered, motioning the frightened woman toward him.

With a whimper, Casey darted toward him—toward the safety of the light.

"You're going to be all right," he assured her, pulling her close.

She was staring at him strangely, the sight of his glowing hand holding a burning knife. "What's happening?" she asked, her body quivering.

"There'll be time for answers later," he said, moving them back toward the door. "Right now, we need to get out of here."

One of the pale-skinned creatures took to the air, averting its gaze from the knife's glow.

"You'll go nowhere!"

It dropped to a crouch before them, and Remy threw Casey back against the door, shielding her with his body as it lunged.

"You should have listened," it hissed.

Remy could hear Casey fiddling with the door behind him as he brought the knife blade up, burying it in the black, leathery flesh of the creature's shoulder.

"Guess you should've killed me when you had the chance," Remy growled, giving the blade a nasty twist, feeling the muscle shred through the wooden hilt, the stink of cooking meat wafting through the air.

The beast tossed its head back and howled in agony, its arms flailing. One of its leathery wings slashed the air, catching Remy across the face, sending him to his knees.

The world spun and he fought to stay conscious. He still managed to hold the knife, but the agony in his hand had begun to spread down his arm as his angelic nature took the opportunity to try and reclaim what had once belonged to it.

A sudden blast of damp, cold air on his neck stimulated his senses, and he saw that Casey had managed to get the door open and was reaching to pull him out onto the back porch. Tyger exploded out from the shadows, the cat's eyes wide with panic as he made his escape.

Typical, the angel thought offhandedly. *Every cat for himself.*

Remy scrambled to his feet, moving the glowing blade about to find his enemies. He saw them, clustered in a bunch, digging through the leather satchel that had once contained the sacred scrolls.

"They're not here," one of the abominations bellowed. They all turned their malevolent gazes toward him.

"The scrolls," his injured adversary hissed, stepping aside as the others surged in Remy's direction. They were manipulating the shadows now, shielding their eyes from the knife's ethereal glow. "Don't let him get away."

Remy was already backing out the door, but he had to slow them down long enough for he and Casey to get away. Carefully, he channeled a little more of his power into the knife; then, pulling back his arm, he let it fly, watching as the burning blade embedded itself in the skull of the lead attacker with a hollow-sounding thud.

The creature's eyes bugged from his head as he fell backward into the arms of his unholy brethren.

Remy smiled, watching the angelic energy continue to burn, sputtering and sparking as if ready to explode.

Which is exactly what it did.

The room was suddenly filled with the brilliance of Heaven and the screeches of the winged creatures as the glorious release of light seared their every sense.

"Mr. Chandler, come on!" he heard Casey yell from the steps below.

It was still raining hard, and the cool air made the

blistered skin on his hand throb as he threw himself down the stairs. They ran through the backyard and down the narrow alley between Casey's building and the one next door.

"Mr. Chandler, please tell me what . . ."

"Remy," he said, as he opened the gate to the street with his good hand. "After what we've gone through tonight, you should be calling me Remy."

The porch light suddenly went on and the front door opened to reveal an elderly woman, her hair adorned with bright pink curlers.

"Oh, shit, it's Mrs. McGovern," Casey whispered.

"What the hell is going on up there? Do you think it's funny waking an old woman up at this time of night? I'm gonna call the cops and we'll see how fucking funny it is!"

Casey started back toward the porch to explain herself, but Remy caught her by the arm.

"No time for that," he said, dragging her across the street, toward the car.

Her protests were interrupted by the roar of an explosion as an undulating cloud of solid black burst through the roof of the South Boston home.

"Go! Go! Go!" Remy yelled, pushing her to the car.

Mrs. McGovern was out of her house in a flash, ranting and raving. Like sharks to blood, the creatures within the cloud of shadow couldn't pass up an innocent victim. The mass, blacker than the darkest night, dropped from the sky, enveloping the old woman before she even had a chance to scream.

Remy and Casey had reached the car, slamming the doors closed in unison.

"She's going to be so pissed," Casey muttered as she snapped her seat belt in place.

"I don't think that's really going to matter now," Remy said, starting the car and slamming it into drive.

He pulled out of the spot with a screech of tires, grabbing the rearview mirror to see if they were being followed.

Of course they were.

He wasn't sure exactly where he was going as he turned up and down the streets of Southie. All he knew was that they had to get away; the human race was depending on him. If he didn't find the scrolls and convince the Angel of Death to snap out of it, the Apocalypse would be called down and the world would end.

And he really didn't want to see that happen. He'd grown quite fond of the place over the years.

"Oh, my God, they're behind us!" Casey suddenly screamed, twisting around in her seat as she gazed out the back window.

Remy looked to the rearview mirror again. There was nothing but blackness behind them, as if somebody had placed a blanket of black velvet over the back of his car.

"Hang on," he said, gunning the engine, trying to move faster than the cloud of shadow. It was late on a weeknight, and luckily the streets were practically deserted. They were back on Atlantic Ave. now, and moving in the direction of Government Center. His eyes darted to his mirror again.

"We may have lost . . ." the angel began, but something dropped from the sky upon the roof of the car.

He jerked the wheel to one side, causing the car to swerve, and the bloody body of Mrs. McGovern slid down the windshield onto the hood, her eyes wide and still alive with agony beyond imagining. Trailing streaks of blood, she slid off the hood, and then the car bounced obscenely as she fell under the tires.

Casey started to scream hysterically, but Remy couldn't stop. He had to keep going, for there was no way these creatures were going to let them survive once they knew that he didn't have the scrolls.

And suddenly, he knew where he was going, as if his subconscious had taken over the reins for a moment and provided them with a way out of their current predicament.

He was the only person that could pull their asses from the fire.

They were nearing the Public Garden now, and Casey had become oddly quiet, hands covering her face. But then the faint light of the city seeping into the car through the torrential rain began to diminish, and Remy flinched at the sudden nails-on-a-blackboard sound of claws dragging, dragging across the roof of the Toyota.

"Oh, God. Oh, God. Oh, God," Casey began to repeat over and over again, peering out from behind her fingers at the encroaching shadows.

"Hang on," Remy called as he banged a sharp left into a narrow public alley, barely missing a large green Dumpster.

"Get ready," he said, over the sound of flapping wings.

"Ready for what?" Casey cried, the panic in her tone intensifying. "Ready for fucking what?"

Remy slammed on the brakes as he spun the wheel, sending the car fishtailing toward the back entrance of a brick building on the left-hand side of the alley.

"Get out now!" he yelled as he fumbled with his own seat belt.

She nearly flew out the door, then raced around the car to join him in front of a large metal door painted an ugly shade of maroon. Remy pounded on the door.

"Francis, open up. It's me!"

The light of the streetlamp began to dim and the sounds of flapping wings seemed to be coming from all around them. Remy glanced over his shoulder to see his car swallowed up in the advancing wave of darkness.

He pressed Casey against the metal door in front of him and continued to pound. *Where is he?* he wondered, his own sense of panic beginning to build.

"Where are the scrolls?" came a nasty voice from behind them.

Remy recognized it as the one he had stabbed back at Casey's apartment. He spun around to face the encroaching shadow, putting himself between the darkness and the girl.

"Francis!" he screamed, one last time as a skeletal hand reached from the roiling ebony mass.

Voices within the cloud of blackness began to chatter excitedly, then suddenly he was falling backward, landing in a heap atop Casey as the metal door was pulled open.

A tall, balding figure with horn-rimmed glasses, wearing only a T-shirt, boxer shorts, and a frayed terry cloth bathrobe stepped over them, aiming a pump-action shotgun into the darkness outside.

The weapon roared, and the creatures in the darkness screamed in pain as each shot found its target. Plumes of orange fire erupted from the barrel, and like the purifying rays of the sun, it burnt away the darkness and all those concealed within its folds.

Remy lifted his head to see that the last shot had been fired, and that now only the legitimate night remained. He helped Casey up from the ground.

The man in the bathrobe turned, smoldering shotgun by his side, a look of distaste on his face.

"Remy Chandler," he snarled, reaching into the pocket of his bathrobe and removing the nub of a cigar.

"Hey, Francis."

The man lifted a finger to the blackened end of the cigar and ignited it with an orange spark of flame. He took a puff, letting the smoke swirl above his head.

"What crap have you managed to drag me through this time?"

CHAPTER TWELVE

It wasn't like Remy to doze off, but the dry warmth of Francis' basement abode worked its magic. Sitting in the beat-up leather recliner, Remy felt his eyes grow impossibly heavy.

And then they were closed.

He found himself at the desert train station again.

It was dark and a freezing-cold sleet sliced down from the bruise-colored sky. The sound of rain hitting the fragile wooden canopy that draped over the station was nearly deafening.

But Remy didn't know what deafening was until the locomotive suddenly appeared before him, like some great leviathan surging up from the depths, its whistle wailing like the death cries of a world not yet ready to pass from life.

The great train nestled into the station, its unnerving appearance causing him to stumble back against the station wall. It released a long, hissing exhalation of foul-smelling steam, the surface of its black metal body glistening wetly in the gloom.

Carefully, he walked to the edge of the platform and, turning his head to the left, gazed down the length of cars that made up the train's serpentine body. A sound like the throb of a pulse emanated from the train, and Remy was compelled to walk along the platform, searching for signs of riders. He stood upon his toes, peering in through the dusty windows at the rows of seats, and saw that the cars were empty.

The throbbing pulse of the train quickened, and he began to wonder if the monstrous conveyance was about to move on when he heard the racket of movement coming from a freight car attached to the last of the passenger coaches.

Remy went closer, the thumping of activity intensifying. He approached the car, reaching for the latch, desperate to satisfy his curiosity. But before his hand could close upon it, the sliding wooden door began to shake. He could hear the clatter of hooves and the neighing of horses from inside.

He stepped back, just as the door exploded outward, the force of the blast sending him sprawling into a wooden bench. The air was filled with the stench of acrid smoke, and something else. A wild scent . . . an animal smell mingled with the reek of electricity.

Remy wiped dust and dirt from his eyes as he raised his head, and in the clearing haze he saw that he was no longer alone upon the platform. And he saw that the train had indeed been carrying passengers, though he wished with all his heart that it hadn't been the case.

The four figures sat astride their mounts, watching him through the whirling smoke and dust. He knew who they were, even though he'd never met them before.

War, clad in a black leather duster, a red scarf wrapped around the lower part of his face, his eyes hidden in the shadows cast by a wide-brimmed Stetson, sat upon a steed the color of drying blood. To his left, sitting erect in a pearl saddle upon a mount blacker than coal, was Famine. She was adorned in flowing robes of white, her face emotionless and cold, like that of a china doll. But her eyes, they were dark and deep and hungry for the life of the world. To the right of War stood a horse more dead than alive, raw, open sores covering its emaciated body. Its eyes were the color of pus, and a thick drool leaked from its lipless mouth. Pestilence slouched in the saddle, his nearly naked form cadaverous and pale, a swarm of blackflies forming a perverted halo around his skull-like head. And on the end was the most fearsome of the riders, this one's steed appearing healthy and strong, and its muscular flesh as white as winter mountains. The rider Death wore a suit of armor that looked as though it had been crafted from the bones of some great beast. Piercing eyes that blazed a fiery red peered out from inside the darkness of the horseman's horned helmet.

Remy slowly got to his feet, his gaze never leaving the riders clustered before him.

The white steed lifted its head, sniffing the rain-filled air, and brayed, its cries causing a rumble of thunder and a flash of lightning so bright that it seemed to illuminate the world.

Remy shielded his eyes from the searing light, and when he dropped his hands, the monstrous train was gone, as if it had never been there at all. A broad expanse of empty desert spread out from the platform, and when he looked to his left he saw that the riders were now all pointed in that direction, gazing out over the flat, barren plain that seemed to go on forever.

Thunder rumbled again, and the rain continued to fall. One by one, the Horsemen guided their mounts from the platform, down onto the desert floor. They rode side by side, a relaxed gait soon turning into a gallop, as the Four Horsemen of the Apocalypse headed across the desert.

The end of the world was their purpose.

The rattle of the ancient furnace kicking over woke Remy with a start, hands clawing on to the armrests of the leather recliner in a death grip.

"Oh, shit," he said, gulping air as the final vision of the Horsemen riding away across the desert slowly left his thoughts, like the last scene in a movie as it came to a close.

"Anyone ever tell you how cute you look when you're sleeping?" Francis asked, standing before him with two steaming mugs of coffee.

"How long was I out?" Remy asked, reaching for the offered cup.

"Not long," Francis stated, taking a sip from his drink. "Couple'a minutes, more or less."

"Where's Casey?" the angel asked, looking around.

"Over there in the beanbag chair," the man in the terry cloth robe said, hooking his thumb toward the corner of the room. Remy moved to the edge of his seat to look. The young woman seemed tiny, curled up in the center of the large, fluorescent green beanbag.

"She all right?" he asked, bringing the cup to his mouth, first inhaling the invigorating fumes and then taking an eager sip of the hot liquid. It had been too long since his last cup, and he felt as though he might be going through withdrawal.

The coffee was strong, some of the strongest in existence. But what would you expect from beans nurtured in the surprisingly fertile soils of Hell's southern regions. And Francis was always sure to brew a pot when Remy came around.

Francis wasn't at all what he appeared to be, a theme that had become pretty popular of late. At one time he had been one of the most honored angels in the Choir Virtues—a Guardian angel of the highest order—but he had been one of the many seduced by the words of Lucifer, joining the side of the Morningstar during the war in Heaven. Finally seeing the error of his misguided allegiance, the Guardian angel threw himself before the Almighty, demanding the harshest punishment for his sins.

Francis—then called Fraciel—expected death, but received much worse.

Taking advantage of the warrior's skills as Guardian, the Almighty assigned him the duty of watching over those angels banished to Hell after the war. It was his job to make certain that they stayed exactly where they had been sent. Occasionally a fallen angel—now a demon after its time in the infernal depths—would escape to earth. It was up to Francis to send them back.

The apartment building that he lived in and managed was built at a nexus where the barriers between the earthly planes and Hell were very thin. Those who lived in the apartments above were all former sinners, who, after countless millennia, had earned a chance to leave the infernal realm on a kind of parole, required to do a certain amount of good before being allowed to pass on to the next plane.

"She seems fine," Francis answered. He grabbed a wooden chair from beneath a tiny kitchen set and dragged it into the room, sitting down in front of Remy. "Now, would you mind telling me how the fuck you got involved with the Black Choir?"

Remy looked at him, perplexed. "Who?"

"The Black Choir . . . the Shunned. Angels denied a place in both Heaven and Hell for trying to play both sides during the Great War."

"The Black Choir," Remy said, a chill of unease racing up his spine as he recalled the sight of the former angels, twisted by their damnation. "Is that what they're calling themselves these days?"

"Yep," Francis said with a nod. "The Almighty didn't

want them and neither did Lucifer. They're stuck in the middle, belonging to no one and perpetually pissed. I'm surprised you still look as good as you do."

Remy held out his injured hand, examining the blistered flesh. Despite the extent of the injury, he had already started to heal. "Would you believe I came up against them twice today?"

"Yeah, and I went to seven o'clock Mass this morning," Francis said, making a disbelieving face as he had another swig of coffee.

"How was the homily?" the angel asked.

"It was good, all about big fucking liars."

"I'm not lying."

"So tell me, then," Francis said. "How did you manage to piss off the Black Choir?"

Remy had some more coffee, the Hell-grown brew coursing through his veins, making his heart race like he'd just run the Boston Marathon. "Good coffee," he said, placing the nearly empty mug down on the floor beside the recliner.

Francis held out his mug, toasting him. "Got the beans fresh my last trip to Hell. Think it might be a little stronger than usual."

Remy glanced at Casey, then back to his friend. "Israfil is missing," he stated flatly.

"Missing?" Francis asked. "What, exactly, do you mean by *missing*?"

"You haven't felt it?" Remy asked. "That hint in the air that things aren't quite the way they're supposed to be?"

Francis thought a moment. "Didn't realize it was anything like this." He adjusted his black-rimmed glasses. "And you're looking for him?"

Remy nodded. "Hired by Nathanuel. He came to my office and everything."

"No shit," Francis said with wonder.

He continued to nod. "Started poking around a bit, getting wheels in motion, when the Black Choir shows up for the first time today—well, yesterday now, I guess—and tries to discourage me from continuing with the case."

Francis leaned back in the wooden chair, crossing his legs, letting one of his corduroy slippers dangle from his foot. "So what, you're guessing that somebody doesn't want Israfil to be found?"

"Right. Somebody wants to bring about the Apocalypse."

Francis whistled through his teeth, bringing his coffee cup up toward his mouth. "Man, you sure get involved in some interesting shit."

"Don't I, though?" Remy agreed.

"So where does Sleeping Beauty come into the picture?" Francis asked, motioning with his bald head to the corner of the room where Casey slept.

"It appears that Israfil became fascinated with the human species, wanted to experience it for himself, and melded with a guy who was dying of a brain tumor."

"You're kiddin'," Francis said, his voice a shocked whisper.

"Nope. He even went out and got himself a girlfriend." Remy looked over to the dozing Casey.

"Now I've heard friggin' everything. That's fucking nuts."

Remy went on. "But it didn't take long before there was trouble in paradise. Looks as though the two natures didn't mix so well—caused a little bit of a problem for our friend the Angel of Death when it came time to do his work."

Francis was quiet, soaking it all in as he gazed off into space.

"You've gotta find him," he finally said, focusing on his friend.

"No kidding," Remy said. "That's what I've been trying to do in between fallen-angel attacks."

Remy stood, his entire body thrumming. Francis' brew had certainly done the trick, giving him much more than a second wind. Even his hand was feeling better.

"What can I do?" Francis asked, standing as well.

"I'm going to need you to watch her," he said, both of them looking at Casey. "Somehow they found out her connection to Israfil. The Black Choir didn't know that I would be at her place. They came looking for the scrolls."

Remy approached the woman, who had started to stir. She came awake suddenly, eyes wide with fear as the memories of what she'd just gone through flooded her thoughts.

"Oh, my God," she said, eyes darting around the boiler room space.

"Shhhh, it's all right." Remy reached out, running his hand along her arm. "We're with a friend now." He moved so she could see Francis standing there. The man gave her a salute.

"Look, I know you probably have a lot of questions," Remy continued.

"What were those things?" she suddenly asked, struggling to sit up in the shapeless chair. The questions started to spill from her, the sense of anxiety growing. "What do they have to do with Jon . . . with you? I don't fucking understand any of this."

"Calm down," Remy said. "Take some deep breaths. I don't expect you to understand what's going on, but I need you to trust me. Something very bad is going to happen if I don't find Jon soon."

Casey listened, her breathing coming in trembling gasps.

"I need you to tell me everything about the night he

left—every single detail, no matter how unimportant it might seem."

She repositioned herself in the chair, bringing her legs up underneath her. "I'll try," she said, running her fingers through her dark hair, mentally preparing herself. "Do you think I could have something to drink?"

"You want some coffee?" Francis asked.

Remy gave the man a stern look. "She cannot drink your coffee," he stated firmly. "Just bring her some water."

"No need to get snippy," Francis said, walking into the quaint kitchen area. "Sometimes it just doesn't pay to be sociable."

Shaking his head, Remy returned his attention to the girl. "He's getting you some water."

"Thanks," she said, struggling to find a smile. "That night was sort of like a lot of nights around that time. I'd come home from work and Jon would be locked in his study."

"Here ya go, sweetheart," Francis said, handing her a full glass of water.

She took it from him and had a large sip right away.

"And he was in the study that night when you got in?"

Casey wiped her mouth with the back of her hand. "Yes, I could hear him in there, talking to himself."

"Any idea what he was saying?"

"It was all muffled, but he sounded upset. I could hear him moving around, pacing . . . the desk drawers slamming," she said, her gaze distant as she relived the past.

She sipped some more water. "I was about to start making supper when I heard the door unlock and he came out. I was kind of shocked to see him. . . . It had been days."

Francis tightened the belt on his bathrobe. "So you

were okay with your boyfriend locking himself in a room for days on end?"

"Francis," Remy scolded.

"I'm just asking," he retorted defensively.

"It's all right," Casey said. "I sort of have a pattern when it comes to relationships. The weird ones with issues are always drawn to me."

"Hit the jackpot with the last one," Francis grumbled beneath his breath.

"I think it might be wise for you to go sit over there," Remy said, turning his gaze to the vacated recliner.

"Yeah, yeah, yeah," Francis said. "It's okay to save your ass from the Black Choir, but try and help you out with a case and it's a capital fucking offense."

Remy sighed, returning his full attention to Casey. "So, he finally left his study. . . ."

"Yeah, he looked awful. I wanted to go to him . . . you know, to comfort him . . . but something prevented me."

"Were you afraid of him?" Remy asked in his calmest of voices.

At first she looked shocked, hurt, but then he saw the realization dawn upon her face. "Yes, yes I was. At that moment, I was afraid of him." Casey started to cry. "Isn't that awful? Going through whatever it was he was going through, and I was too afraid to comfort him."

Remy tried to keep her in the moment. "Did he say anything?"

Casey sniffed, bringing her hand up to wipe her running nose. "He just said he was going out, and he went."

"Did he take anything with him?" Remy asked. "Something to show that he maybe wasn't planning on coming back?"

Slowly, she shook her head. "He stared at me for a minute after telling me that he was going, and then he left." Casey paused, her gaze cloudy, and then Remy watched her expression change.

"What is it? Did you think of something?"

"His briefcase," she said, eyes focused back on him.

"What about his briefcase?"

"He had it with him, but the only time he carried that was when he was going to work . . . to school."

Remy was on his feet. "I think I'd like to check out Jon's office at Mass Tech."

The woman got off the beanbag chair. "I can take you," she said.

"No," Remy said firmly.

She looked as though she'd been struck. "Why?"

"You're just going to have to trust me," the angel explained. "It would be best if you stayed with Francis."

Francis waved from the recliner. "Don't worry, I don't bite."

"He's kind of . . . y'know, weird," she said speaking softly so that only Remy could hear.

"Yeah, you're right about that, but there isn't anybody that I'd trust your safety with more. Please do what I ask."

"I'm gonna cry if you keep this up," Francis yelled from his seat.

"We're all going to be crying if I don't find what I'm looking for," Remy said, fishing his car keys from his pocket.

"You might want to think about changing your location," Remy told his friend as he walked to the door. "The Black Choir knows we're here, remember."

"Good point." Francis opened the door for him. It was still raining hard outside. "Safe house?"

"Probably the best bet." Remy turned the collar of his jacket up as he prepared for his run to the car.

"I'll give you a call when we're settled," Francis told him.

Remy darted out into the downpour.

"Hey, Chandler," Francis called to him.

Remy stopped at the car, opening the door as he waited to hear what Francis had to say.

"I know it's tough, but don't do anything stupid."

He wished he could've made that kind of promise, but those times had long passed.

Stupid may have been all that he had left.

The rain was coming down in a diagonal sheet now, but it was late enough—*or was it early?*—that traffic was still relatively light.

He wasn't far from the city campus of Massachusetts Technology and drove a little bit faster than he should, but time was of the essence, as his last dream of the Horsemen had shown him.

Remy found his phone and dialed Lazarus' number. The immortal answered on the third ring.

"You all right?" the man asked.

"It's all relative," Remy answered.

"What's up?" Lazarus wanted to know.

"I'm going to need you to back up Francis," he said.

"Something in motion?"

"Yeah, you could say that," Remy replied. "Somebody's out to start the Apocalypse, and they're looking for the scrolls," he said, speaking louder than normal to be heard over the steady deluge of water that was battering his car.

"Well, we're still here, so they haven't had any luck, I'd guess," Lazarus said.

"Yeah, but not for want of trying. Israfil's girlfriend and I were attacked by the Black Choir at her apartment. They were the same ones who roughed me up at the office. I don't think they're smart enough to be doing this on their own, so I'm guessing they're taking orders from somebody else."

"The Black Choir?" Lazarus sounded surprised. "You'd have to be wielding some serious power to keep them on a leash."

"That's what I'm afraid of," Remy said, as he drove over the Harvard Bridge into Cambridge. "I think somebody is very serious about ending the world, and I doubt there's anything they wouldn't do to accomplish their goals."

"What can I do?" the immortal asked.

"Go to the safe house, give Francis a hand with protecting the girl. I'm going to check out where Israfil's human aspect was working before he up and disappeared."

"Got it," Lazarus said, but before Remy could end the call, the man began speaking again. "It . . . it's close to happening, isn't it, Remy?" Lazarus said, a hint of something that could very well have been fear tainting his voice.

"Closest we've ever been, I think," Remy said. "And we're not out of the woods yet, by far."

"Thanks for sugarcoating things for me," Lazarus said, the two of them briefly laughing before wrapping up their conversation.

No matter how many times he tried to squelch it, Remy couldn't get the idea from his mind: It was the closest the world had ever come to ending. The Horsemen were already here, waiting for the seals on the scrolls to be broken. And even though they had yet to be given the official go-ahead, their influence upon the world could still be felt.

The intensity of the weather was only a minor example. He'd had the radio on earlier as he drove, but was forced to turn it off as stories of startling world events were reported. India and Pakistan were on the brink of a nuclear exchange, and North Korea had amassed troops and weaponry on the line of demarcation with

South Korea. And then there was the spread of famine in Africa, reaching epidemic proportions with hundreds of thousands on the verge of death, and the outbreak of a mutated strain of flu in Los Angeles.

The Horsemen were most definitely here, and the only member of the dark riders not exuding his influence was Death. Remy hoped that he had enough time to keep it that way.

Remy finally reached Mass Tech and parked his car in front of the Dryfuss Library Building. He had taken Madeline here for some business seminars years ago, and knew that there was a system of tunnels beneath the college that connected just about all the buildings on campus. He figured he'd have the least amount of trouble getting in through the library, even at this late hour.

He was right, getting inside the library through a side door, and easily avoiding contact with a security guard by willing himself unseen. Finding a mounted wall map of the tunnel system and the buildings that it connected, Remy found the one that he was looking for and headed in that direction.

The Mahut Building was where the Department of Brain and Cognitive Sciences was located, and the offices of its teachers and professors were conveniently on the lower level.

He reached the building quickly and headed down a well-lit hallway, certain from what he recalled of the map that the faculty offices were just up ahead and around the corner.

There was a sudden crash, followed by what sounded like barking coming from behind a closed door on Remy's right. His eyes darted around, searching for shadows, but he didn't see a thing. Cautiously, he walked up to the door and, cupping his hands over his eyes, peered through the window.

It was a large laboratory, the entire back of the room lined with cages, and inside the cages, monkeys. Rhesus monkeys, he believed they were called. They were often used in medical experimentation. Most of the animals were asleep, but he saw that one of them was awake, standing up as it clutched the thin metal bars of its cage. It was looking directly at him as he peered through the window glass.

Remy's heart had been racing, but now that he knew the source of the odd sounds, he found himself calming a bit. He moved on down the hall, turning the corner into a short corridor with offices on either side, and began looking for Professor Stall's name.

He found the office at the end of the hallway, beside a custodian's closet. It was locked. If time hadn't been in such short supply, he would have picked the lock, but this needed to be done quickly.

Remy placed the flat of his hand against the door, just above the knob, and started to push. There was a loud crack, and the door swung into the office, pieces of the jamb dropping down onto the carpeted floor. He quickly entered, closing the door the best he could behind him.

He had to make this fast. He didn't know how early the staff was required to show up, but since there were animals to feed, he figured it had to be relatively early. Pulling the chain on the desk lamp, Remy began his search. First he went through the drawers in the old-fashioned wooden desk, removing all the contents—files, books, lecture notes—but came up with nothing.

He stood, surveying the office, his eyes darting about, searching every corner. In a small space between an old file cabinet and the wall, Remy found a leather briefcase like the one Casey said Jon had taken with him that night.

He snatched it from the floor and laid it down upon the desk, rummaging through every pocket and compartment, but the briefcase was empty.

"Damn it," he swore beneath his breath. For a moment, he thought he'd been close.

A rumble like the sound of an oncoming train filled the cramped quarters, momentarily returning him to alert, but then he realized, as he felt the warm current of air on his legs from the heating duct in the wall behind the desk, that it was only the sound of the heat coming on.

There was something odd in the smell of the heat.

He doubted that anyone else would have noticed, but there was no mistaking the smell of dried papyrus, no matter how slight. He dropped down to the floor to peer into the heating duct, the forced warm air, drying the moisture of his eyes.

The spark of excitement he felt upon finding the briefcase was back again, and he quickly searched the desk for something that would enable him to investigate further. In a top drawer he found a letter opener. Kneeling down, he used the flat tip of the blade to unscrew the metal grate in the wall.

Pulling the black grate away, he tentatively put his hand inside the warm duct and began to feel around. At first all he found were large clumps of dust and grit, and he was about to give up when the side of his hand brushed up against something rough.

Remy got down on his belly, looking into the darkness, and extended his reach even farther into the duct; there was definitely something there. Carefully, he felt around with fingertips, and then one by one, he withdrew the ancient scrolls, five in total. A scroll for each Horseman, giving them permission to unleash their full fury; the fifth a final edict from the Almighty stating that it was time for it all to be brought to a close.

Without the fifth opened, hope still remained alive.

Th-th-that's all folks! Remy heard the voice of a cartoon pig stutter as he gazed upon the ancient documents laid out before him on the floor. He felt some of the enormous weight of responsibility resting upon his shoulders lighten, but not all.

He carried the scrolls to the desk and began to place them inside the empty briefcase. The fifth he put in the pocket in the lining of his coat. Buckling the straps of the leather satchel, his eyes scanned the office one last time, desperate for some little thing that could send him down the right path to finding Israfil before whomever was pulling the Black Choirs' strings found him first.

The heat blowing from the grate caused the papers tacked to a bulletin board above it to flutter in the warm currents of air, revealing a hint of something familiar beneath them. With nothing to lose, Remy approached the bulletin board, lifting one of the fluttering pieces of paper higher to see what was tacked there. It was an old photograph of a small beach house at dusk, the sun setting beautifully in the background.

It was a nice picture, and Remy wondered if Jon or Israfil had taken it.

He suddenly recalled the watercolor painting and the framed photograph hanging on the wall of Casey and Jon's living room. They too were of a beach house. Stepping closer to the board, Remy began to lift up more of the papers, finding even more photographs beneath. Sensing that he might be on to something, he removed the first layer of documents to reveal a sort of collage dedicated to the quaint piece of beach property.

Across the top of the board was tacked a heading that read, A LITTLE PIECE OF HEAVEN.

It felt as if a trap door had been sprung and the floor was dropping out from beneath him.

"I know where you are," Remy said, feeling his pulse quicken and his heart begin to race. He removed one of the yellowed Polaroids and stared at it.

"I know."

He shoved the picture into his coat pocket, grabbed the briefcase from the desk, and left the office. He would first hook up with Francis and Lazarus to find a safe place to store the scrolls, and then they would . . .

Remy froze as he turned the corner to the long corridor that would lead him back to the tunnel.

Listening.

Where before he'd heard the cry of a single lab animal, now he was hearing the cries of what sounded like hundreds. He listened to their frenzied voices, trying to decipher the cause of their panic.

Slowly, he began to walk down the hall, toward the laboratory door. He was surprised to see that it was open, and that someone was standing in the center of the room.

Somebody he knew. Somebody he would not have expected to see here in a million years, but then again, a few days ago he would never have expected to see him in his office either.

The angel's name was Galgaliel, and once he was a brother to Remy.

"Why are you here, Seraphim?" Remy asked the angel, who was clad entirely in black, his pale complexion almost corpselike in its appearance.

Galgaliel had been staring at the caged animals, and he slowly turned his attention toward Remy. "I think you have found something that we've been looking for," the angel said, the look in his pitch-black eyes more chilling than the inhospitable fall weather outside, as more pieces of the enormous puzzle began to drop into place with foreboding precision.

Remy turned to head toward the tunnel system, clutching the satchel beneath his arm. If he could lose the Seraphim in the miles of passages beneath the college, he just might make it out in one piece.

The problem was getting that opportunity.

Galgaliel appeared in front of him, wings of speckled brown spread wide, blocking his way before he was even aware that the angel had left the laboratory. He lashed out, a savage blow hurling Remy backward.

"Give that to me!" the Seraphim demanded, pointing to the briefcase.

Head ringing, feeling the pulse of his heart in his swelling lip, Remy got to his feet, but Galgaliel was there before he could recover. The angel grabbed hold of the briefcase, attempting to wrest it from his hands, but Remy held on tightly.

"Do you truly understand what you're doing?" he asked, struggling to hold on to the case. "Whose wrath you will incur?"

Galgaliel hit him again, and he lost his grip on the briefcase as he was propelled back into the laboratory.

The animals were berserk, the sounds of their howls and screeches nearly deafening in the confined space, the stink of their fear nauseating.

Remy climbed to his feet as he watched the Seraphim bending down to pick something up from the ground where it had fallen.

The beach house photograph.

His hand quickly checked his pocket and found it empty.

Galgaliel stared at the frozen image, the corners of his mouth twitching in what could have been an attempt at a smile, before sliding the photograph into a side pocket on the briefcase.

Remy's thoughts hummed with the possibilities of what he could do to the Seraphim, and the likelihood of failure, when Galgaliel turned his attention toward the cages.

"This is the one who wishes you harm," the Seraphim said, speaking in the tongue of the wild so that all would understand. "The one that wishes to cut your flesh and open your bellies."

The cages rattled with the ferocity of the animals' panic.

"That is, unless you harm him first."

And with his final words, Galgaliel flapped his majestic wings, stirring a moaning wind as tendrils of crackling angelic energy coursed from his fingertips to caress the cages.

One after another, the doors exploded open and the animals once confined within bounded toward Remy.

Eyes blinded with madness and malice.

CHAPTER THIRTEEN

Galgaliel left the lab, the door slamming closed behind him with a deafening finality as the monkeys swarmed.

They were insane, eyes wild, teeth bared, grayish-colored fur puffed up with aggression, making strange barking sounds as they charged, slapping at the ground with elongated fingers.

Remy lifted his arm to shield himself from their assault. They bounced off his body, weighing much more than he would have believed. It was like being hit with multiple bags of wet laundry.

Knocked backward by the shrieking mass, Remy slammed against a table in the far corner of the room. Beakers tumbled over, rolling to the edge and off into oblivion to crash upon the floor. He spun around, looking for something—anything—to defend himself with. There was a metal folding chair leaning against the wall, and he grabbed it, placing it out in front of himself as a sort of shield. All he needed now was a whip.

But the chair wasn't enough.

Where there had been only monkeys before, now he was faced with a wave of furious animal life: rats, mice, rabbits, pigeons, and cats had formed a seething wave, with the sole focus of doing him harm.

Their cries were deafening; a miasma of shrieks, snorts, and wails. Brandishing the chair to keep them at bay, he tried to speak to them, to appeal to an area of their small brains not inflamed by the words of the renegade Seraphim, but they wouldn't listen—couldn't listen—their simple thought processes stuck on the response of survival.

To remain alive, they had to kill him.

The monkeys saw their moment, taking hold of his makeshift weapon, pulling it from his grasp, and tossing it away.

And then they were upon him.

Remy struggled to remain standing as he was engulfed by the swarm; a writhing mass of fur and claws, driven by fear and hate, biting, clawing, and ripping at his beleaguered form. But the weight of the assault was too great, and he stumbled back, his heels crushing the tiny bodies of those that scurried excitedly below his feet. The pigeons dove for his eyes, pointed beaks darting forward to peck at the soft flesh of his face. Remy waved his arms, one of his hands reaching out to wrap around a bird's neck, squeezing it with all his might, feeling the hollow bones beneath the thin layer of feathers and flesh snap and pop within his grasp. The monkeys screeched all the louder as he threw the broken yet still twitching body to the floor.

But no matter how many he disabled, there were ten more to take their places.

Finally, he lost his footing on the bodies and blood of the rodents, his feet sliding out from beneath him as he fell backward to the cold linoleum floor. He rolled onto his side, curling up into a ball, attempting to protect his face. Remy didn't know how much more of this he could take. His entire body was bleeding; deep scratches and bites weeping freely, the scent and taste of his blood further exciting the fury of the attacking menagerie.

Remy didn't want to hurt the poor beasts, feeling a certain amount of sympathy toward their pitiful existence, but at that moment his options were severely limited.

He could either lie there, his body gradually being ripped to pieces, and in the meantime the scrolls were being opened, readying the apocalypse, or . . .

Or he could again awaken his angelic nature.

It was like opening a Pandora's box; he knew it would be like this since he'd summoned his inner power back at Casey's apartment. It became easier to call upon it, and the humanity he worked so hard to build was slowly eroding.

Something forced its way beneath his hand, sinking its teeth into the flesh of his neck.

But what choice do I have?

Remy delved deep within himself, like plunging from high rocks into the freezing embrace of a furious ocean. But he didn't have far to go. The power was there, waiting for him like an addiction.

It knew that he would be calling upon it again. And the angel beckoned to it, calling the force of Heaven to his side.

The power of God's will surged through him like lightning. Remy's body trembled with the ferocity of his disappointment and hate, while tears of happiness streamed down his face.

For once again—even for the briefest of moments— he was complete.

There was a searing flash of brilliance, and the stinking aroma of cooked fur and flesh filled the air, along with screams of animals in pain.

The fire alarms sounded as an artificial rain was released to douse the source of the intense heat, turning to steam as it touched his body.

Remy knelt upon the floor, rocking with the pulse of the power that coursed freely through him. The animals had withdrawn, forming a cautious circle around his glowing form.

Despite the water from above, it felt as if he were on fire and his delicate human shell was wracked with pain. He could feel blisters forming, the fluids of his fragile body brought to boil from the intensity of the power that wanted so much to be released.

But to do that would be to give it all away, everything that he'd worked so hard to build.

And he did not want that.

Remy yanked back upon the psychic reins, restraining the primal powers of creation bestowed upon him by God, attempting once again to place it under his control.

The power fought him, the intensity of the light radiating from his body growing. He could smell his own flesh burning now and felt himself grow nauseous from the stench of his fragility, but he did not allow it to deter him. He continued to fight the wild, angelic nature, and finally his perseverance was rewarded, as the brilliance thrown from his body began to subside, and he managed to place his Heavenly aspect beneath his control.

He pitched forward, the cool touch of the water-covered floor feeling good against his scorched skin. Slowly he lifted his head, seeing that the animals, despite their injuries, were still waiting.

Waiting for the opportunity to pick up where they'd left off.

Remy struggled to focus through blurry eyes as the animals—their coats singed and blackened—silently started toward their prey. He wondered if they could overtake him if he made a run for the door. It was worth a chance, and he tensed his legs in preparation to spring, when the laboratory door flew open, smashing off the wall with such force that it cracked the glass window and dug an angry gouge in the plaster wall behind it.

Francis.

The animals bellowed; their cries unified into one all-encompassing shriek of fury as they started to move forward.

"You might want to move your ass," the former Guardian angel said over the constant ringing of the fire alarm. He pulled a gun from a holster beneath his arm and started to fire at the advancing animals, as he reached out and yanked Remy up from the floor.

"Not that I don't appreciate the save, but what are you doing here?"

He didn't answer right away, continuing to fire at the wave of animal life that kept swarming over the motionless, but not lifeless, bodies of their fallen comrades.

"What the fuck's gotten into them?" he asked as they backed toward the door. "It's saccharin, isn't it," he said, aiming his weapon and firing again. "I knew it. It doesn't give you cancer—it makes you fucking nuts."

They reached the door. Remy grabbed the knob and pulled it closed behind them, shutting in the swarm of living things that surged across the flooded linoleum floor.

"We might want to think about getting out of here before the fire department and the police show up," Francis said, putting the gun back into the shoulder holster beneath his arm.

Remy agreed with a nod, and lurched toward the doorway that would take them into the tunnels. He felt stronger already as he led the way past walls lined with student lockers painted a fluorescent yellow.

"Is that a sunburn?" Francis asked.

Remy glared.

"You let it out . . ." his friend suddenly said.

"Let's not talk about that now. Where's Casey?" he asked.

They had reached a set of stairs that led up from the tunnels and into a back garden section of the college property. They took the stairs two at a time, coming out into the early morning.

No surprise, it was still raining.

"We've got a problem," Francis suddenly said, and Remy stopped. In the distance they could hear the wail of sirens.

"What kind of problem?"

"I brought the girl to the safe house like you asked, and then Lazarus showed up."

Remy nodded. "Yeah, I asked him to. For backup."

Francis brought his long-fingered hand up to his face, stroking his chin. Remy noticed a line of dark bruising along his friend's jaw.

"He wasn't alone," the fallen angel explained. "He brought some Seraphim, and after they kicked the crap out of me—I'm fine by the way—they took the girl and left."

Remy clenched his fists, feeling his anger surge and his concern for the sake of the world begin to intensify. "Son of a bitch, he's part of this. Lazarus is part of this."

"Looks to be," Francis said softly, unhappy that one they had trusted in the past had turned against them.

"It explains how they knew where to find us—the Black Choir in Southie, me here." Remy stopped talking as something slowly rose to the surface of his thoughts. The look on his face must have been something awful.

"What's up?" Francis asked cautiously.

"I think I figured out where Israfil is, and I bet they have too," Remy said.

"So, what, the Seraphim are behind all this?" Francis asked, his face screwed up with confusion. "Why the fuck would they want to start the Apocalypse?"

Remy shrugged, shaking his head. "I found the scrolls in Jon's office, but it was a Seraphim who caused my little predicament back in the lab, after he relieved me of the scrolls."

"So you had the scrolls, but you lost them?"

"Yeah, mostly."

"Mostly?" Francis asked.

Remy reached inside his coat pocket. "Hope it wasn't too damaged by my momentary physical change," he said, pulling the rolled piece of parchment from the inside pocket of his coat.

The scroll appeared a bit singed, but the seal remained intact.

"I hid one, just in case."

"Sneaky for an angel," Francis said, a sly smile creeping across his features. "Are you sure you never fell?"

Remy placed the scroll back inside his coat to protect it from the rain.

"So what do you do now?" Francis asked.

They headed across the garden in the direction of Remy's car.

"I don't really have many choices," he said. "I either try to stop them or I don't. I think you know which one I'm going to pick."

"Need any help?" Francis asked.

Remy turned his head to look at him. "Yeah, that would be greatly appreciated."

"*De nada*," Francis said. "So where to, then?"

"We've bought ourselves some time with the scroll," Remy said, patting his coat, as they came up to his car. "There are a few things I have to do first, but then we're heading for the Cape."

"Excellent," Francis replied, pulling his own keys from the pocket of his dress pants and turning in the direction of his own car. "Been meaning to get there all season."

CHAPTER FOURTEEN

Four years ago: before he had a name

The black Labrador puppy plopped his tiny, nine-week-old butt down upon the newspaper in the open wooden box and tilted his head quizzically up at the man staring down at him.

His brothers and sisters were playing roughly in another corner of the birthing box, growling and barking at one another, uninterested in their new visitor.

It was as if they could not see him. But he was there, standing above him.

The puppy did not understand why, but he was fascinated by this one.

There had been others that had come to look at them, males and females, young and old, but none had interested him like this.

"Hello there," the man said, and the puppy could understand the words as if they had come from one of his own kind.

"*Hello*," the puppy responded with a yip.

"You're a cute one, aren't you?" The man slowly reached down with one of his large hands, allowing the puppy to sniff.

He liked his smell and licked one of the man's fingers in affection before lifting one of his paws and placing it within the man's hand.

"My name is Remy," the human said.

The puppy barked, not yet having a true name. In the language of dogs, he informed the man that he was fifth-born of seven.

"Well, Fifth-Born of Seven," Remy said to him. "How would you like to become part of my pack? Me, a female, and you."

The pup turned his gaze toward his brothers and sisters, who were still playing roughly in the corner. First of seven had seven of seven pinned to the floor and was biting her ear, while the other barked excitedly.

"Leave pack?" the puppy asked, lifting his head to look back up at the man.

"Leave this pack to become part of another," Remy answered. "They'll all be leaving this box soon as well to go to other packs."

Fifth-Born of Seven thought about this for a moment.

"Sad," the pup whined.

"Yes, for a bit, but you will be very much loved in your new pack."

"You love?" the pup asked Remy.

The man smiled, showing off his large teeth. The master of the pack for sure, the pup knew.

"I will love you very much," Remy said, and Fifth-Born of Seven knew that this one's words were true, and that he would love this man very much in return.

"Female?" the puppy asked, sniffing the air for traces of her. He could smell her scent on the man's clothes. That too was a pleasant smell.

"I know she will love you too."

The puppy climbed to all fours and turned his head to look at his brothers and sisters at play.

He knew he would miss them at first, and wondered if they, in turn, would miss him.

"Will you join my pack?" Remy asked him again.

The puppy turned away from the old pack to look at the new.

"*Yes,*" he barked, his tail wagging in equal parts excitement and fear.

Remy smiled again and bent forward, picking him up and removing him from the box where he had come into the world.

It was a big world outside the box, filled with new smells and frightening noises, but as he nestled into the crook of the human called Remy's arm, he sensed that this was the beginning of something wonderful, and that there was no reason for him to be afraid.

"You'll need a name," Remy said as they left the only world Fifth-Born of Seven had ever known.

He held the puppy out before him. Their eyes connected, and the pup waited to hear what he would be called.

"I think your name will be Marlowe," the male said, and kissed him gently on top of his head before returning him to the crook of his arm.

"*Marlowe,*" the pup repeated, his eyes suddenly very heavy, the need for sleep overwhelming him.

"*Good name,*" Marlowe agreed, not having the strength—or the will—to remain awake any longer. Feeling perfectly at ease, he fell fast asleep, dreaming of running very fast.

And of how very much he would be loved.

"*Where?*" Marlowe asked from the backseat of the car.

"I told you already," Remy said, trying not to sound annoyed. He'd told the dog their destination at least ten times since he'd returned home to quickly change his charred clothes and pick up the animal.

"Ashlie's house. You're going to Ashlie's house."

Marlowe grumbled something Remy didn't quite

catch, but he was sure it had to do with his displeasure of being left behind yet again.

The Bergs lived on Mount Vernon Street, which was only the next street over, and they could very easily have walked, but the rain had yet to let up. It was nice that Ashlie's parents shared her love of Marlowe. They had no problem at all taking care of him for Remy, especially knowing how difficult things had been for him since his *mother* had fallen ill.

Remy double-parked in front of the Bergs' brownstone, then opened the back door, standing in the rain, waiting for Marlowe to exit.

"C'mon boy," he said, urging the dog out. "We're going to see Ashlie now."

Marlowe didn't move.

Remy leaned in to the car. "What's wrong?"

"I go," Marlowe said, refusing to make eye contact with him.

"You can't come with me, pal. It's too dangerous."

"No," the dog said stubbornly, draping his head over the back of the seat.

The heavy rain thrummed against the metal roof as Remy stood, half in and half out of the downpour.

"Listen," he finally said in his firmest tone. "I don't have time to fool around right now. It's very important that I get to where I'm going so I can take care of business and come back to get you."

Marlowe lifted his head to look him in the eyes.

"When?" the dog asked.

"As soon as I'm done," he explained. "I have to go and help Casey and her friend . . . and then I'll come back. Okay?"

The dog thought for a moment.

"Must come back," Marlowe said, and Remy could sense genuine sadness emanating from the animal's words. *"Pack gone. Just Marlowe. All alone."*

Remy reached into the car, tenderly rubbing the side of his best friend's face. "I'm not going to leave you alone," he promised the animal. "Nobody's going to break up our pack, okay?"

Marlowe's tail flopped feebly.

"Let's go in and see Ashlie. The sooner I leave, the sooner I can come back and get you."

The dog's mood seemed to brighten a little bit.

"*Park?*" he asked hopefully.

Remy chuckled at the animal's attempt at blackmail. "Sure, you get out of the car now and I'll take you to the Common when I get back. Deal?"

Remy held out his hand to the Labrador and Marlowe lifted his paw to be shaken.

The deal was struck.

"C'mon, pal," Remy said, extracting himself from the backseat.

"*Remy,*" Marlowe called to him.

He stopped, crouching to look into the backseat of the car.

"*Love you,*" the dog declared.

"Love you too," the angel responded in kind.

And satisfied by this answer, Marlowe jumped out of the car and trotted up the steps to the Bergs' front door.

Remy knew how the dog was thinking: The quicker they got this business out of the way, the quicker he could come back and take him for his walk.

It was a plan that Remy could get behind. He only hoped that when this was finished, there'd be a world—never mind just a park—to come back to.

Remy kept the good-byes brief, but as he turned to leave the brownstone, Ashlie's mother threw her arms around him in a hug, kissing him lightly on the cheek, whispering in his ear to be strong.

He continued down the steps, hoping that he did have it within himself to be as strong as he was sure he would need to be.

He was just about ready to drive away when he heard a horn behind him and saw a car pull up, flashing its headlights. He got out of the car, slamming his door closed, and approached the car. The window slowly lowered and Steve Mulvehill looked out at him, cigarette dangling from his mouth.

"Get in for a minute," the homicide detective said.

Remy thought that the man looked like hell; his face unshaven, dark circles beneath swollen eyes.

He went around to climb in on the passenger's side. "What's up?" he asked, an involuntary shiver running along his spine as rainwater trickled down his neck as he sat in the front seat.

Mulvehill reached inside his raincoat pocket and came out with a folded piece of paper. "Got the information on that Cape Cod property you were looking for. It was sold by the original owner about four years ago."

It was sold *before* Israfil took control of Jon Stall's life.

Remy took the offered paper, reading the address scrawled there. "Thanks. You didn't have to drive over here. You could've just called me."

His friend gazed out the windshield, the wipers on high to keep up with the intensity of rain that was falling. Despite the speed, the blades were still having a difficult time.

"Yeah, I know, but I wanted to talk to you . . . before you left." Mulvehill took a long pull from his cigarette as he looked at him. "I should go with you," he said.

Remy shook his head. "Thanks, but no. This isn't for you."

"Angel shit?" the detective asked.

"Angel shit," Remy answered with a nod. "It's better

that you stay here. I have no idea how this is going to work out."

It was Remy's turn to gaze out the front window, the wipers going back and forth in a mesmerizing beat.

"Things are bad, aren't they?" Mulvehill commented.

"Yeah, they are," Remy replied.

"Be honest with me," Mulvehill said. "Do you think we've got a chance?"

"Failure's not an option," Remy told his friend, forcing a smile on his face. "Get a bottle of Glenlivit, and when I get back, we'll go up on the roof and I'll tell you all about it."

Mulvehill nodded, smoking his cigarette down to nothing. "Don't stand me up," the detective said finally. "You know how much I hate to drink alone."

Remy laughed as he pulled the latch and opened the car door. "What the hell are you talking about? You always drink alone." He got out into the rain.

"Yeah, you're right," Mulvehill agreed. "All the more for me that way." The detective smiled at him. "Watch your ass, angel," he said, putting the car in drive, starting to pull away.

Remy closed the door, standing in the early morning rain, watching as his friend continued down Mount Vernon Street, taking a right and disappearing from view. He wondered briefly if it would be the last time he'd see Steven Mulvehill, before dismissing the dispiriting thought.

Hurrying to his car, he glanced at his watch. It was getting late, but he still had one more stop to make.

One final good-bye that had to be said.

CHAPTER FIFTEEN

Somerville, Massachusetts, 1972

Madeline knew that he wasn't asleep; after fifteen years of being married to Remy, she could tell these things.

They had finished making love a little while ago, but she found that sleep was eluding her as well this cool summer night.

It was dark in their one-bedroom apartment, and the light curtains that hung in front of the window billowed in the night breeze, looking like a ghost from any number of scary movies she'd seen throughout the years.

"Hey," she said, her voice sounding intrusive in the still of the dark.

"Hey back," he answered.

"What's wrong—not sleeping tonight?" Madeline rolled onto her side, throwing her naked leg over her husband's lower body. She snuggled her face in the crook of his neck, breathing in his scent. He smelled faintly of cinnamon and some other spices she couldn't quite remember.

Madeline remembered when she'd first asked him about the aroma, not too long after he'd told her what he was . . . *had been*.

He'd told her that that was just how angels smelled.

It was fine by her; it reminded her of fall in New England which was her favorite time of year.

Madeline kissed his neck.

"What's your story?" he asked. "I'm not keeping you up, am I? I could go in the living room and read if . . ."

She patted his muscular chest. "Shhhhhhh," she told him. "It's all right, I just can't seem to sleep either."

The room momentarily returned to quiet.

"Want to fool around again?" she asked him, taking the skin of his neck in her teeth.

Remy chuckled, putting his arm around her and pulling her closer to him. She never felt as safe as she did when he held her.

"I was just about ready to put myself to sleep when I made the mistake of listening."

For a second she didn't understand, but then remembered that Remy still retained the gifts of his kind, the ability to hear those praying to their gods.

"Did you hear something that bothered you?" she asked.

"Worse," he said. "I heard something that made me think."

"What was it?"

"It was a guy, older guy from the sound of his voice, whose wife is dying. He was begging God to help, promising anything just so that his wife wouldn't die."

"That's sad."

"Yeah, it is, and it made me think of us . . . of you, and what if . . ."

Remy gently moved her over and sat up, throwing his legs over the side of the bed.

"Hey," Madeline said consolingly. She hugged him from behind, liking the feeling of her bare breasts pressing against the warmth of his back. "I'm fine, nothing's wrong with me. No need to think this way."

She kissed his shoulder blade and hugged him tighter.

"But I do need to think that way. I'm not like you, Madeline, and no matter how much I want to be, I never will be like you."

"Don't talk like that, please," she said. "You're my husband and I love you very much, and I don't want you to ever forget that. Yeah, you're different. So what? My girlfriend Ginny's husband is Armenian. Big friggin' deal."

Remy turned around on the bed, taking her into his arms. He brought his face down and kissed her long and passionately on the mouth, both their tongues hungrily searching out each other's.

He broke their kiss and looked lovingly into her eyes. In the dark his eyes had a golden glint, the flecks of color reflecting in the faint light of the bedroom.

"Hearing that man's prayers," he said, his voice an emotional whisper. "It reminded me of how fragile you are."

Madeline couldn't remember the last time she had seen her husband so upset. She pulled him close, wrapping her arms around him, a bandage to his emotional wounds.

"I don't want you to think about that stuff," she said, running her hands through his hair.

He started to protest, but she brought her lips around, placing them firmly over his in a kiss that forced him to be silent.

Remy broke her lock upon his mouth, again looking into her gaze.

"I just don't know what I would do if . . ."

She didn't want to hear it anymore, and using all her strength, forced the man she loved back down onto the bed and crawled naked atop him before he could even think about escaping her.

"There are other things to think about now," she

said, grinding her lower body into his, feeling him respond.

His hands drew her down to him, and they kissed.

Within moments, they were making fevered love again, their cries and moans of pleasure drowning out the prayers of the needy traveling in the night.

She looked so frail.

Remy stood beside his wife's bed, watching her as she slept.

Her eyes slowly came open, as if somehow alerted to his presence, and she turned her head upon the pillow, looked at him, and smiled.

"Hey," she said, her voice no stronger than a whisper.

"Hey," he said back, moving closer to her bedside. He reached out, taking her hand in his. Again he was disturbed by how cold it felt, how artificial the skin that he had kissed and adored every inch of felt beneath his touch.

"How are you feeling?" he asked, bending down to place a kiss upon her brow. He regretted the stupid question as soon as it left his lips.

"Been better," she said, closing her eyes with an exhausted sigh.

The wind moaned outside, throwing the rain violently against the window.

"Listen to that," she said. "Still pretty bad out?"

"Yeah," he said. "No sign of letting up either."

"It'll make the flowers grow," she said, smiling with her eyes closed, forever the optimist.

He squeezed her hand in response. She loved the springtime, the flowers in bloom. It was like a knife to his heart to think that she had seen her last.

"Always liked nights like this," she said, turning her head to look up at him. "Sitting on the couch, curled up under a blanket, watching something . . . anything on TV, no matter how good or bad. It was good . . . just being there with you."

The pain was excruciating, like nothing he'd ever felt before. He'd thought about this pain, what it would be like, and never imagined the full fury of its strength.

He would have taken the burning pain of his true form asserting itself repeatedly over the next seven years instead of having to endure this now.

"You look awful," she said, weakly squeezing his fingers in return. "At least I have an excuse."

He didn't know how much to say, how much to tell her.

"It's obvious that you haven't found him yet," Madeline said. "Because I'm still here."

Remy didn't get sick; it wasn't possible for him, but he certainly felt sick then, everything about him breaking down. He felt as though he were dying.

Dying along with her.

"I'm close," he said. "I . . . I think it might be done today."

Something broke loose within his chest, something jagged and sharp, spinning around inside, ripping him to bloody bits.

"That's a good thing," she said.

He stared at her with panicked eyes. Everything he had feared was coming true, as if he were being punished.

Penance for my sins.

"It is," she said to him firmly. "I'm tired, Remy, tired of fighting to keep this poor old body afloat. I'm done now. I've had my life . . . my greatest love. I can leave satisfied."

His eyes burned like pieces of the sun jammed into the fleshy sockets, but he did not cry. He never could cry.

It was the only human aspect he could not surrender to. It would have hurt far too much to be *that* human, and he was unsure if he was *that* strong.

"Do this for me, Remy Chandler," she said. "One last thing to show how much you love me."

He brought her hand . . . her poor, cold hand that had once pulsed with so much love, to his mouth and laid his lips upon it. "Anything for you," he said, eyes afire.

"Find him," Madeline said, her voice growing progressively weaker. "Put things back the way they're supposed to be."

Her face twisted up slightly, and he knew that she was in pain. And it killed him to know that there was nothing that he could do to take it away.

Except.

He reached down to her, gently taking her frail form into his arms, and he saw his life with her flash before the theater of his mind. Such a short, wonderful life they had shared, and he wouldn't have traded it for anything.

"I have to go now," he said to her.

Madeline swallowed, a dry click in her throat. Her eyes had closed, but she forced them open. "Tell the baby that I love him very much . . . but that I have to go, and that I'll miss him. Will you do that for me?"

He nodded, his body feeling as though it would simply dissolve, everything that he was disintegrating to dust and blowing away on the wind.

"I will," he said.

"Try to make him understand, I . . . I don't want him to be mad."

"He won't be mad," Remy told her. "He'll miss you very much. . . . I'll . . ."

His voice wouldn't work; it had rotted away, silencing him.

"You have to go," she said, and she pulled her hand

feebly away. Madeline closed her eyes, turning her face so as not to look at him. "I'm ready, and so are you."

He leaned forward again, placing his lips upon her head.

"I love you, Madeline Chandler," he said, finding his voice again.

"And I you, Remy Chandler," his wife said, turning her face so that their lips could touch again. "My love . . . my angel."

And he knew at that moment, if Madeline were able, she would have left the world right then, surrendering what little life remained in her fragile form, ascending to become part of the stuff that composed the universe.

But she couldn't.

She was asleep again as he stepped back from her bed, remembering this last sad sight of her, before turning toward the door.

Francis stood respectfully in the entry, hands folded, bald head bowed.

He slowly lifted his face to look at Remy. "Are we ready?" the former Guardian angel asked.

"Yeah," Remy said, the plaintive cries of imprisoned souls urging him on to the last leg of his journey.

"We all are."

CHAPTER SIXTEEN

They took Francis' car, the black Land Rover barreling down Route 3 on the way to the Cape.

It was sort of eerie, Remy thought, looking out the windows; the roads were nearly empty, despite the time of morning. It was rush hour, and traffic should have been at the max, especially on the other side, leading toward Boston.

"It's almost as if they can sense something's going to happen," Francis suddenly said, picking up on his vibe. The Guardian looked across at him. "Like they're just waiting for the other shoe to drop."

They'd had the radio on when they first hit the road, turning it off less than ten minutes into the journey. They didn't need to know how close the world was to the end.

It was pressure that they could live without.

"There're some CDs in the glove compartment," the fallen angel said to him. "Take your pick."

Remy pushed the button and opened the compartment.

To say that Francis' taste in music was eclectic was an understatement. Remy found examples of rock, pop, soul, hip-hop, and even some country, each new CD case uncovered providing him with another surprise.

"Barry Manilow?" Remy said, holding it up.

The fallen angel shrugged. "He writes the songs that make the whole world sing."

Remy decided that some Sinatra would be just the thing to calm his nerves. He placed the disc into the car's player, the Rover's high-end stereo system immersing them in the songs of Old Blue Eyes, as they drove on to inevitable conflict.

They continued on Route 3, and the closer they got to the Cape, the harder it seemed to rain. It wasn't long before they were the only vehicle on the road.

"I know how you feel about guns," Francis suddenly said, interrupting Remy's rumination on the words to "I've Got You Under My Skin." "But I stopped off at my storage bin and picked up some items that might come in handy."

"What kind of items?" Remy asked.

Francis reached out and turned the volume down. "Items that will be beneficial in dealing with the Black Choir, not to mention the Seraphim."

Remy didn't like the idea of weapons, or violence, for that matter, but he knew that there wasn't likely to be any choice. Whoever was responsible for what was going on wasn't about to allow them to waltz in and break up their plans.

Violence was inevitable.

Gazing out through the rain-spattered windshield, Remy again saw another sign of the impending Apocalypse. The Sagamore Bridge was empty of traffic, and they passed over the Cape Cod Canal without ever slowing down.

"That doesn't happen too often," Francis said, increasing the speed of his wiper blades to keep up with the watery onslaught.

Remy recalled the hours sitting in the summer traffic leading up to the bridge; how Madeline swore, year after year, that it was the last time that they would do it. But every year they had returned, seduced by the beauty of the Cape.

It took his wife's illness, not the seemingly never-ending traffic, to finally stop their visits.

They continued off the bridge up Route 6 to Well-fleet. Remy could feel a knot of anxiety growing in the pit of his stomach.

For about five seconds, after his final words with Madeline, he'd seriously considered just calling it quits, returning to Beacon Hill, picking up Marlowe, and going home to wait it out.

Losing the one you love had the ability to make you think some really stupid things. It had taken four seconds to come to this conclusion, and another second to berate himself for wasting time.

"How we doing?" Francis interrupted Remy's thoughts. They were on a long stretch of road, undeveloped property that wasn't likely to remain that way on either side.

Remy unfolded the map he'd printed out from Map-Quest earlier and gave it a quick perusal. "Ravenbrook Lane should be coming up on our right," he said, and before too long, Francis pulled the car over and turned off the Land Rover's engine.

"We're here," he said, leaning his bald head against the driver's-side window, gazing out at the weather. "So much for it clearing up."

Remy observed that even though it was morning, it seemed as dark as night here. "Figures," he said. "You finally get to come to the Cape and it's raining."

"Isn't it always that way, though?" Francis asked.

"Isn't it?" Remy responded in kind.

They got out of the SUV, going around to the back of the vehicle. Francis used his key to open the hatch-back and put down the gate. He reached inside the back, throwing aside a blanket and opening a storage compartment.

"Now, I want you to be nice to these," Francis said, pulling out the items that were wrapped in a navy blue blanket. "They're quite valuable."

He set the blanket down on the gate and carefully began to unwrap it.

Remy had sensed them as soon as Francis opened the hatchback, like a tiny, musical voice singing from somewhere far off in the distance.

The two swords appeared ancient; their once-resplendent surfaces tarnished nearly black by the passing of years. He found himself stepping back, away from the blades.

It wasn't often that swords forged in the fires of God's fury showed up minus their owners.

"How did you come by these?" he asked, not able to take his eyes from the weapons.

"They were part of a cache of Heavenly weapons that supposedly went missing during the war," Francis explained. "Haven't a clue what happened to the others. These two were found in an archeological dig in Lebanon fifty or so years ago." The fallen angel stared lovingly at the blades. "Do you know how many bad guys I had to kill in order to afford these babies?"

Remy scowled. He'd never appreciated Francis' extracurricular activities as a hired assassin.

"Take your pick," his friend told him.

It had been thousands of years since he'd last wielded a sword, and he had sworn that he'd never do it again.

The weapons whispered to him of what they could accomplish in his hand; the enemies that would fall before their righteous power.

"I don't mean to rush you," Francis said over the

hissing whispers of the weaponry. "But there's this thing called the Apocalypse we're trying to avoid."

Francis was right, and he had no choice this time.

"I'll take this one," Remy said as he reached down to the blanket, taking a tarnished blade by the hilt.

And the sword began to sing.

In the hands of any other, the sword would have been just that, performing as such, but in the hands of a member of God's Heavenly host, it was so much more.

The blade vibrated in his grasp, the heavy accumulation of tarnish and grime burning away in a snaking trail of oily smoke. He could feel the weapon attempting to make contact with his true nature, and silenced the communication with his mind.

"I think it likes you," Francis said.

Remy stared at the weapon in his hand. It had started to glow, sparks of yellow flame leaping from the blade's edge as he passed it through the air.

Francis claimed his own weapon, but with little effect. The blade remained the same, its surface dark and stained. The sword did not react to him, for he had fallen from the grace of the Creator.

"Not as pretty as yours, but it'll do," he said, slicing the air with the weapon, trying it out. "Oh yeah, take one of these too."

There was a smaller package wrapped within the blanket, and Francis flipped it open to reveal two ornate daggers. "The two sort of go together," he explained, handing Remy a knife with similar markings to those on the hilt of his sword.

Not sure where he should put it, Remy slid the knife through his belt, looking down to make sure that it would stay. It did.

"All right, then," he said with a sigh. "Should we give this a shot?"

Francis adjusted his glasses and hefted his sword. He had put his knife in the inside pocket of his suit jacket. "Yeah, what the fuck? Already made the drive."

They walked side by side—swords in hand—down the dirt driveway that led to a small cottage. They'd willed themselves invisible. If anyone had seen them, the police would have been called immediately, reporting that there were two crazy people walking down the street with swords.

It was a traditional-style Cape dwelling, with unpainted, weathered shingles, a carved American eagle hanging above the front door, and lobster traps decoratively placed against the house on either side of the steps.

"Quaint," Francis said, changing his sword from one hand to the other.

"Yeah, I'm sure it's what every angel dreams of having," Remy said, looking around for any sign that they might not have been alone. The smell of the ocean was heavy in the breeze, the wind whipping the rain nearly horizontal.

"We going in?" Francis asked. The lenses of his glasses covered with raindrops, and Remy had to wonder how he could possibly see.

"I was thinking we should," Remy said, moving toward the front steps.

Francis followed, reaching ahead of him to take hold of the doorknob. "Allow me," he said, and he gave it a quick twist, an expression of surprise blooming on his face as the door opened easily.

"Look at that," he said. "I think we're expected."

The fallen angel threw open the door and bounded inside, his sword at the ready.

Remy followed, eyes darting around the living room as he closed the door behind him. A leather couch, a love seat, and three chairs, along with a coffee table and two end tables with matching lamps, made up the furnishings. Nothing looked out of place.

The house smelled stale, as if it had already been closed up tightly for the season.

Francis lowered his sword and headed toward the kitchen.

Remy closed his eyes and took in a deep breath, searching for a scent—any hint—that a member of his kind was there.

He didn't have long to wait.

"Hey, Remy," Francis called from the other room.

He continued through the living room and down a short brick corridor to a spacious kitchen that seemed much larger than it should. Francis stood beside a marble-topped island, gazing out through the glass sliding door at a wooden patio deck, and the beach beyond it.

Something was wrong with the beach.

It appeared to be low tide, but it was the lowest tide he had ever seen.

Multiple figures were standing upon what had once been the ocean floor, their attention riveted to the house.

"You think they're waiting for us?" Francis asked.

Remy looked at the sword in his hand; it had started to glow brighter, the golden flames sparking higher.

"I think we should go down and ask," he said.

Francis looked through the glass of the sliding door. He made a face and shrugged. "Works for me."

Remy pulled open the sliding glass door to the deck outside.

The wind howled off of what used to be the ocean, the intensity of the rain like tiny pinpricks upon their exposed flesh.

Francis removed his horn-rimmed glasses and put them inside his shirt pocket.

They walked across the deck, down some steps, and crossed a small yard. Francis opened a gate at the end of the property and then the two of them descended a short flight of wooden steps to the beach below.

The closer they got, the more disturbing it all became. The ground that had once been the ocean floor was revealed to the world; seaweed and rocks and refuse that had lain at the bottom of the sea for years, exposed, as well as thousands of examples of ocean life writhing and flopping about in their death throes.

But their suffering went on and on, for they could not die.

An ominous rumble of thunder reverberated along the coastline. A white flash that resembled more the blast of a nuclear weapon than lightning illuminated the distant horizon, and Remy gasped at what he saw.

The Horsemen.

They were giants, sitting astride their equally enormous mounts, waiting for the signals to unleash their intent. And then they were gone, lost in the gloom of the never-ending storm.

But Remy knew that they were still there, patiently waiting for the festivities to begin.

"I won't ask if you saw that," Francis said, staring straight ahead as they made their way toward the group of figures waiting for them on the beach.

Remy was about to warn Francis to be on his guard when he saw it from the corner of his eye. A patch of what he thought to be part of the storm-blackened sky dropped down suddenly, flowing toward them.

"Watch it!" Remy managed, as the patch of darkness expanded, enveloping them both in its freezing embrace.

The shadow was all-encompassing, but the sword that Remy carried provided them with a small area of light.

He and Francis stood back to back, swords raised. They were silent, tensed, and ready, listening to the scuttling and rustling of their opponents beyond the small circle of light.

"Did I mention how much I hate these guys?" Francis asked, as the first of the Black Choir emerged from its hiding place within the concealing shadows.

It crawled along the ground, malformed wings folded upon its back. It saw Francis and stopped, a spark of fear in its jaundiced eyes. The Guardian between Pandemonium and Earth was not someone that anyone—fallen or exalted—truly cared to mess with.

Remy had always believed that it was a good thing that Francis was on his side.

The Choir member's flesh appeared injured, its body speckled with open wounds, exposing muscle and bone.

An aftereffect of Francis' special shotgun blasts from the previous night, Remy guessed, raising his sword and bringing it down upon the vile creature's back.

The demonic angel shrieked as the burning blade cut into its pale, loathsome flesh. It flipped onto its injury with an animalistic hiss, grabbing the sword blade with both hands before Remy could withdraw it.

"A blade of God in the hands of one who has shunned the glory of its master," the fallen angel screamed, the flesh of its fingers blackening as it tried to hold on to his sword.

Remy tugged on the blade.

Other members of the Choir emerged from the black, some flying, others charging. They had their own weapons as well, nasty blades and clubs that looked as though they had been formed from the shadows where they made their home.

Francis met their attack head-on, his tarnished blade not having as dire an effect, but the sharpness of its edge proving to be more than devastating. The screams of the injured Black Choir were deafening.

Using all his strength, Remy yanked on his weapon, watching the charred and blackened fingers of his opponent break away with a snapping-kindling sound. He spun around to assist his friend, the glow of the blade seeming to instill in the Choir a certain level of fear.

"Wish mine did that," Francis said, bringing his blade down upon the skull of a fallen angel that suddenly swooped from the darkness above, nearly cleaving it in two.

But the angel did not die, and neither did any of its brethren.

"You cannot stop us, deserter of the faith," one of the Choir moaned, charging from the shadows to rip at Remy's face. He turned his body around as it leapt upon his back. "The danger of what you have done will be shown, and humanity will pay the price."

Remy didn't understand what the abomination was going on about. He thrust back with his sword, feeling the glowing blade pass through the emaciated flesh of its stomach before biting into the spinal column. The Choir member cried out in pain, attempting to take flight from its perch upon his shoulders, but the blade was stuck firm, and all it could do was struggle to free itself.

"Let me help you with that," Francis said, coming to aid him, his own sword cutting deeply into the Choir member's chest, knocking it back.

Remy pulled his blade free with a grunt of thanks and turned his attention to the next wave of attack.

The Choir were burnt, cut, and mutilated, but still they came.

"Why?" Remy asked, his anger fueling his fury, causing him to remember—and embrace—the warrior's high that he had attempted to escape for so very long. "Why would you risk this? The end of all things would result in your deaths as well!"

The Choir halted their actions, clumping together to glare at him with pain-filled eyes from the shadows that shifted like thick smoke.

"We would risk anything to be forgiven," one of them said in a chilling whisper, as if merely saying the words could result in some form of punishment. "To again be allowed in His presence."

They all bowed their heads in reverence, praying for it to be so.

"Forgiven?" Remy asked.

Francis stood beside him, his friend's face spattered with the lifeblood of their enemies. "Somebody's been feeding them a lie," the Guardian said.

"Who told you this?" Remy demanded to know. "Who told you that God would forgive you if . . ."

There was a sudden, searing flash of white.

The Black Choir screamed in agony as their pale skin was burnt from their bodies, Remy's and Francis' own cries of pain joining with the creatures of shadow.

Remy fell to his knees, shielding his eyes from the pulsing emanations. He could barely make out the shape of someone within the white fire, searing light streaming from its outstretched hands like the rays of the sun.

It was the light of the divine; the power of God given to those who served His most holy cause. If Remy had been merely human, it would have burned his flesh and turned his bones to ash. It was another painful reminder of what he truly was, and could never hope to be.

The Choir's screams had ceased, but now Remy's ears were filled with the agonized moans of his friend.

The light of the divine burned him worse, for he had fallen from the grace of God.

"Stop it!" Remy screamed, feeling around until his hands found Francis' thrashing body. Remy threw himself atop the Guardian, blocking his body from the destructive effects of the holy glow.

The power of Heaven roiled inside him, awakened by the purity of the light. Remy could feel it stirring, trying to push aside the humanity he had worked so hard to emulate. "Show yourself to me!" he demanded of their attacker.

And the light was extinguished as quickly as it was ignited, returning the world to darkness and gloom. The remains of what had been the Black Choir lay about Remy, the blackened bodies still twitching with life. He lifted himself from atop Francis, who was curled into a quivering ball on the dry ocean floor, his body smoldering from the touch of the divine emanations.

"Are you all right?" Remy asked, reaching out to grip his friend's shoulder. A portion of his jacket crumbled beneath his hand.

Francis shivered and lifted his head. "Fucking awesome," he managed, his teeth chattering as if painfully cold.

Remy squeezed his upper arm reassuringly, and climbed to his feet to face his foes.

The Seraphim stood together, and he was reminded of the last time he had seen them, when they had come to his office to ask for his help.

He should have known better.

"Hello, Remiel," Nathanuel said, the rain vaporizing

as it touched him, forming a billowing mist about his human guise. "We've been waiting."

Remy felt his anger surge, the angelic fury that was at his core straining to be released, but he managed to hold it at bay.

But for how long?

Once these Seraphim—Nathanuel, Galgaliel, Haniel, and Zophiel—had been his brothers, but now, as he looked at the mayhem around him, the distance between him and them grew even greater. He strode across the wet sand toward the gathering of angels, stopping briefly to let a crab skitter across his path as it searched for a place to hide until things returned to normal.

If they returned to normal.

"What are you doing?" he asked, spreading his arms out before him. He looked to the left of the Seraphim, his eyes falling upon the shrinking form of Lazarus, standing off to the side with Casey Burke, trying not to be noticed. Casey was bound and gagged, her eyes pleading with Remy to free her from this madness.

"Laz? So you are a part of this, too?" he asked the immortal who he had once thought of as his friend.

Lazarus squeezed his eyes shut and shook his head from side to side. "No!" he screamed, his body trembling with suppressed anger. "Don't you judge me," he growled, refusing to look at Remy. "Don't you dare judge me."

Casey whimpered and tried to pull away, but Lazarus viciously yanked her back, forcing her to her knees. Her eyes were on Remy, pleading, and he wished he knew what to do.

It was all so much bigger than he had imagined.

"You're responsible . . . for all of this," Remy said, turning his attention to Nathanuel, contempt oozing from his every word.

The Seraphim leader seemed taken aback. "Oh, no, Remiel," he said with a shake of his head. "It is you who are responsible, as is he."

Nathanuel and the Seraphim stepped to one side to reveal a lone figure dressed in a sopping wet Grateful Dead T-shirt and jeans, kneeling in the sand as if deep in prayer.

Remy had no doubts that this was Israfil, in the guise of Jon Stall.

"What did you do to him?" Remy asked, watching as the man muttered beneath his breath, rocking from side to side, so lost in his own place that he didn't seem aware of where he was and what was happening to him.

The Seraphim chief stared at the man, a snarl forming on his smooth, pale features. "He did it to himself," the angel said. "Seduced by the infection that is humanity." Nathanuel turned his attention back to Remy. "And it has nearly destroyed him."

He couldn't believe his ears. "And for that, you allow the world to be brought to the edge of the Apocalypse."

Nathanuel smiled, that same cold, predatory smile that had disturbed Remy so in his office.

"To the edge, and beyond," the angel said coolly. "The Almighty must be shown the danger of desiring humanity . . . of longing for what He has denied us, the first and most loving of His creations."

Remy laughed, a horrified sound lacking any trace of humor. "You're going to allow the world to end because you're jealous?" he asked, his voice growing louder with indignation. "Because the Almighty saw fit to give humanity a spark of His divinity . . . a soul?"

The Seraphim simply stared.

"You're out of your fucking mind," Remy snarled.

"No," Nathanuel stated, his dark eyes sparking with

anger. "This whole place is out of its . . . *fucking mind*, and the contagion must be quelled before it can spread any further."

"What are you so afraid of?" Remy asked, striding toward the angel, fists clenched. "Are you afraid that more of your kind . . . *our* kind will want to be like them? Are you afraid that you and your ideas about what it means to serve the Creator will become obsolete?"

Enormous wings of the purest white unfurled from Nathanuel's back, one of the feathered appendages extending to viciously swat Remy aside before he could get too close.

Remy fell the ground against the slime-covered rocks, the seaweeds, and the fish gasping for life—or death. His mouth filled with the taste of copper, blossoms of color exploding before his eyes.

"You dare speak to me of loyalty?" the Seraphim leader growled. "You, who deserted your duty to walk amongst the animals? You are no better than the Grigori filth."

Remy slowly rose, wiping scarlet from his mouth with the back of his hand. "At least the Grigori don't conspire with the enemy," he said as he spit a wad of blood in the direction of the still-twitching remains of the Black Choir.

"Desperate times require desperate measures," Nathanuel proclaimed. "Is that not right, Lazarus? The Black Choir would have destroyed this world themselves if it meant getting back into His good graces. They yearn so desperately to be forgiven."

"Let me guess," Remy said, nodding toward Lazarus, who still refused to meet his gaze. "You promised him that he would finally get to die."

Nathanuel covered his mouth with a thin white hand, feigning surprise. "So devious . . . it's almost as if I were human."

Remy heard the sound of a labored laugh behind him and turned his head slightly to see that Francis had managed to rise to his feet, tarnished blade of Heaven still clutched in his blistered hand.

"I always said you were a prick, Nathanuel," the fallen angel spat. "And this just shows what an excellent judge of character I am."

The Guardian's exposed flesh was an angry red, covered in oozing sores, and he swayed a bit as if the ground beneath his feet was moving. Remy backed toward him, retrieving the dagger that Francis had given him earlier from his belt.

"Where's your sword?" Francis asked him.

"Dropped it somewhere back there," Remy replied, getting used to the feel of the knife in his hand.

"You just can't have anything nice, can you?"

Remy didn't have the opportunity to respond, for Nathanuel's voice rang out.

"Take them!"

And his three Seraphim soldiers were upon them, pulling swords from within the folds of their flowing coats. Francis threw himself into the fray with little hesitation, his blade thrust deflected by Zophiel's own. The Seraphim spread their wings, shrieking their excitement. It had been too long since these warriors of Heaven had seen conflict, since they had spilled the blood of their enemies.

From the corner of his eye, as he attempted to keep Galgaliel and Haniel away with his knife, Remy saw Francis fall. The flat of Zophiel's blade struck the Guardian with a vicious blow to the head that sent him sprawling. Distracted by the sight, his Seraphim foes attacked as one, driving Remy down to the cold, wet sand, tearing the knife from his grasp.

"So much less than you were," Nathanuel said,

contempt dripping from every word as he stood over him.

Remy tried to climb to his feet, but Nathanuel slashed at him with his wings, driving him to his belly.

"Stay down, Remiel," the Seraphim ordered. "Things are too far along for you to prevent them now." The Seraphim chief arched his back, furling his wings, and they disappeared from sight as he paced before him. "I believe you still have something that we need," he said slyly, looking over his shoulder.

As Haniel roughly searched his clothing, Remy smiled, knowing that at last he had the upper hand.

But his superiority was all too short-lived.

"Master, we have it," Galgaliel called out, and Remy lifted his head to see Zophiel removing the fifth scroll of the Apocalypse from inside the jacket of a struggling Francis.

Remy watched in horror as Galgaliel handed the delicate piece of parchment to his master.

"We doubted you would be so foolish as to bring it with you," Nathanuel said, holding the potentially destructive document in his hand. "But we were obviously wrong."

Remy stared at Francis in disbelief. "You couldn't have left it in the car?"

Francis weakly swatted off Zophiel and Galgaliel, pushing himself up onto his hands and knees. "Yeah, but I thought we'd be able to use it as a bargaining chip," he said, shaking his head to clear away the cobwebs. "I'll admit; it wasn't one of my better ideas." The Guardian made an attempt to stand, but the Seraphim shrieked their displeasure, beating him back down to the ground with their powerful wings.

Nathanuel held the final scroll in his pale, delicate hand, devouring it with his cold black eyes. In it he saw his plans come to fruition, and the pleasure that it brought to his face was most chilling.

"All right, then," Nathanuel said. "Let us commence."

It was the most human Remy had ever seen the Seraphim chief look.

CHAPTER SEVENTEEN

The Seraphim loomed over Remy and Francis, attack dogs from Heaven, making sure that they stayed on their knees in the sand, as Nathanuel approached Jon Stall with the scroll.

The rains continued to fall, the nearly black sky slashed with glowing jags of lightning, followed by roars of rolling thunder.

The Horsemen are growing impatient, Remy thought, watching as the Seraphim chief stood over the pathetic wreck of a man who was once one of the most powerful angelic beings in all the Choirs.

Nathanuel lifted a beckoning hand, and Galgaliel moved toward him. From within his flowing black coat, he produced the leather briefcase. He reached inside, gingerly removing the other four scrolls, and carefully laid them down upon the sand in front of Israfil.

Remy could feel it churning in the air, the impending end of all things. Every fiber of his being screamed for him to do something, but no, he had to wait.

Wait for an opportunity.

He only hoped it wouldn't be too long in coming, for there didn't seem to be much time left for the world. He looked to the Heavens, searching for a sign from God, anything that indicated He would step in and make things right. But he could see nothing, and it didn't surprise him in the least.

God is funny that way, Remy mused, *that whole working-in-mysterious-ways business defined in moments like this*. He could picture the Almighty watching this whole scene unfolding, a big bowl of popcorn—or the Heavenly equivalent—on His lap, dying to know how it would all turn out.

"It's time, Israfil," Remy heard Nathanuel say, his statement punctuated with a flash of lightning and a clap of thunder. The Seraphim leader still held the last scroll, the final message from God, in his thin, pale hand.

Israfil didn't seem to hear the angel. He continued to rock from side to side, whispering beneath his breath.

Nathanuel stepped closer and poked him with the toe of his black shoe. "Do you hear me, Israfil? It is time to slough off your masquerade of flesh and bring closure to this failed experiment."

Israfil rocked all the faster, his voice growing louder, and finally Remy could understand his words. He was apologizing, saying over and over again how sorry he was to have caused so much pain and suffering.

"You can end the pain." Nathanuel squatted beside him and spoke into his ear. "All you need do is open the scrolls."

The Seraphim chief touched the final scroll to Israfil's chest, urging him on. "The constant barrage of sadness, pain, and suffering—I don't know how you can stand it, especially now."

Israfil's prayers for forgiveness intensified, as if attempting to drown out the angel's words.

"Take it," Nathanuel ordered, poking him with the scroll. "Take it and fulfill your final purpose. End the experiment. Do the humane thing and free them all from their misery."

The man's swaying movements began to cease, and Remy felt the pounding of his own heart intensify. Slowly, Israfil turned his haunted features toward the angel kneeling beside him.

"I wanted to know what it was like," he said, voice trembling. "I just wanted to know, but I never expected . . ." He shook his head, teary eyes wide in disbelief. "So much beauty and happiness . . . but also so much ugliness and pain."

Nathanuel reached out a tender hand, cupping the side of Israfil's face. "It's chaos, my brother, unrelenting chaos, and it is up to you to bring order to it."

There was a look in the eyes of the Angel of Death, as if the Seraphim's words had somehow permeated a thick fog that surrounded his thoughts. He took the scroll from Nathanuel in a trembling hand.

"Israfil, no!" Remy screamed, lunging toward him. "It doesn't have to end. It doesn't have to be like this."

Galgaliel pounced upon Remy, forcing him back down to his knees, driving his face toward the sand.

Scroll in hand, Israfil looked at Remy. . . . No, it was Jon Stall who looked out through bleary eyes, and for a moment, Remy thought that there might be hope.

But the moment was fleeting.

And as if on cue, Nathanuel lunged at Remy. "Silence!" he thundered, grabbing Remy's face roughly in his hands, forcing him to meet the Seraphim's scowling gaze. "I despise this world, this miserable ball of dirt with its ragged emotions and savagery," he said. "How the Creator can muster such affection for mankind, I cannot even begin to understand. These are the creations that followed us, the Heavenly Choirs? *This* is how the Almighty intended to improve upon *us*? It's enough to make me doubt His sanity.

"Lucifer Morningstar was right, but he let his righteous indignation get in his way. Now it's my turn.

Now *I* can prove our supreme worth to Him." He shoved Remy aside and turned back to the Angel of Death. "Proceed, Israfil," he urged. "It is for the best."

Stunned by the Seraphim chief's rantings, Remy watched as Israfil slowly turned toward Nathanuel. "There has to be another way," he whispered.

From where he knelt in the sand, Remy could see the struggle within the cage of fragile flesh and bone, the two opposing natures—angelic and human—warring for control. It was a pathetic sight to see a being of Heaven, once so strong, reduced to this quivering mass.

Nathanuel saw it too and shot Remy a hate-filled glance. "You are the one to blame for this," he said, gesturing toward the Angel of Death, contempt dripping from his words. "You who have chosen a path other than service to the Almighty. Living amongst these lowly animals, walking in the mud of this planet, it was never meant for those of us who have soared above the spires of Heaven."

"The pain will just go on and on, brother," Nathanuel said quietly, almost compassionately, to Israfil. "We will be doing them a favor."

Israfil's eyes turned to the scrolls and then quickly looked away.

With a sigh of exasperation, Nathanuel turned to Lazarus. "The female, bring her to me," he ordered.

And Lazarus did as he was told, clearly so desperate to be free of his accursed life that there was nothing he wouldn't do.

Nathanuel grabbed Casey, and Remy could see the amusement on his face as he studied her fear-filled eyes. The Seraphim chief removed the gag from her mouth and freed her hands. She sputtered and coughed, fluids leaking from her mouth and nose.

"Jon," she gasped as she rushed to Israfil's side. "What's happening?" She wrapped her arms around him, the desperation obvious in her voice. "I . . . I don't understand. Who are these people? Why are they doing this?"

"Everything is going to be all right," Israfil promised in a gentle voice.

But Remy knew it was a lie.

Nathanuel suddenly reached down and grabbed a handful of Casey's dark hair, yanking her away.

"It is not all right, brother," he said, forcing her to look at Israfil before violently twisting her head to one side, breaking her neck with a muffled snap.

To Remy the sound seemed louder than any clap of thunder, and he watched with numbed horror as Nathanuel let Casey's body drop to the ocean floor at Israfil's feet, twitching and flopping about like the fish deprived of their watery habitat.

Deprived of death.

"No! No! No!" Remy screamed, his fingers digging deep into the wet sand, prying up a rock that he had noticed the last time his face had been pushed to the ground in subjugation.

An opportunity? Perhaps, no matter how small.

He made an attempt to charge forward again, and when the growling Galgaliel grasped the back of his neck in a grip like iron, Remy spun around, smashing the rock into the angel's face as hard as he could. Blood exploded from his pulverized nose as the angel released his hold, both hands going to his damaged face.

Remy didn't hesitate, scrambling across the exposed ocean floor toward Israfil, who still knelt before the body of the woman he had loved.

"Listen to me!" Remy yelled as Zophiel descended

from the sky with a birdlike cry. He dropped to his belly as the angel soared over his head, outstretched hands just missing him, as Remy continued to crawl closer.

"Think about what you're doing. He's asking you to end it all. . . . To bring about the Apocalypse. Don't do it, no matter how bad you think it is. . . . It isn't time for that."

Israfil's face was slack, gazing down on the quivering body of the woman who had helped him attain his humanity, and Remy had to wonder if he was even hearing him.

Nathanuel was suddenly there in front of him. He reached down, grabbing Remy by the throat, pulling him up from the ground.

"There will be none of that, Remiel," Nathanuel said, holding him aloft as he turned his attention to the Angel of Death. "Israfil has a duty to fulfill."

Remy tried to scream, tried to get the Death Angel's attention, but all he could manage was a strangled gasp.

"Show me your human compassion," Nathanuel urged Israfil. "Put a world filled with so much suffering out of its misery."

The Angel of Death tore his gaze from Casey's body, and Remy saw by his expression that any chance of reaching him was now gone. He turned to the scrolls lying before him in the sand, and without a moment's hesitation, picked up the first.

"That's it," Nathanuel urged. Israfil held the scroll out before him and with one quick movement, broke the waxen seal with a deafening snap.

The foul weather immediately intensified, the thunder roaring and wind whipping, and the sky illuminated in an unearthly light.

Still held in Nathanuel's grip, Remy managed to twist his head toward the horizon to see the enormous shapes of the Horsemen as their mounts moved inexorably closer.

The Seraphim chief pulled him close, forcing Remy to meet his gaze. "It has begun," he said triumphantly over the sounds of the advancing Apocalypse, and then he tossed him aside like a piece of garbage.

Harmless.

Remy landed on his back in the sand, the winds raging about him. As he prepared to stand, his hand fell upon something warm; something that sang of the glory of battles to be won in the name of the Lord God.

He saw the sword that Francis had given him partially buried beneath the whipping sands, and picked it up. Searching the beach for his friend, he found the former Guardian curled in a ball upon the ground, Haniel and Zophiel looming over him like vultures.

It looked as though it was solely up to him.

Through the storm, Remy saw Israfil, another of the scrolls held aloft, Nathanuel by his side, urging him on. Struggling against the hurricane-force winds, Remy started toward them, only to have his progress stopped by a hand falling roughly upon his shoulder.

He was spun around, coming face to face with a grinning Galgaliel, his face spattered with blood from his broken nose. The Seraphim slowly shook his head from side to side, sporting an evil grin far too wide for his face.

Remy raised his sword, but the warrior of Heaven was faster, taking hold of his arm before he could carry through. Galgaliel pried the weapon from his grasp, nearly breaking his fingers in the process.

"What have we here?" the angel asked, his voice nasal from the injury to his nose. He hefted the weight of the blade in his own hand. "A weapon of Heaven in the hands of one who has forsaken it? For shame."

Haniel and Zophiel had come to watch, their dark eyes glistening in anticipation of Remy's impending doom.

Galgaliel pushed Remy to the ground and raised the sword above his head. Remy could do nothing but watch as the fiery blade began its descent, his mind filled with the painful thoughts of how he had failed everyone and everything that he had ever loved.

How he had failed the world.

At first he mistook the sound for thunder, but as one of Galgaliel's black eyes suddenly erupted from his skull in an explosion of crimson, he realized that it was something far more deadly.

The angel lurched to one side, the swing of the heavy blade going wild and cutting into the wet ground, before his body pitched forward to land in a flailing pile.

Haniel and Zophiel looked around in complete dismay. Through the rain and blowing sand, Remy saw Francis, pistol in hand. The Guardian aimed, firing at the remaining Seraphim. Unfurling their wings, the two escaped into the air.

Francis limped over to where Remy still lay, reaching down to help him to his feet.

"Bullets forged from metals mined in Hell," he yelled by way of explanation over the cries of the storm, and holding out the old-fashioned Colt pistol. "The metal travels through their blood like poison. It won't kill them right now, due to the circumstances and all, but they'll sure wish they were dead."

"And you couldn't have used that earlier?" Remy asked.

"Wanted to wait for them to get here first," Francis

said, leaning in close to Remy's ear, trying to be heard above the din of the coming Apocalypse.

Remy pulled back, not sure what his friend was talking about, and saw that Francis was pointing up to what had once been the shore's edge. Remy looked in that direction and saw that they were no longer alone. A line of armed individuals stood waiting for a sign.

"Who are they?" Remy asked his friend.

"Grigori," Francis said, a sly smile snaking over his battered features. "Had a talk with them before I picked you up at the rest home. I suggested it might be in their best interest to give us a hand."

A flash of lightning, as if the world were being split in half, again lit up the sky, the thunderclap that followed causing a shock wave that shook the ground beneath their feet. The Horsemen were closer; their mounts reared back, pawing at the sky with hooves that trailed fire.

The sky had started to glow with an eerie light, as if the lightning had somehow ignited the atmosphere. And with this new illumination, Remy witnessed yet another disturbing sight.

The two remaining Seraphim, Haniel and Zophiel, now stood with a newly risen Black Choir. The fallen angels' bodies were little more than charred and blackened skeletons, the framework of their once-leathery wings jutting from their backs like spiny appendages. A thick, ebony aura radiated from what remained of their desiccated flesh, like steam rising from melting ice.

Beyond the Seraphim and their monstrous army, Remy could see that Israfil still knelt upon the beach, opening the scrolls one at a time. As near as Remy could tell, only two remained.

"Go," Francis said. "Do what you have to. We'll take care of these freaks."

Remy pushed himself against the raging elements, rushing toward the kneeling figure. Israfil appeared deep in concentration, his mind set upon the most deadly of tasks.

Remy experienced a sudden wave of panic as he came to the disturbing realization that Nathanuel was no longer beside the Death Angel. He was hidden somewhere in the storm, but still Remy pushed on.

What choice did he have?

The remaining Seraphim made a move in Remy's direction, but Francis would have none of that.

He opened fire with his pistol, using up bullets that cost him close to a thousand bucks apiece as if they were nothing more than dime-store caps. He thought about all the jobs that he'd taken, besides his responsibilities of guarding the gateway between Hell and Earth, all the creeps he had to put down for the count, in order to make that kind of money.

It was money that he'd been setting aside for a rainy day.

And Francis couldn't imagine it raining any harder than this.

The bullets did their job, the projectiles tearing into the flesh of the divine beings with devastating results.

It stopped them from chasing Remy, turning their attention to Francis.

"If you were looking to capture their attention, I believe you've done it," said a voice standing beside him.

Francis turned to see that the Grigori had left their places on the old shore to join him, each of them brandishing the guns, knives, and swords that he had provided, and which he hoped would be returned to his personal collection once everything had settled.

Sariel admired the ancient blade. It didn't glow any more than Francis' had, but would still hack off a limb if necessary.

"It's been quite some time since I've participated in battle," the Grigori leader said to the fallen Guardian, watching as the Black Choir began to stalk toward them.

"It's just like riding a bike," Francis said, charging to meet their enemies halfway. "Only a lot more bloody."

And he felt the bloodlust upon him; his thoughts returning to the day that he had fought at the side of the Morningstar, for a cause that he was foolish enough to believe was right.

The Black Choir had retrieved their own weapons from the ground, lurching at him and the Grigori soldiers, the first line of defense between them, the Seraphim, and the end of the world.

Even more frantic than before, the Choir came at them, blackened abominations roaring in rage, their weapons raised to cut them down. Francis moved among them, firing his pistol and lashing out with his sword.

Cutting a Choir member in half that had attempted to brain him with a spiked mace, Francis chanced a quick glance around to see how the Grigori were faring. Their leader's words about their inactivity in the combat area had worried him a bit at first, but seeing them in action now, Francis realized that his concerns were unfounded.

The Grigori were taking to violence like a ducks to water. But that didn't mean the battle was won yet.

The Choir were frantic, sensing a threat to their absolution. Francis had to laugh as he fired his pistol into the face of one of the pathetic creatures, obliterating its head in an explosion of blackened skull. He found it a riot that they actually believed that God would look favorably upon them for their contributions to the end of the world.

Almost as amusing as the brief idea he'd had tickling his mind that maybe he'd make some points with the big guy upstairs for helping to avert this catastrophe of such enormous proportions.

Yeah, and someday soon my fucking hair will grow back.

Francis looked around him, through the storm and creeping black fog. It was like a scene plucked from the pits he was forced to police, a little slice of Hell here on Earth.

The Choir were locked in vicious combat with the Grigori; shrieks of rage and terror filled the air, mingling with the scent of angels' blood.

Whether it be of the fallen or not, once it was spilled, it all smelled the same.

He loaded the last of his special bullets from his coat pocket into the revolver, just as three Choirs loped out from a cloud of black. Not to waste any more valuable ammunition, he stuck the gun in the waistband of his slacks and decided to deal with the abominations old school. He brought the blade down upon the shoulder of one, nearly cutting the former angel in two from collar to groin. Drawing back the weapon, he parried a blow by another of the beasts, and pulling the dagger from the inside coat pocket of his suit coat, plunged it deep between its charcoal-black eyes.

The final member of the three sized him up. It switched a short sword from one hand to the other as it eyed him, a charred lip raised in a snarl to reveal teeth like blackened corn. Finding that he had a limited reserve of patience, Francis simply pulled the gun from his waistband and shot the creature in the face, satisfied to waste the bullet if only to move things along.

Squinting against the driving rains, he searched for

signs of the remaining Seraphim soldiers. He was certain that he'd hit at least one of them. Lifting his nose to the air, he sniffed for a hint of their scent, but it was no use; the stink of spilled angel blood was everywhere—Grigori, Black Choir, and Seraphim, all mixing together in a nauseating miasma that tainted the air.

In the distance, but far closer than moments ago, the mounts belonging to the Four Horsemen pawed at the earth impatiently, sending tremors through the ground that caused him to stumble.

"Shit," Francis hissed, caught off balance.

It was then that the Seraphim chose to make their move, descending out of the sky, wings spread as they glided down to attack him. Francis spun around, aiming his weapon, but Zophiel's movements were a blur, his Heavenly blade slicing through the flesh and bone of his wrist.

"Son of a bitch," the Guardian cursed as he watched his hand, still holding the pistol, sail through air.

The angels dropped in front of him, both holding weapons that cut the gloom with their unearthly fire.

Clutching his bleeding wrist tightly to his chest, Francis eyed one and then the other.

"Well, now that we're about even, what's say we get this bullshit over with?"

Remy Chandler was dying.

With each step he took closer to the Angel of Death, he felt more of his humanity being stripped away.

An aura of death hung around the kneeling Israfil as he picked up the fourth scroll, and, holding it out before him, broke the seal. Again there came a flash, and the deafening sounds of the Horsemen as they moved closer filled the air.

The winds howled and moaned, snatching at his clothes as if trying to hold him back, but Remy fought against it, falling to his hands and knees, crawling toward the kneeling angel through the muddy sand.

"Israfil, listen to me," he begged, yelling to be heard. "Yes, there's pain and sadness and misery here. . . . But there's also happiness and wonder . . . and the strength to fight through the misery."

But Israfil ignored his words, reaching for the fifth and final scroll.

"Is this what Casey would have wanted?" Remy continued. "Would she have wanted to see it all end because you weren't strong enough to deal with her loss?"

Israfil's fingers seemed to hesitate over the final scroll, the Almighty's permission to unleash the Horsemen and bring about the end of the world. He looked toward Remy, tears running down cheeks scoured by the wind, sand, and rain.

"Remiel," he whispered. "How do they do it? . . . How do *you* do it?" he asked, his voice a dry croak. "It hurts so much. I thought it would be a lark . . . something to break up the never-ending monotony of my existence, but it ended up as so much more."

Israfil paused, lowering his head.

"So much more."

"Don't do this," Remy said, inching closer. "Nathanuel is insane, jealous of God's love for His complicated and, yes, seriously flawed children."

Israfil shuddered, dropping the scroll as his body pitched forward into the sand.

"It hurts so damn much," he moaned.

"Let it go," Remy said, reaching out for the scroll. "Shed your human skin and return to the form that would know what you are doing is wrong." His fingers brushed against the ancient parchment. He almost had it, and then something had him.

Remy found himself suddenly airborne, viciously yanked away and hauled up into the sky.

"Can you hear it, Remiel?" Nathanuel spoke in his ear to be heard over the raging storm and the flapping of his wings. "It is the death cry of humanity."

Remy thrashed in the Seraphim's grasp as the angel's wings took them steadily higher.

"And there's nothing you can do about it."

CHAPTER EIGHTEEN

She saw the riders.

They sat upon their colored horses at the horizon, waiting to begin the death of the world.

But in the sky, above the giants of the Apocalypse, two figures were locked in struggle. One had powerful wings of blinding white, and the other seemed to be just a man, willing to fight the forces of Heaven itself for what he believed.

Just a man, but in fact, so much more.

Madeline gasped for breath, her eyes opening wide as she looked about the semidarkness of her room, the disturbing images that she suspected were so much more beginning to fade away, replaced with the reality of her present condition.

She was still alive.

And though numbed with pain medication, fed through an IV hanging beside her bed, Madeline knew that her life should have come to an end hours, if not days, ago.

Her husband had gone to take care of that problem.

She remembered her dream.

Or was it a vision?

Madeline was suddenly afraid for him; wishing that he were there with her, by her side and holding her hand as she finally slipped away.

But he couldn't be. He needed to be elsewhere in order to make things right, in order for her, and so many others, to finally be allowed to go.

Remy had told her that he could hear them. Call them what you want: spirit, soul, inner self. He'd said that he could hear them trapped within prisons of flesh, begging to be free.

He said it was the saddest sound he had ever heard.

She saw the image flash within her mind again. The giants of the Apocalypse, her husband above them, locked in struggle with one of his former kind.

Madeline reached across, removed the IV needle from her arm, and pulled the oxygen line from her nose. Delving into a reserve of strength that she didn't know she had, she rose from her bed and shuffled barefoot across the cold tile floor to the window.

The storm was ferocious, the wind spattering heavy rains against the panes of glass. She saw herself there, reflected against the glass in the darkness beyond the storm, a reflection of who she had once been.

When she was healthy and full of life.

The reflection provided her with the strength necessary, and she lifted her arm, placing her hand against the cool glass surface.

She thought of her husband, the angel that had come into her life and given her so much, and about how much she loved him.

A love strong enough to hold back the end of the world.

Nathanuel's hands burned him like fire.

"You embrace this pathetic existence as if born to it," Nathanuel growled, his face monstrous in the light of the eerily glowing sky.

Remy clung to the front of the Seraphim's coat, frantically holding on.

Nathanuel pressed his hand against the side of Remy's face, and searing pain coursed through his body as the flesh was burned away to reveal something else, something hidden beneath.

"You know what you are and where you truly belong, but still you run from it . . . hide from it in this suit of flesh and blood."

The smell of his burning humanity filled his lungs, choking Remy with its acrid stench. The Seraphim chief was incredibly strong, as if feeding on the encroaching catastrophe. And as they hovered above the deliverers of the end, held aloft by the beating of Nathanuel's powerful wings, he reached down, taking hold of Remy's hands, and began to peel his fingers away from their desperate hold on his coat.

Remy glared defiantly at the one he once called brother, his hold more and more precarious with each passing second. And just as he was about to fall, Nathanuel caught hold of his wrist.

"You love them so much," Nathanuel cooed, dangling him above the world, a moment's respite from what Remy knew was inevitable. "Then go to them."

The Seraphim released him, and Remy began to fall.

Is this how it ends? he wondered as he tumbled to the earth, a victim of gravity's pull.

Was it all for nothing?

Something stirred deep within himself in response to his question.

Something that yearned for sweet release.

And it answered him . . .

"No."

Marlowe watched helplessly as his master fell.

There was nothing he could do to help, and that angered the dog. He tossed his head back, howling his discontent.

The dog awakened with a start, unsure at first of where he was. He lifted his head and sniffed the air.

"What's the matter, boy?" Ashlie asked him, scooting over on the overstuffed sofa where they had been watching television to put her arm gently around him. "It's all right," she said soothingly as she patted his neck and kissed the top of his head. "It's only the storm. Remy will be back soon to take you home."

She lay against his side, as he rested his chin between his paws with a heavy sigh, afraid to drift off again.

So he listened to the sound of the storm raging outside and whined pitifully at the memory that roused him from his slumber.

A dream of his master falling from the sky.

He didn't remember passing out, but then, how else could he explain it?

Remy was back in Heaven.

But it was a Heaven of the past; a Heaven that he'd tried so hard to forget because it didn't really exist anymore.

From a gentle hilltop called Serenity he gazed down into the verdant valley of Awe, repulsed by the scene of violence that now overran the once-peaceful lowland.

Angel against angel, brother against brother; he listened to the cries of warfare, sounds that did not belong in a place such as this.

Though disgusted by what was transpiring below him, Remy found himself drawn toward the unfolding scene of carnage, moving down the sloping hill toward the raging battle.

And the closer he got, the more frightened he became, for he remembered this day.

Stepping over bodies of those with whom he had once soared through the skies in service to the All-Father, Remy continued toward the center of battle.

Few remained standing, the last of the Morningstar's forces against one lone figure that fought with an unbridled fury for the glory of God.

Adorned in armor of gold, wings spattered with the blood of the vanquished, the angel set upon the last of his adversaries, his cries of fury mingling with the screams of those who fell beneath the savagery of his onslaught.

And then all was quiet as the last of the Morningstar's army joined the rest of the dead.

Remy stood on the outskirts of the circle of death, staring at the back of the winged figure as he slowly started to turn, alerted to Remy's presence. He wanted to avert his eyes from the sight of a Heavenly being capable of such brutality in the Lord's name, but he couldn't, his vision riveted to the sight of the warrior angel—a Seraphim.

The angel faced him, his features stained with the blood of the lives he had taken, and Remy felt immediately sickened by the sight.

Sickened by the sight of Remiel of the holy host Seraphim.

Sickened by the sight of *himself*.

"Is this where it began?" Remiel asked.

Remy stepped back, but the heel of his shoe caught on the chest plate of an angel killed in battle, and he fell to the ground.

"I'm not you anymore," he stated, crawling backward to get away.

The angel stared down at the dead lying about his feet. "Is that what you tell yourself? Does it take away the pain of what you were . . . of what you are?"

Remy didn't want to hear this; he didn't want to be in this place again. He got to his feet and tried to walk away. A gentle breeze blew across the plain, carrying the sweet scent of Heaven's blossoming trees and flowers, tainted with the hint of death.

"You can't change what you are, Remiel," the warrior angel called after him.

Remy stopped, the words like an arrow shot into his back.

"You are of the host Seraphim, a soldier of the Almighty, and you have a sacred duty."

Remy turned to find his warrior self directly behind him.

"I'm not part of this anymore," he told the angel. "I gave it up. . . . I left it behind for something else."

Remiel laughed. It was a sad laugh, heavy with sorrow.

"And now that it is threatened, as was Heaven. Will you walk away from that as well, or will you fight for what you have loved?"

"What I *do* love," Remy whispered, surprised as the words left his mouth. Staccato images of the life he'd led upon the earth flashed through his mind; the painful and sometimes wonderful steps he had taken on the long path of learning to be human.

Ending with Madeline and Marlowe.

Suddenly, he felt their strength flowing through him, and he knew what he had to do.

"You terrify me," he said to himself.

Remiel nodded. "You were a thing to be feared."

They were silent for a moment, standing on the corpse-strewn battlefield.

"Will you embrace your true nature and become that force again?" Remiel asked. "Or will you let it all die?"

Remy closed his eyes, seeing the faces of those he loved there in the darkness.

Is there even a question?

*   *   *

It was difficult, if not downright impossible, to fight two opponents with the use of only one hand.

But it didn't keep Francis from trying.

Bleeding stump still pressed against his chest, he eyed the two Seraphim, sword held firmly in the other hand.

"So what made you go along with your boss's crazy plan?" he asked, through gritted teeth, fighting against the throbbing pain in his wrist. "I mean, Seraphim, always so straight and serious. What makes you suddenly decide to go against God?"

The normally expressionless faces of the pair began to show signs of wear—a slight twitch around the eyes of one; the beginnings of a frown on the other.

"You seemed smarter than that," Francis continued, aiming his tarnished blade at one and then the other. "You'd think that after the business with the Morningstar . . ."

He'd struck a nerve.

Haniel was the first to attack, wings opened to their full extent as he leapt into the air. Francis stumbled back, keeping one eye on the soaring warrior and the other on Haniel's partner.

And as if on cue, Zophiel lunged from the ground, crackling blade aiming for the Guardian's chest. Francis swatted the Seraphim's blade aside with his own, and flicked blood from his still-bleeding stump into the face of his angelic attacker.

The angel screamed, stumbling back as if he'd had acid thrown into his eyes. It wasn't acid, but the next best thing.

The blood of a fallen angel.

Haniel swooped down from the sky with a roar. Francis barely avoided being cleaved in two as the arc of the Seraphim's blade bit a chunk from the shoulder of his already injured arm. Francis dropped to his knees, his head beginning to swim. Losing as much blood as he had usually had that sort of effect.

Haniel touched down, going to the aid of his brother, helping him to wipe the noxious blood from his eyes.

"Well, isn't that sweet," Francis chided, jamming his bloody stump into the ground, the jolt of excruciating pain keeping him from falling forward, unconscious.

The Seraphim cursed in a language older than creation, and they started toward him again.

Something rumbled and flashed in the fog-enshrouded sky above his head, and on reflex Francis turned his eyes to the Heavens. At first he saw nothing, only the roiling clouds and whipping rain, but then he saw it, an area of the sky above him, growing steadily brighter.

Something was coming.

He looked back to the Seraphim, almost upon him now. They had smiles on their twisted faces. They thought they had him.

He didn't have the heart to tell them otherwise.

"Heads up," the fallen Guardian said, as the Seraphim ignored his warning, raising their weapons to hack him to bits.

The Angel of Death knew that it was wrong.

As he knelt upon the sand, holding the last sacred scroll, the cold, wet dampness seeping through the knees of his jeans, he knew that it had all gone terribly, terribly wrong.

It had been an experiment, a flight of fancy to help him better understand the Creator's favorites. How was he to know it would come to something like this?

Israfil had merged with Jon Stall, and everything that the college professor had been became a part of him. How exciting it was to feel things the way humans did—to be so deliciously fragile.

He held the parchment in his hands, his thumb tracing the uneven surface of the waxen seal. *So fragile*, he thought.

They were beautiful creatures, filled with so much love and feeling, and yet capable of such savagery. It was as if God had taken every characteristic imaginable and rolled them into one complex life form.

It's obvious that humans are what He was working up to, Israfil mused, barely noticing the wind and heavy rain that fell upon his kneeling form.

Thunder rumbled, and he chanced a quick glance behind him. Through the thick, roiling mists he caught a glimpse of them, the beings created by the Lord of Lords to end it all. He could sense their impatience. Never had they been so fully awakened.

All he had to do was break the last seal.

In a way, it would be a blessing for the world and its inhabitants, he told himself. There was just so much chaos and suffering here. He'd never realized that until he had become a part of Jon, and Jon a part of him.

His eyes strayed to Casey, lying on her side, eyes wide open, her soul crying to be released. If he listened—*truly listened*—he could hear others like her, millions of souls begging to be free.

I should do it for her—for Casey, he thought.

Nathanuel believed they were being merciful by extinguishing their grievous lives, taking away their despair, for they could not do it themselves.

All he had to do was break the last seal.

At first, Israfil believed it to be just another sound created by the raging storm, but when he heard it again, it captured his attention, distracting him from his tortured thoughts.

The sound . . . *the word*, was soft yet firm in its conviction, and there was no mistaking where it had come from.

Casey continued to stare at him, her eyes wide from the intensity of her trauma. A dark line of blood oozed from the corner of her mouth to be absorbed by the sand beneath her face. And though her mouth barely moved, he heard the word slip from it again.

"Don't."

He tore his gaze from the woman he had loved, sensing that he was no longer alone, to look upon the frightening visage of Nathanuel as he drifted down from the turbulent sky.

"What are you waiting for?" he asked, touching down in a crouch, voice dripping with impatience. "The time has never been more right."

And as if on cue, there was a cacophonous roar of thunder and something fell from the sky, hitting the ground in an explosion of brilliance that could only be described as divine.

Remy allowed himself to fall, feeling his body change as he dropped from the sky.

The closer he got to the earth, the less human he became. Engulfed in Heavenly fire, the facade he had worked so hard to build dissolved away to reveal what he'd tried to conceal.

What he'd worked so hard to forget.

He should have known better; he should have known his true self would always be there, patiently waiting for a time when it would be needed. He couldn't hide from what he was, even after all these long years on this planet.

There was a little pain as the flesh of his masquerade burned away to reveal the truth beneath, but it had less to do with the physical and far more to do with the emotional. Remy loved what he had become, what he had made for himself over the millennia, and was sad to see it go.

The angel Remiel hit the waterless ocean floor in an explosion of fire, the heat of his transformation so intense that the sand around him crystallized. He emerged from the smoldering crater wearing his combat armor of gold, the same armor he had worn when fighting the last of his battles against the legion of Lucifer Morningstar.

When he had decided to give up Heaven.

The rain hissed and steamed as it fell upon him, and he stretched his wings of creamy white, fanning the air. If there was one thing he didn't mind about the transformation, it was having his wings back again.

"Looking good, pal," he heard a familiar voice say weakly, and he looked to see Francis emerging from beneath the smoldering bodies of Haniel and Zophiel.

Remiel extended his hand, sensing an aspect of the Creator nearby, and called it to him. The sword that he had carried down to the beach leapt up from where it had been dropped, spinning through the air, casting off flecks of Heavenly fire as it came to him.

The grip of the sword nestled neatly in the palm of his hand as the beating of his powerful wings carried him across the beach toward what he was sure would be the final confrontation.

Praying to a God to whom he had not spoken in quite some time that he was not too late.

CHAPTER NINETEEN

The angel Remiel emerged from the storm, screaming the name of his enemy.

The Seraphim chief crouched over the limp form of Israfil, the Angel of Death seemingly protecting the final sacred scroll with his body.

"Nathanuel!" Remiel raged, the fury of his voice carried on the moaning winds of storm.

He saw it all in a bizarre form of slow motion, Nathanuel tearing his gaze away from the beleaguered Angel of Death, a look of such extreme hatred on his normally emotionless face, shockingly morphing into a twisted smile.

"Remiel," he said, stepping over Israfil, his awesome wings flowing open from his back. And from within his coat he produced a sword. "How nice it is to truly see you again."

Touching down upon the sand, Remiel studied his foe. It was all coming back to him; everything that he'd tried for so long to forget.

The violence he and others like him were capable of.

"I've waited too long for you to be able stop me," Nathanuel growled, springing at him with blurring speed. His blade cut the air, glancing off the shoulder plating of Remiel's armor, a spray of sparks shooting into the air as he sidestepped the attack. "I've been patient—till now."

Remiel reacted in kind, spinning to attack, swinging his blade toward the Seraphim chief's side. The angel twisted his body, angling it in such a way that only his raincoat's flap was cut by the passing of Remiel's blade.

Nathanuel jumped into the air, a raptor's scream upon his lips as he brought his sword down in a hacking motion. Remiel jumped back, narrowly avoiding the crackling blade of Heaven as it gouged the drying ocean floor.

The storm raged around them, the intensity of their conflict seemingly reflected in the intensity of the weather. And as they fought, their Heavenly blades casting flecks of godly light, a jagged hole was torn in the thick curtain of fog to reveal the Horsemen, moving closer still. The four giants sat upon their colored horses, as if drawn toward the struggle playing out beneath them, as if looking for a little entertainment before beginning the work of ending the world.

Time was fleeting, and Remiel knew that what little sanity Israfil maintained was a fragile thing indeed.

"Look at them, Remiel," Nathanuel shrieked above the relentless clanging of their striking sword blades. "Have you ever seen a more awesome sight?"

"It's not their time, Nathanuel," he responded, driven back across the beach by the Seraphim chief's relentless onslaught. "That will be a time of His choosing, not yours."

Remiel lowered his sword, inciting his brother to come closer.

Nathanuel lunged, as Remiel allowed the fiery blade to pass dangerously close, skimming along the side of his breastplate, before lowering his arm and trapping the blade against his side.

The expression upon Nathanuel's face was priceless.

"You let me get too close," Remiel said, driving his forehead into the Seraphim leader's face. "A big mistake."

Remiel swiped the balled pommel of his own sword across the Seraphim's face, knocking him backward to the ground.

Nathanuel's grip torn from his sword, Remiel now stood above the chieftain of the host Seraphim, a blade forged in Heaven in each of his hands.

"If you're smart, you'll stay where you are," Remiel raged, doing everything in his power to keep the angelic fury that raged within him at bay. *It would be so easy*, Remiel thought. *To let it out, to satisfy its voracious hunger.*

So easy.

Remiel pulled back upon the rage, painfully repressing what had once been second nature to him.

But not anymore.

"Listen to me," he warned, turning away from the Seraphim chief, hoping—praying—that he was wise enough to stay down. That this could all be brought to a close with a minimal amount of violence.

And someday pigs would fly.

The hideously disfigured creatures that had once been Seraphim surged from the shifting fog. Haniel and Zophiel's burnt and blackened bodies, scarred by his fiery descent, rasped and rustled as they grappled to restrain him.

Remiel roared, one of his swords arcing down, taking away one of Haniel's arms. He brought his other sword up and across, slicing through Zophiel's midsection, causing steaming entrails to spill out onto the ground. But still they came at him, taking hold of his arms, preventing him from using his blades further.

The Seraphim tried to speak, to whisper ominous threats in his ear, but all he could hear were choking rasps.

Prying the weapons from his hands, they turned him roughly around to face the approaching Nathanuel. Twin lines of blood trailed from each nostril of the Seraphim leader's nose. He held a dagger in one hand while dabbing at the blood that streamed from his nose.

His fingers stained crimson, Nathanuel's eyes grew wide and his entire body began to tremble.

"What will it take for you to understand?" the Seraphim leader asked, bringing the tips of his fingers to his mouth, tasting his blood. "The travesty of this world has gone on long enough. It ends here and now. . . . Despite your actions."

"It ends when I deem it over," said a voice that froze the Seraphim where he stood.

Taken aback, Nathanuel turned to see the form of Israfil emerging from the fog. In one hand he held the still-unopened final scroll, in the other a vintage Colt pistol. "What is this?" Israfil asked, his expression of surprise turning to one of absolute revulsion as he caught sight of Francis looming behind the linchpin of his plans.

"With them all dead and gone . . . He'll love us best," Nathanuel said, attempting one last time to convince the Angel of Death that his plans were just.

Israfil aimed the pistol, firing off a shot before the Seraphim could speak again. The Hell-made bullet hit him in the center of his forehead, his eyes turning upward as if attempting to see the extent of the damage that had been done to him.

Nathanuel fell backward to the ground.

Remiel flexed his wings, shrugging off the injured Seraphim soldiers, and was about to put them down when further shots rang out. Jumping aside, he saw that Francis had snatched the pistol away from Israfil and was firing with coldhearted efficiency, taking out those Seraphim loyal to Nathanuel.

"Not dead yet, but they will be," Francis said as his legs grew unsteady and he dropped down to the ground. "Think I'll take a seat."

He had torn off his suit coat sleeve and tied it tightly around the stump of his hand to stop the bleeding.

"Soon as Israfil gets his shit together, we'll be all set."

Remiel approached the Angel of Death, who stood staring off into the mist-enshrouded distance. He was pale and trembling, skin burnt a bright pink in many places. His eyes had started to leak a dark-colored ooze.

The body he inhabited was breaking down.

"I just wanted the pain to go away. As much for myself as for the world." Israfil turned his dripping eyes to Remiel. "But I kept hearing your voice, telling me that it wasn't the time."

An ominous rumble shook the air, and they both looked out through the fog to see the Horsemen growing restless. Death, in his armor of bone, upon his horse of the purest white, had left the line of his brethren, as if urging his master, the Angel of Death, to get on with it.

"They're waiting for you to decide," Remiel said.

"There's still a part of me fighting to end it . . . to drop the curtain on it all, to take away its pain, and I'm not sure I have the strength to fight it much longer."

Remiel moved closer to the angel. Israfil stared at him—as if seeing him for the first time. "Look at you," he said, voice no stronger than a whisper. "I never believed I would see you this way again."

"He looks good," Francis said. He was lying on his

back now, his speech starting to slur. He'd lost quite a bit of blood. "Don't you think he looks good? I remember when I looked as good . . . better."

"We're done here," Israfil said. "But I'm not sure that I'm strong enough to do what still needs to be done."

The angel swayed, buffeted by the storm, his human shell looking worse with the passing seconds.

"Will you help me, Remiel?" he asked. "Will you help me return it to the way it's supposed to be?"

For a brief moment of selfishness, Remy hesitated. *How much more can I give?*

Israfil waited for his answer, and it was as if the angel suddenly knew the cause of his reticence.

"I'm sorry," the Angel of Death said, tears of black flowing more freely down his gaunt face.

Remiel shook his head, steeling himself for what had been asked of him. "There's no reason to be sorry," he said firmly. "This is how it's supposed to be . . . how it has to be."

And with those words, Israfil gathered what remained of his strength and turned. He walked toward the horizon, across the sand, which was until recently beneath the ocean, heading toward the riders of the Apocalypse.

And Remiel followed.

They stood side by side, gazing up at the awesome sight, at the personification of the world's last days. The harbingers of the end.

"Are we ready?" Israfil said wearily.

"As ready as I'll ever be," Remiel answered, laying a hand upon Israfil's shoulder, lending him his strength.

Israfil seemed to take a moment, as if wanting to hold onto this moment—this fragility—for as long as he was able.

Remiel squeezed his shoulder tighter, signaling that it was time.

Israfil gasped, an awful gurgling sound filling his throat as he turned his face up to the crying Heavens, and left the body of Jon Stall. The human shell that the Angel of Death had inhabited these past months dropped to the ground, a marionette whose strings had been cut.

Israfil floated in the air like smoke, his ethereal form weak and undefined, as if part of what he was had atrophied.

They both stared at the abandoned body lying upon the ground.

"His soul is still trapped inside," Israfil said sadly, his voice like a cool fall breeze rustling through the leaves.

"Like so many others."

"Yes," Israfil agreed. "But first things first."

In his angelic form again, the Angel of Death spread immaterial wings the color of smoke and flowed toward Remiel.

"Your strength to mine," the angel whispered as Israfil's essence merged with his own.

Remiel tensed as the angel flowed into him, instinctively reacting to the invasion. His wings flapped wildly, fighting the attempt of another being to take up residence within him. He imagined that this was what the human Jon Stall must have experienced as he surrendered the last of his life, giving over his body to the curious Angel of Death.

And Remiel was suddenly filled with an awesome and fearful power. His body began to glow; crackling energy hummed and throbbed through him, leaping from the ends of his fingers, from the tips of his wings. He had always known the Death Angel was powerful, but never could he have imagined the magnitude.

All at once he saw the world—saw it as Israfil did—and he was in awe of it. Every living thing, down to the smallest microbe, anything that undulated, squirmed, swam, flew, or walked upon it; he saw it all as he was reconnected to the life pulse of the planet.

The power at his disposal was immeasurable, a wild and terrible force, but he handled it with ease and grace, taming it with a gentle yet firm thought, pulling it to his side, demanding its obedience.

And the power of death obliged.

He took to the air, powerful wings tossing off arcs of crackling energy as he soared upward toward the fearsome representatives of the Apocalypse.

Hovering in the air before them, the force of one of Heaven's most powerful radiating from his body, Remiel was able to capture the attention of the unearthly beings. They turned their awesome gazes upon him, waiting.

"Not today," he told them. He was suddenly aware of the sacred scrolls lying upon the beach below, seals regrowing upon the open parchment like fresh skin over an open wound, in preparation for a time when they truly would be needed.

At first he wasn't sure if they had heard him, the fearsome aspects of the end, continuing to study him as he floated in the air, little more than an annoying insect to them, he was sure.

The way they stared, it was as if they were giving him a chance to reconsider—to change his mind. But the being that was both Remiel of the Seraphim and Israfil the Angel of Death held strong to their decision.

The world would not end this day.

And after a time, the Horsemen of the Apocalypse came to realize that their presence was no longer required, and one at a time, they turned away from the world, returning to that otherworldly realm, where fearful beings such as this awaited the time when they would be called again.

And their duty to the one that created them, done.

Remiel watched as they receded into the horizon, the storm that had blanketed the region since their summoning drawn along behind them, clearing the sky so that the sun was allowed to shine again.

Riding the winds above the Cape, Remy heard the roar of the ocean as it rushed in to reclaim the land that belonged beneath it. He thought briefly about Francis, whom he had left lying on the beach, but pushed the concern from his mind. The former Guardian could take care of himself, and there were other, far more pressing matters still to be concerned with.

The balance needed to be restored, the inevitability of death returned to the world.

The being that was both Remiel and the Death Angel floated in the darkness of space, just above the vaporous atmosphere, attuned to the heartbeat of a world.

Remiel knew he should be in awe of what he witnessed below him, a beautiful blue marble nestled in a black velvet blanket of stars, vibrant with life, but there was something about sharing his body with the Angel of Death that dampened his enthusiasm.

There was a job to be done; one that Israfil had been derelict to perform for at least a week's time. Remiel dreaded what was to follow, but there was no other way if the balance was to be restored.

He fixed his gaze upon the earth, his every preternatural sense awakening at once, making the planet aware of the Angel of Death's return. Desperate for release, everything that had been destined to meet its end but couldn't cried out in one powerful voice, calling for his attention.

The power inside him was nearly overwhelming, and for one brief moment, Remiel suspected that he knew what it must feel like to be God, or as close to one as his kind was ever likely to be. The power inside him began to grow, intensifying toward release. Knowing what he was now capable of, and what he was about to do, Remiel experienced painful pangs of fear.

As well as guilt.

Floating above the earth, he extended his arms and let the Angel of Death's purpose flow through his body. He felt it move inside him, building at his core, spreading up from his torso and down his arms into his hands. A sort of ethereal webbing flowed out from his fingertips and drifted down to cover the world.

Still connected to his hands, he felt it all—vibrating up through the membranous net, the thrumming heartbeat of the planet.

He saw them all, each and every thing: the large and small, the human as well as the inhuman, the sick and the suffering.

"Come to me," Remiel said, his voice an odd mixture of his own and the angel Israfil's. Given permission to go on, the life forces were released from their places of confinement, flowing up from the planet to collect within the vast netting he had cast about the world.

As the souls were collected, he saw the existences that had once belonged to them, entire life experiences flashing before him in the blink of an eye.

Life, in all its myriad shapes and sizes.

The souls of humanity, what stories they had to tell.

From birth to death, and everything in between, he saw it all.

Tales of lifetimes, better than anything that could be crafted by the world's most skilled authors. The sadness and the joys, the hatreds and the loves: it was all there, everything that defined them as a species, that set them apart from all other of God's creations.

Their humanness was intoxicating.

And among the seemingly countless existences, he found a life of joy that spoke to him in a voice so familiar. It sang of life filled with accomplishment and the sweetest of loves between man and woman.

Remiel knew this life, for he had been honored to be part of it, overjoyed to be accepted into the loving embrace of one of the Almighty's most blessed creations.

To love and to be loved was the greatest of His gifts, and Remiel reveled in the honor that he had been allowed to experience.

He did not want to let this life go. He wanted to hold on to it—keep it, like a precious stone, admiring its beauty and complexity for all eternity.

But the Angel of Death had other plans.

Israfil stirred within Remiel, his strength and purpose regained. Reassuming his mantle, Israfil emerged in an explosion of brilliance, like the dawning of creation, leaving Remiel alone in the darkness of space, suddenly no longer connected to the lives of those souls that had been harvested.

What a horrible and empty sensation to be cut off from an experience so vast, so intimate.

And he drifted in the cold of space, feeling so very alone.

Yearning for the touch of the world he had saved, and all the beauty it offered, Remiel moved closer to the planet, allowing its pull to draw him from space, pulling him back to the place he had adopted as his home so very long ago.

He fell to the world again, plunging deep into the restored ocean of the Cape.

Remiel emerged from the boiling sea, flapping the excess water from his cooling wings as he walked up onto the shore. Francis was waiting for him on shore, along with Sariel and other surviving members of the host Grigori.

"Thought you might've . . . y'know, gone back or

something," the former Guardian insinuated, gesturing with his chin to the glorious blue sky above.

"No," Remiel answered, noticing that Francis had found his missing appendage. "Your hand?" he questioned.

"Yeah, found it just before the water came back," he said, flexing his fingers. "Good thing, too. I don't think I'd look as hot with a hook."

Remiel managed a fleeting smile before turning his attention to the Grigori. Their clothes were torn and stained, and they stank of violence. There was a gleam of excitement in the survivors' eyes.

"I didn't expect to see you here," Remiel said to them.

Sariel stared out over the ocean.

"This is our world whether we like it or not—at least until the Lord calls us home. And until we hear His call, we aren't about to allow something to happen to it."

The fallen angel suddenly seemed distracted, glancing down at the Rolex watch that had somehow managed to remain intact upon his wrist. "Look at the time," he said casually. "We're having a little party tonight," he explained. "Celebrating the world not ending and all."

He and his followers began to walk away. "You're welcome to come." He nodded toward Francis. "You and your winged friend."

The Grigori chuckled as they continued up the beach.

Francis waved good-bye, a smile beaming upon his features.

"He's such a dick," Francis said, still smiling as he continued to wave. "Pretty good in a fight, though. Not a fucking Black Choir to be found. Doubt they're all dead—we couldn't be so fucking lucky—but at least they're not around giving us a pain in the balls."

Remiel looked about the beach, the roar of the surf behind him. "The bodies?" he asked.

Francis shrugged. "Taken by the sea, with most of my friggin' weapons, I guess." He placed a hand over his brow, looking out over the restless ocean. "Wasn't much time to move them when the water came back."

"And Lazarus?"

"Lost sight of him after the shit hit the fan," Francis said with disgust. "Doubt he's dead. Think we should look for him?"

The Seraphim shook his head. "He'll turn up eventually, and besides, he'll have worse than us to deal with now. The guilt over what he has done will be torment beyond anything we could ever do to him."

"Yeah, I guess, but I'd still like to kill the bastard a few times. Y'know, to get even." The Guardian paused, checking out the reddish line where his hand had been reconnected to his wrist. "So everything is taken care of?" he asked offhandedly.

Remiel remembered what it was like to touch the world and to bring death back to it, but sensed that the memory would be fleeting. How could one being hope to retain memories so vast? There was only so much of the experience one mind could contain. He recalled the lives and endings of those connected with his life: Peter Mountgomery, Carol Weir, Casey Burke, ready to let the memories go with the seemingly countless others.

But there was one in particular that he would not allow himself to forget.

"Yes," he answered, feeling so terribly alone. "It's been taken care of."

Francis accepted his answer with a satisfied nod. He removed his glasses from the pocket of his tattered shirt and held them up to the sun. Somehow they had remained unbroken. "So, do we want to get out of here?" he asked, adjusting the glasses to his face.

"I think we're done," Remiel said, although the thought of what he was returning to was more painful than anything he had experienced thus far.

In a way, for him the world *had* come to an end.

"So is that your new look?" Francis asked.

Remiel stared at himself, at the pale brightness of his exposed skin, of the golden armor, the feeling of wings upon his back. It was time to again abandon what he had already believed discarded forever. It just went to prove that forever wasn't as infinite as he would have liked to believe.

He closed his eyes, concentrating on assuming his human appearance. It was painful; his angelic nature was again fully expressed, and did not care to be cast aside, but he was stronger and not in any mood to be played with. He felt his wings grow smaller, receding into the flesh of his back; the golden armor melted away, returning from whence it came in some long-forgotten Heavenly armory.

Human in appearance again, but so much less than he had been.

The angelic nature existed just below the surface, so much closer than before, dormant for now, eagerly awaiting the next opportunity to exert itself.

Remy looked down at his human guise, surprised to see that he was naked, his clothes burned away by the intensity of his transformation.

"Let me borrow your suit coat," he said, as Francis removed the ragged, bloodstained jacket.

"Don't get it dirty," he joked as Remy covered his naked body.

"I think I've got a pair of sweats in the car," he added, as the two of them quickly started up the beach to where they had parked. It was all they would need, to be found like this by the locals, beaten, nearly naked and spattered with blood.

Remy sensed them immediately, the hair on the back of his neck tingling, a lingering aftereffect of having recently assumed his full angelic semblance. He turned around to see them silently coming up from behind them, three beings beyond comprehension. It had been at least a millennium since he had seen them. They appeared as perpetually rolling balls of energy, their rounded, seething surfaces—like the skin of the sun—covered with unblinking eyes.

They were quite the sight.

Francis turned and immediately dropped to the ground, hands going to his eyes, temporarily blinded. It was not meant for the unclean—those of the fallen persuasion—to gaze upon the majesty of the Heavenly host known as Thrones.

Remy's angelic nature stirred, eager to emerge and interact with the representatives from Heaven that served the Almighty directly, but Remy would have none of it. He'd had just about all he could stomach of Heaven and its representatives.

"What the hell do they want?" Francis asked, burying his head in the sand.

Remy stared at the center Throne, unsure of which set of eyes to look into. He didn't think that it really mattered.

"I haven't a clue," he answered. "Right now they seem content to just stare."

"I imagine they'd be good at that," Francis added.

"*Greetings, warrior of Heaven,*" a voice like the tuning of the world's largest orchestra boomed inside his head for only him to hear. "*We bring you glad tidings from He Who Is the Father of All Things.*"

"Greetings," Remy responded, to be polite.

"Are they talking to you?" Francis asked, still looking away. "Are they talking to you inside your head? I fucking hate that."

"The Lord of Lords has bid us find you, for you have performed a great service to the Kingdom of Heaven."

"I only did what I had to do," he told the divine entities.

"The Creator asks for your return to the City of Light— for the honor to sit at His right hand."

At mention of the privilege that was to be bestowed upon him, the Thrones' energy forms blazed all the brighter, the music of the spheres that blared inside his skull nearly deafening.

"No, thank you," Remy told them.

The light of the three beings immediately dimmed, multiple sets of eyes suddenly squinted, scrutinizing him.

"This is not an offer to be refused," the Throne leader proclaimed.

"But I am refusing it," Remy informed it. "Tell the Creator thank you, but my place isn't in Heaven anymore. It's here, on this world with the crazy inhabitants that He created. Thanks, but no."

And Remy turned his back on them, these representatives of God's will. He reached down, pulling Francis up by the arm as he passed.

"Are you sure that's smart?" Francis asked, eyes tightly closed against the blinding Heavenly glare.

"It's how it is," Remy answered.

He could feel them coming up behind him, their presence causing the nerve endings in his spine to painfully twitch. He didn't turn around.

"He will not be happy," the Throne bellowed inside his skull. Remy felt a trickle of warmth—blood—slowly begin to leak from his nose down onto his lip.

So fragile. So human.

"And if I go with you, neither will I."

The sound of displeasure that only he could hear grew to a brain-hemorrhage-inducing crescendo before dramatically falling silent.

Remy turned his head slightly to see that the emissaries from Heaven were no longer there.

"Are they gone?" Francis asked, cautiously opening his eyes a crack. Seeing that they had indeed left, he removed his glasses, rubbing his eyes. "I think they burned out my fucking corneas. All I can see is spots. Think you're gonna have to drive home."

Remy didn't mind; he enjoyed driving. Some of his best thinking was done while behind the wheel. Coming up from the beach, into the backyard of Jon Stall's former summer home, they walked along the side of the house and up the dirt driveway to where the Land Rover was parked.

"Let me see about those sweats," Francis said, going to the back of the Land Rover.

Remy went around to the driver's side and opened the door.

"Here," Francis called, tossing him the gray sweatpants.

He slipped them on, not feeling quite as naked, when he heard the trill of a cell phone from inside the vehicle.

"Not mine—lost it on the beach somewhere when I was getting my hand chopped off and shit," Francis said, fiddling with his glasses.

Remy stared across the driver's seat to the passenger's side, recalling that he'd taken his wet coat off when getting into the Rover to start their trip.

The incessant trilling was coming from inside his coat pocket.

Francis had moved around to the passenger's side

to get in. He opened the door, reaching inside Remy's coat pocket to remove the ringing cell phone. He offered it to him.

Remy took the phone and flipped it open, already certain that he knew from where the call was coming.

CRESTHAVEN, said the black letters on the tiny screen, and he felt the weight of the world—of the universe itself—fall down upon him.

The phone stopped its noise, but started again with only a moment's pause. He placed the phone on the dashboard as he climbed up into driver's seat, behind the wheel.

"Aren't you going to take that?" his friend asked, handing him the car keys.

"No," he said as he put the key in the ignition and turned the engine over. "I already know what they're going to tell me."

For him, the world had come to an end. The Apocalypse *had* happened.

What more was there to say?

EPILOGUE

Four months later

They'd had snow overnight; about three inches, Remy figured, as they trudged down the winter-covered walkway through the Mount Auburn Cemetery.

It was still relatively early, the sun just over the rise, but he hadn't been sleeping much these days, and it helped him to get out and do things.

Helped to take his mind off missing her so much.

And besides, Marlowe could use the exercise.

The dog barked happily, his jet-black fur a severe contrast with the snow as he romped through the powdery white stuff on the trail of something that didn't hibernate through Boston's winter months.

"What is it?" Remy yelled to the dog, wanting to be a part of his excitement.

"Squirrel!" Marlowe answered, stopping for a moment, tail wagging like mad, before bounding toward the base of a large oak tree.

"Awesome, but remember what we said about not doing your business here, all right?"

"Right," the dog grumbled, more concerned with the squirrel's scent. But the Labrador had been really good about such things, after it had been explained to him a few times that this was a special place where people came to remember those who had gone away.

Remy didn't need this place to remind him; she was on his mind nearly every moment of every day and night.

It was pretty here just about any time of the year, but breathtaking after a new snow; the trees, headstones, and monuments draped in a puffy covering of cotton white.

Madeline loved this time of year, a New Englander through and through. She'd often talked about how it just wouldn't seem right without snow, that she'd lose her ability to gauge the passage of time without the seasons.

The passage of time; Remy had never been more aware of it.

He glanced around, making sure that Marlowe hadn't gotten himself into any mischief. The Labrador was getting dangerously close to a frozen pond, so he whistled shrilly to get the animal's attention.

"C'mon, pal," he hollered. "Back this way."

Marlowe stopped and turned in his direction. Remy could practically hear the gears moving around inside the animal's blocky head as he thought about whether or not he was going to acknowledge the request. He sniffed around beneath a willow tree for a little bit more before finally choosing to bound across a stretch of chest-deep snow yet untouched by man or beast.

The defiler smiled in a cloud of white as he made his way toward Remy.

Remy had no choice but to laugh at the sight. Marlowe loved it here, looking forward to their daily visits, lately even more than their walks to the Common.

He guessed it probably had something to do with Madeline being here as well.

"*Run fast,*" Marlowe said, bringing himself to a skidding stop just before the path he was on. "*Run fast in snow.*" There was a fine coating of ice crystals stuck to the Labrador's whiskers and powdered snow on his muzzle.

"You certainly do," Remy praised. "I bet you're the fastest dog on the planet."

"*Yes,*" the dog agreed. In his mind, at that moment, he was the fastest dog around. There was no other reason for him to believe otherwise.

Rather like the world.

Remy didn't think humanity realized how close they'd come to the end. They had just convinced themselves that everything had been naturally occurring mayhem, and with a little perseverance, they'd made it through just fine.

Just like they always did.

Humans thought very highly of themselves and their abilities to hang in there. It was one of the things he'd learned to admire about them. Their optimism was amazing.

Even Steven Mulvehill, knowing more than most, chalked up weeks of the Angel of Death being missing— and the nearly devastating effects that followed—as a bit of a rough patch.

But things seemed to have evened out.

Remy had been willing to tell him, during the last of their rooftop drinking sessions, before it got too cold, about what had gone on at the Cape, but Steven didn't want to know. He'd made his comment about knowing too much, poured himself a double, and changed the subject to the Patriots' chances of making it to the Super Bowl.

Remy had to respect the man's decision not to know. Whatever helped to make it through the day was perfectly fine with him.

"Are you going to come with me to visit Madeline?" Remy asked the dog, who was now rolling on his back in the snow, legs flailing in the air.

"Not Madeline," Marlowe answered indignantly, climbing to his feet before shaking off the icy powder.

"No, not Madeline," Remy corrected himself.

They went through this at least a few times every week. The Labrador didn't quite grasp the concept of burial, even though he'd been in attendance at Madeline's graveside ceremony. Remy recalled something the animal had said as they bid their final good-byes while standing beside the mahogany coffin. In his simple way, he had told Remy that the female—that Madeline—was not in the box because he could not smell her there. Later on that evening, when the mourners who had stopped by the house for coffee and something to eat had finally left, out of curiosity he'd asked the animal to explain himself in more detail. It was difficult for him, but Marlowe explained that the female couldn't be in the box because she was there with them.

Remy still hadn't understood, and frustrated with his master, Marlowe had left the room, only to return pulling a tattered blanket that he often slept on. He left again, returning with a filthy stuffed teddy bear with half of its face missing. Marlowe had been ready to leave once more when Remy stopped him, asking what he was doing.

And the dog explained that Madeline hadn't been put into the ground because he could still smell her there. It took a moment, but Remy realized that the items that Marlowe had brought out to him were all items that Madeline had given to him, that had once belonged to her.

Her scent was on these things—permeating the house—and as far as Marlowe was concerned, Madeline had not left them; just her physical presence was missing.

"Coming?" he asked the dog, continuing down the

path that would soon turn, taking them around a slight bend to an area of the cemetery that would be shaded by large pines in the summer months, but now would be laden with snow.

Marlowe bounded up ahead of him. It pleased him that the dog was doing so well with Madeline's loss. Now if only he could adjust as well.

He missed her more today than the day before, and the day before that. It didn't seem to be getting any better. Everything he saw, everything he read or listened to or did, reminded him of her and how much she had filled up his life.

But now she was gone, the one horrible inevitability that he'd always known would come from the joy of being with her. And though he had tried to be ready, tried to steel himself against the predetermined, nothing could have prepared him for the bottomless feeling of emptiness that was with him his every conscious moment.

Marlowe's sudden excited barking startled him from his funk, and he sped up down the snow-covered walkway, hoping that the rambunctious Labrador hadn't gotten himself into trouble with a groundskeeper or an early morning visitor to one of the other graves.

What Remy saw, as he rounded the corner, peering beneath the snow-weighted branches of an old pine, was like nothing he could ever have been prepared for.

"*Look, Remy! Look!*" Marlowe barked, sniffing the large patch of green grass that had replaced the snowfall around his wife's resting place.

Remy slowly approached, taking it all in, piece by piece.

It didn't stop with the grass. The trees in the general vicinity of the grave were filled with leaves, providing a gentle shadow across the face of the headstone.

The headstone.

A snaking vine had grown up over the marble surface; delicate purple flowers had bloomed in such a way as to encircle Madeline's name carved upon the stone. And below the grave marker, the ground had erupted in an explosion of color. Every kind of flower imaginable had sprung up from the earth, as if what had been buried there was the seed for all things beautiful.

Remy smiled, thinking that there could very well be some truth to it.

The area around his wife's grave was lush with life. Fragrant bushes, flowers, and plants of every conceivable variety had been given permission to ignore the inhospitable touch of winter and were allowed to bloom around her place of eternal slumber, in celebration of her life and in a show of gratitude for what he had done.

Although he could not sense him, Remy knew who was responsible. Israfil had been here.

Soaking in the signs of life, he turned back to the grave and slowly knelt down before the marble marker.

MADELINE CHANDLER: BELOVED, the inscribed words read, now embellished by the tiny purple flowers. He reached out, laying his hand upon the face of the stone, and was surprised at how warm it felt.

"Would you look at this?" he asked, imagining her somewhere close by. "Someone must be pretty darn special to deserve this sort of treatment."

He stroked the letters of her name, recalling the countless times he'd marveled at the touch of her skin, the feeling of her as he held her in his arms.

Missing her. Always missing her.

Marlowe had come to stand beside him, showing the marble headstone more attention than he ever had before.

"What do you think of this, bud?" he asked the dog, patting his square head. "Pretty nice, isn't it?"

The Labrador did not answer, instead closing his eyes and tilting his snout up to a very, un-winterlike breeze.

"*She's here,*" Marlowe said.

And for a moment, he too could sense her. Remy could hear her in the rustle of leaves, smell her in the fragrance of the hundreds of flowers that bloomed in her honor, feel the warmth of her through the lush grass that he knelt upon.

And the tears that he'd held on to for so long began to flow, running down his face, as he basked in the loving presence.

Marlowe had been right, Remy thought, patting the dog's side as he lay beside him atop his wife's grave.

Madeline was indeed here—all around them, in fact.

And she couldn't have looked more beautiful.

Read on for an excerpt from
the next Remy Chandler novel,

DANCING ON THE
HEAD OF A PIN

Available now from Roc.

It wasn't easy being human.

And it was never more obvious to Remy Chandler than it was now, as he stared across the desk at the foul thing pretending to be a man.

He was bulky, wearing a loose-fitting leather jacket with only a wife beater beneath. Anyone who saw him on the street, picking up the newspaper and a few lottery tickets at the corner store, would think him to be one of *those* neighborhood types—y'know, just rough around the edges.

Rough around the edges didn't even begin to describe what this thing was.

"Is it all here?" he asked, his dry, raw voice echoing slightly in the cavernous warehouse. He snatched up a roll of dirty bills held together with a thick elastic band.

"Yeah," Remy said with a slight nod. "Just like you asked."

The thing posing as a man called himself Eddie, and as much as it pained Remy to admit it, they had once been the same, brothers of Heaven.

Angels.

But that was long ago, before the fall. What separated Remy from Eddie now was damnation. Remy had chosen to abandon the glories of Heaven; Eddie had been cast out for choosing to fight on the losing team.

For challenging the authority of the All-Powerful, Eddie and all the others who had fought on the side of the Morningstar were banished to Hell until the Lord deemed that the first phase of their suffering was at an end. After a time in Hell they were brought to Earth to serve the remainder of their penance, earning forgiveness for their transgressions against the Almighty.

But His absolution was not easily given.

Remy wasn't sure what the Supreme Being was trying to say by forcing Heavenly creatures who once served His glory to live amongst the lowly beasts that caused the rift between the Son of the Morning and the Source of All Things to begin with. What he did know was that many of the fallen angels, those Denizens of the pits, chose not to lead a quiet life of contemplation, and instead continued their downward spiral into depravity.

They hadn't left Hell at all, really; they'd just brought a little piece of it with them.

Eddie sniffed the roll and smiled. "Smells about right," he said, and chuckled, shifting his bulk in the metal chair.

He reached down to the floor and lifted a white hard-foam cooler onto the desk before Remy. An undulating cloud of mist rose from the dry ice inside as he lifted the lid.

"They're all yours," Eddie said, reaching into the grayish fog and pulling out two eyeballs, delicately held between the thumb and index finger of each hand. "Here's a neat trick." He held the eyes before his own. "You can look through them—see a person as they truly are."

Remy had the urge to stop him, but what would be the use? Eddie would learn the truth sooner or later.

"Are you a good man or a bad man, my friend?" Eddie asked with a chuckle.

As if gazing through a pair of binoculars, he fixed the eyes upon Remy, and the response was immediate. Remy couldn't decide whether it was a look of fear or revulsion that appeared upon the fallen angel's face, not that it really mattered.

The twin orbs dropped from his fingers, falling back into the frothy mist of the cooler, and Eddie began to reach for something at his back.

Remy lunged up and over the desk, wrapping his right hand around the fallen angel's throat, driving him backward.

"Fucking Seraphim," Eddie gurgled as Remy slammed him against the wall, catching his wrist with his free hand before the fallen could use the dull black blade.

Remy could sense evil coming off the knife in waves. A blade like that in the right hands could do a lot of damage, but he doubted that Eddie was anything more than a common thug in the Denizen hierarchy, a parasite feeding off the sadness of the world.

So much for redemption, eh, Eddie?

"I'll take your eyes too," he hissed, froth spewing from his angry mouth.

"Is that any way for someone looking for God's forgiveness to talk?" Remy asked, allowing the holy fire of the Seraphim within himself a chance to flow through his body, igniting the hand that held Eddie's black blade at bay.

Remy's true nature clawed at its internal confines, yearning to be released, desperate for him to shed his mask of humanity. Since he had averted the Apocalypse just a few short months ago, this power he had worked so hard to suppress had become far too easy to set free. He fought the urge to let the power of Heaven burn away his human guise and assert its full potential.

He had to wonder if there would ever come a day when he was no longer strong enough to hold it back, when he would be too weak to be human anymore.

Eddie's scream and the sound of the knife blade clattering to the floor pulled Remy from his troubling thoughts. The stink of burning flesh wafted into his nostrils as he pulled back on the power, his angelic nature momentarily struggling as he exerted his full control.

Remy released the Denizen, and he fell to the floor clutching at his injured hand. "What did you do to him?" he asked the former angel, glancing quickly to the cooler, struggling to control his anger.

Eddie cowered on the floor, holding his blackened appendage close, flecks of burned flesh raining down to litter the floor like blighted snow. The fallen slowly lifted his face, and Remy saw both pain and fear in his eyes.

Remy pointed at the cooler still resting on the desk. "Don't make me ask you again."

"He . . . he gave himself freely," Eddie stammered.

Remy was amazed. Though he was faced with the threat of further pain, the lies still flowed from this Denizen's mouth. It was typical of their kind, the time spent in Hell shaping them into things of deception.

His angelic nature surged forward, like a pit bull testing the strength of its chain. Remy reached down, grabbed Eddie by the front of his leather jacket, and yanked him to his feet.

"Where is he?"

Eddie's eyes shifted suddenly to the right, his fear becoming something else.

Anticipation?

And then Remy sensed that they were no longer alone. Still gripping the fallen angel by the front of his jacket, he spun him around, as two more Denizens emerged from the shadows of the warehouse, guns in hand. Eddie didn't even have time to protest before the bullets punched into his body.

Tossing his Denizen shield aside, Remy darted for the cover of some crates stacked in the corner of the large, open space. More bullets ricocheted off the concrete floor around him, while others burrowed deep into the wood of his cover.

The fury of his Seraphim nature roiled to be loosed, and he tried to ignore it. It would be so simple to set it free, to burn away the skin of humanity that he had worked so hard to maintain, leaving only the soldier of Heaven to deal with the foul betrayers of God's trust.

So easy not to be human anymore, to no longer feel the agony of his loss.

Madeline is dead.

It happened at the most peculiar times: taking a shower, grocery shopping, walking the dog, trying not to be shot. It was always there, eager to remind him just how much it hurt to lose the love of his life, making him relive the most painful experience of his existence.

Three more shots brought him back to reality, allowing him to forget the gnawing pain in his heart for now. He could hear them moving closer.

Where was his backup?

He looked around his hiding place for something to use as a weapon and found an old crowbar beneath an oil-stained tarp. Remy hefted the heavy piece of metal in his hand. It wasn't as deadly as a gun, but it would do in a pinch.

And this was most certainly that.

Holding the crowbar ready, he listened for the

sounds of his attackers, but they had gone strangely silent. Carefully Remy peered out from behind the crates to see a lone figure standing in the center of the open room, two unmoving bodies at his feet.

"Where the hell have you been?" Remy asked Francis as he stepped out from his hiding place.

"Sorry," his friend replied, cleaning the blood from a fierce-looking blade with a white handkerchief. "I ran into a few of their buddies outside having a smoke. Always said that smoking was dangerous."

The bodies of the two fallen angels had already started to burn, their corporeal forms dissolving away to nothing as they ceased to exist. Their time on earth had been their last chance at redemption, and they had failed miserably.

"Learn anything?" Francis asked, sliding the knife into a concealed pocket on the inside of his gray suit jacket.

A pain-wracked moan filled the air, and Remy looked to see that Eddie was somehow still alive, although clearly not for long. He had propped himself against the corrugated metal wall, his breath coming in short, labored gasps. Plumes of smoke, like those from the head of an extinguished match, drifted from the bullet holes in the front of his dirty T-shirt.

"Won't be long now," Francis said, adjusting his black horn-rimmed glasses, the faint light of the warehouse glinting off the top of his bald head.

Remy knelt beside the Denizen, who seemed to be staring off into space, perhaps taking a good long look at the oblivion that awaited him.

"Did you hear that, Eddie?" Remy asked him. "It won't be long now."

Eddie turned his head slightly and looked into Remy's eyes.

"But there might still be a chance for you," Remy

continued. "Do something right before it's over. Tell me where he is . . . the angel whose eyes you tried to sell me. . . . What did you do to him?"

"Fucking Seraphim," Eddie spat, then gasped as a spasm of pain wracked his body.

"Maybe we need the knife?" Francis suggested, pulling open his jacket to expose the hilt of the blade peeking from the top of the pocket.

"I don't think that'll be necessary," Remy said.

"If you say so." Francis shrugged.

"Can you feel it, Eddie?" Remy asked calmly. "That's oblivion barreling down the tracks to meet you. No more chances, pal. You're done, unless . . ."

The smoke from the bullet holes was thicker and carried with it the smell of rotting meat. Eddie tried weakly to staunch the flow with his good hand, but the effort was futile.

"I wanted . . . wanted to go home . . . to Heaven; I really did," Eddie began, his voice quavering. "It gets inside you . . . Hell does, makes it so you never forget." He shook his head quickly. "*I* never forgot. . . . How can you—something like that?"

Remy reached out, gripping the fallen angel's shoulder. The leather of his jacket was hot. "Where is he, Eddie?"

"He said he couldn't stand it anymore . . . wanted to die. Wanted to pay for his sins."

The words ended in an awful scream as flames shot from the dying angel's wounds, expanding across his torso, up his chest, and down his legs. Remy managed to push himself away from the Denizen as, with a final burst of strength, he surged upward, flailing in the unnatural, hungry fire.

Remy caught Francis pulling a gun from another pocket. "No," he said, his eyes on the dying former creature of Heaven.

Eddie made it halfway across the warehouse before dropping to his knees. His body burned with a pulsing orange glow, the shape within the fire becoming less and less human. Then slowly he raised what remained of an arm, pointing to an area of darkness at the far end of the warehouse before succumbing to the final death, his body pitching forward, nothing more than orange embers burning upon the floor. And within moments those too were gone, leaving behind nothing to show that the fallen angel had ever existed.

"Stubborn prick," Francis growled. "You'd think that after nearly an eternity in Tartarus they'd be ready to leave this evil shit behind them."

The mention of Hell's prison sent an icicle of dread up and down Remy's spine. "You heard him," he said, approaching the spot where Eddie had fallen. "It gets inside you. It changes you, makes it so you can't do the right thing."

"But some do," Francis reminded him.

"Yeah, some do."

Remy continued toward the back of the warehouse and peered into the darkness. There were more crates and some scaffolding, but nothing of any significance that he could see.

"Wonder what they'd pay out there for my eyes," he heard Francis say.

Remy turned to see his friend holding the cooler. He had fished out one of the angel eyes and was looking at it. "Mine are as nice as this—maybe nicer."

"But you're not pure," Remy told him.

"Not right now, but I'm working on it," Francis said as he dropped the eye back into the fog created by the dry ice.

Francis had once been one of the Lord's most powerful Guardian angels, but even the greatest sometimes make mistakes. In the beginning, he had sided with

Lucifer during the rebellion, but soon saw the error of his ways. He threw himself on the mercy of the Creator, begging his master's forgiveness. But the Lord does not forget slights easily and forgives them even less so. Still, He gave the former Guardian angel a special job—custodian of one of the many gateways between Hell and Earth.

Not the nicest of jobs, but better than a stint in Tartarus, and Francis made the best of it, even using some of the deadlier skills he'd learned from his time in the nether regions to become a highly paid assassin.

Yeah, he's working real hard on being pure.

"I think I found something," Remy called to his friend.

He wasn't sure exactly what, but he could feel the hair on his arms and at the back of his neck stand on end as he moved closer to a particular area. The shadows seemed thicker there, almost palpable.

"It's a doorway," Francis said, coming up beside him and sticking his hand inside the thick, inky blackness. "There's another room beyond it."

"Must be where my two friends back there came from," Remy said. He too stuck a hand into the shadows. The darkness was cold and damp, like the bleakest November night.

"Angel magick," Francis observed. "Ain't it something?"

Angel magick had been created by the Watchers, the first of the angelic hosts to be banished to Earth. Even though fallen angels were stronger and more durable than the average human, they were nothing compared to a full-fledged angel. Denizens used the magick as well as weapons chiseled from the black stone walls of Tartarus and smuggled out by parolees to protect their illegal dealings from angels and humans alike.

Use of either was considered a sin against God, but that didn't stop the Denizens.

"I think Eddie answered my question as he died," Remy said.

"Wouldn't be the first Denizen to see the light as their own was being permanently extinguished. So are we going in?"

Remy didn't answer. Instead, he took a deep breath and stepped forward, immersing himself completely in the fluid darkness.

Though brief, the journey through the darkness made Remy think of every bad thing he had ever done, the ebony wetness seeping in through his pores, drawing out the poison, reminding him of how devastated— *lost*—he'd felt since the passing of his wife.

"Well, that was certainly pleasant," Francis said, brushing traces of clinging dark matter from the sleeves of his suit jacket. He adjusted his glasses, a nervous habit, and looked about at their surroundings.

Remy tried to shake off the hungry sadness, but there was little else to occupy his thoughts these days.

Madeline is dead.

"You all right?" Francis was looking at him, the feeling behind the question emphasized by the intensity of his gaze.

"Yeah," Remy lied as he stepped away from the thick patch of shadow. "Where do you think we are?"

Francis shrugged. "Not far from where we started," he said.

They were in a corridor that turned sharply to the right in front of them. To keep his thoughts at bay, Remy began to walk.

"Let's see what we've got down here."

He studied the walls as he went. The entire structure appeared to be made from shadow—from the darkness itself. An eerie inner light, a sort of bioluminescence, dimly illuminated their way from behind the black walls.

The hallway led to a larger room, empty but for a single table, upon which lay the body of an angel. A small cart, its surface littered with bloodstained surgical instruments, was positioned nearby.

Remy could only stare.

Francis had been the first to hear the rumor, a whispering among the unnatural community that the Denizens had acquired a full-fledged angel, and that its most holy body, every inch of it—a thing of great power—was for sale. He'd asked Remy to help him investigate, and the more they poked around—the more rocks and rotted logs they flipped—the more they realized that the disturbing rumor was indeed true.

And here it was, manifested in its true form, feathered wings splayed out beneath its naked, broken body. The angel's flesh had been cut, strips of its skin peeled away to reveal the pink musculature beneath. Most of its hair had been shaved down to the scalp. Its face was a gory mask, two empty black sockets where its eyes had been. The chest had been cut open and the rib cage exposed—an angel's heart was worth an absolute fortune.

Slowly Remy approached, fighting back a wave of revulsion. He did not recognize the angel, or the host from which it had come.

"Do you know him?" he asked Francis, unable to take his eyes from the disturbing vision before him— like some perverted version of dissection for a high school biology class, a creature of Heaven instead of a fetal pig.

Francis remained strangely quiet as he approached the surgical cart and picked up a plastic container. With a finger he flipped off the lid and reached inside.

He pulled out what appeared to be a bloody piece of cloth, but what Remy quickly realized was a large section of flesh flayed from the angel's body.

"He was a Nomad," Francis said, holding the skin in the open palm of one hand, tracing the black tattoo in its center with a finger.

Remy leaned in closer to look and saw that Francis was correct. There was no mistaking the mark worn by the sect of warrior angels that had abandoned their violent ways after the Great War, departing Heaven, disillusioned, very much like himself. In the most archaic version of angelic script, the mark meant "waiting between Heaven and Hell." What the Nomads were waiting for was the real question.

"How could he have ended up like this?" Remy asked, more than disturbed by the sight of something once so magnificent, now so horribly ugly.

"You actually have to ask that?" Francis questioned. "The war screwed a lot of us up. It isn't easy to forget what some of us did back then."

Remy had known it was a stupid question as soon as it had left his lips. He knew he wasn't the only one to turn his back on Heaven. It was just so very rare that he encountered any other expatriates—they tended to keep to themselves.

"He didn't deserve this," Remy said as he reached out to place a hand on the angel's shoulder. The flesh was cold beneath his fingertips, like the feel of a marble altar.

With a wet, sucking gasp, the angel rose to a sitting position, his wings flapping spastically as he took hold of Remy's shoulders in a trembling grip. Remy stared in awe, unable to believe that something so horribly mangled could still be alive.

"The sins live on," the angel gasped, the stink of rot exuding from his lacerated flesh. "They think it done . . . the war, but they deceive themselves, and the deceivers live on, the black secret of their purpose clutched to their breast."

The angel's head lolled upon his shoulders, his body wracked with spasms of excruciating pain.

"I could bear the deceit no longer. . . . My secret sin consumes me. . . ."

The final words left the angel's mouth in a gurgling wheeze, and he began to convulse. Flapping wildly, his damaged wings lifted him from the table but were not strong enough to support him. His damaged body crashed into the smaller table, spilling the bloody instruments. He lay atop the tools that had been used to dissect him, trembling and gasping for air.

"I've seen enough," Francis said coldly. He dropped the angel's flesh and removed a pistol from the holster beneath his arm. "Don't have any idea what he's talking about, secret sin and all, but nothing deserves to suffer like this."

Remy blocked his companion's way.

"What are you doing?" Francis asked, brandishing the weapon.

"I think we can do this another way."

The angel was crying tears of blood, streaks of crimson draining from the blackness of his barren eye sockets.

"We think ourselves so smart . . . so clever, but it will be our ruin, and the ruin of all that we hold dear," the injured creature of Heaven whispered as it writhed in pain upon the floor. "We should be punished. . . . Oh, yes, we deserve so much more than this."

"What's he talking about?" Francis asked. He still had the gun in his hand.

"I don't know, and I don't think we'd get a straight answer if we asked." Remy couldn't wrap his brain around what he was seeing. This pathetic creature appeared to be here by choice. He was not bound or restrained in any way. He was going to let the Denizens have him—cut him up and sell his parts to the highest bidder.

"He's in a lot of pain."

"Then let me stop it," Francis insisted.

Remy knew that the sight of the dying angel was getting to his friend—they were not used to seeing beings of such power in a state like this.

"Let me put him down. It'll be quick and relatively painless . . . less painful than what he's going through now anyway."

Remy shook his head. "It is ugly, but after going through all this"—he gestured about the room, at the operating table, the bloody surgical instruments strewn upon the floor—"he deserves better than that."

The angel had curled himself into a tight ball, his body trembling so severely that it practically blurred the sight of him.

Francis sighed. "What are you going to do?"

"I'm going to help him end it himself," Remy explained. "I'm going to convince him to let go of his guilt . . . his pain, and return to the Source."

How many times since Madeline's passing had he thought of doing that very same thing? To abandon it all, to will himself and all that defined him into nothingness. To return to the energies that shaped the universe and all it entails.

"What makes you think he's going to listen?" Francis asked.

"I don't know if he will, but I have to try." Remy stared at the pathetic sight shaking upon the floor. "I can't imagine that whatever he's done, he hasn't at this point paid for it a hundred times over."

Francis slid the lethal weapon back inside its holster. "So what now?"

"Make sure the building is empty," Remy told him as he knelt beside the tormented angel. "Things could get a little destructive if he abandons this form."

The former Guardian nodded, turning to head back the way they'd come. "Are you going to be all right with this?" he asked from the doorway.

"I'll be fine," Remy replied, gently pulling the angel into his arms, attempting to stifle the bone-breaking spasms that wracked the Heavenly creature's body. "We're just going to have a little talk."

Francis remained in the doorway, unmoving.

"Go on," Remy urged. "I want to get this over with. He's suffered enough."

"I'll see you outside," Francis said over his shoulder as he turned into the hallway of shadow.

Remy leaned forward, his mouth at the angel's ear, and spoke in the language of the Messenger—the language of God's winged creations.

"Are you ready, brother?" he whispered. "Are you ready to let go of the wreckage that is this material form?"

The angel turned his face toward Remy, and he could not help but stare into the sucking black of the empty sockets.

"*I deserve no such thing,*" the angel rasped, clutching the front of Remy's jacket with a bloodstained hand. "*We're no better . . . than those cast down into the inferno.*"

"Let go of your sin, brother," Remy soothed. "Return to the Source and know the forgiveness of—"

The angel suddenly pushed him roughly away. "*I would never dream of tainting the purity of the Source,*" he cried, rising to his knees.

Remy tried to stop him, but the angel moved with surprising swiftness, his hand finding what appeared to be the sharpest of the knives and gripping it tightly.

"No!" Remy reached out to stop the action, but he was swatted aside by one of the angel's flailing wings.

"*I deserve no less,*" the angel spat, and plunged the blade into his heart. He withdrew the knife and repeated the horrific action again, and then again, before falling to his side, legs thrashing as if he were trying to run, as the life left his body.

Remy was stunned. By taking his own life, the angel had damned himself, trapping the life force within the body, to slowly dwindle away as the corpse decayed.

He couldn't bear to see the body of the holy being left to the devices of scavengers. Reaching deep within himself—into the resources of his own suppressed divinity—he laid his hands upon the angel's waxen brow and carefully called upon the power within.

The fiery essence of the Seraphim ignited his hand and spread onto the dead Nomad's body. The fires of Heaven were voracious, consuming the flesh, muscles, bones, and feathers.

Hand still burning with an unearthly orange radiance, Remy pulled the fire back into himself, struggling to stifle the urge to burn away his own human guise and let his angelic identity roam free. And slowly the power was returned to that deep, dark place inside.

A place where it waited for him to abandon the charade that he had begun since leaving the golden plains of Heaven.

Remy rose to his feet, backing toward the exit, watching, waiting for the sign that he was expecting.

The body of the angel lay upon the ground, consumed in holy fire. Its grinning skull peered out at him from within the marigold flame, before collapsing in upon itself with a loud crack like a gunshot. At that point the fire grew larger, burning brighter—hotter—

igniting the floor before spreading to the walls of the chamber, burning away even the shadows.

Satisfied that there would be nothing left for the scavengers to salvage, Remy left the room, the spread of divine flame burning hungrily at his back.

ABOUT THE AUTHOR

Thomas E. Sniegoski is the author of the groundbreaking quartet of teen fantasy novels titled *The Fallen*, which were transformed into an ABC Family miniseries, drawing stellar ratings for the cable network.

With Christopher Golden, he is the coauthor of the dark fantasy series *The Menagerie* as well as the young-readers' fantasy series *OutCast*. Golden and Sniegoski have also cocreated two comic book series, *Talent* and *The Sisterhood*, and wrote the graphic novel *BPRD: Hollow Earth*, a spinoff from the fan-favorite comic book series *Hellboy*.

Sniegoski's other novels include *Force Majeure*, *Hellboy: The God Machine*, and several projects involving the popular television franchises *Buffy the Vampire Slayer* and *Angel*, including both *Buffy* video games.

As a comic book writer, he was responsible for *Stupid, Stupid Rat Tails*, a prequel miniseries to the international hit *Bone*. Sniegoski collaborated with *Bone* creator Jeff Smith on the prequel, making him the only writer Smith has ever asked to work on those characters. He has also written tales featuring such characters as Batman, Daredevil, Wolverine, The Goon, and The Punisher.

His children's book series, *Billy Hooten: Owlboy*, is published by Random House.

Sniegoski was born and raised in Massachusetts, where he still lives with his wife, LeeAnne, and their Labrador retriever, Mulder.

NEW IN TRADE PAPERBACK

WHERE ANGELS FEAR TO TREAD

A REMY CHANDLER NOVEL

by Thomas E. Sniegoski

Six year-old Zoe York has been taken and her mother has come to Remy for help. She shows him crude, childlike drawings that she claims are Zoe's visions of the future, everything leading up to her abduction, and some beyond. Like the picture of a man with wings who would come and save her—a man who is an angel.

Zoe's preternatural gifts have made her a target for those who wish to exploit her power to their own destructive ends. The search will take Remy to dark places he would rather avoid. But to save an innocent, Remy will ally himself with a variety of lesser evils—and his soul may pay the price.

Available wherever books are sold or at penguin.com

Also Available

DANCING ON THE HEAD OF A PIN

A REMY CHANDLER NOVEL

by Thomas E. Sniegoski

Still mourning the loss of his wife, fallen angel
Remy Chandler has immersed himself in
investigating dangerous supernatural cases.
His latest: the theft of a cache of ancient
weaponry stolen from a collector who deals in
antiquities of a dark and dubious nature.
The weapons, Remy knows, were forged eons
ago and imbued with unimaginable power. And if
they fall into the wrong hands, they could be used to
destroy not only Heaven but also Earth.

R0042

AVAILABLE NOW

An anthology of all-new novellas of dark
nights, cruel cities, and paranormal P.I.s—
from four of today's hottest authors.

MEAN STREETS

Includes brand-new stories by

JIM BUTCHER
FEATURING HARRY DRESDEN

KAT RICHARDSON
FEATURING HARPER BLAINE

SIMON R. GREEN
FEATURING JOHN TAYLOR

THOMAS E. SNIEGOSKI
FEATURING REMY CHANDLER

The best paranormal private investigators have
been brought together in a single volume—
and cases don't come any harder than this.

**Available wherever books are sold or
at penguin.com**

THE ULTIMATE IN
SCIENCE FICTION AND FANTASY!

From magical tales of distant worlds to stories of
technological advances beyond the grasp of man, Penguin has
everything you need to stretch your imagination to its limits.

penguin.com

ACE
Get the latest information on favorites like
William Gibson, T.A. Barron, Brian Jacques,
Ursula K. Le Guin, Sharon Shinn, Charlaine Harris,
Patricia Briggs, and Marjorie M. Liu,
as well as updates on the best new authors.

ROC
Escape with Jim Butcher, Harry Turtledove, Anne Bishop,
S.M. Stirling, Simon R. Green, E.E. Knight, Kat Richardson,
Rachel Caine, and many others—plus news on the
latest and hottest in science fiction and fantasy.

DAW
Patrick Rothfuss, Mercedes Lackey, Kristen Britain,
Tanya Huff, Tad Williams, C.J. Cherryh, and many more—
DAW has something to satisfy the cravings of any
science fiction and fantasy lover.
Also visit dawbooks.com.

*Get the best of science fiction and fantasy
at your fingertips!*